The Starlight Monad

Alexander Patten

Alexander
Patten

Signed: _____

A@AlexanderPatten.online

AlexanderPatten.com/books

Preface

This novel began as a short story intended to evoke fantasy vibes within a sci-fi setting. It's a troublesome process determining how many different drafts I actually went through, but four years, two jobs, and six living-situations later, I present this, the First Edition!

The Starlight Monad is about a whole family, not mere isolated individuals. So, each chapter follows one of three Characters: Shran, Liza, or Zieglon.

Astute readers will notice that Chapter Two begins shortly before Chapter One, because it follows a different Character. And likewise in other chapters. To mitigate confusion about my carefully crafted timeline, each Character announces when they see it is a new day.

I'm tempted to delve into detail on the intricacies of planet Tew and The Upper Horizons lore as a whole. But for brevity's sake, know that Tew is the first new planet colonized by Earthlings, in a future where literacy is non-existent.

The Upper Horizons Books: For any questions, please contact a@alexanderpatten.online

First Edition.

ISBN 10: 8-9930096-0-5
ISBN 13: 979-8-9930096-0-5

LCCN: 2025919635

Cover design by Nicholas Shipley

The
Starlight Monad

Section One

Into Starlight

Chapter One

Shran

Friday after breakfast, I looked down the aisle they'd formed, and everything in me but my voice cried out for an escape.

"You lost, Shran," Jaldane called from the front of the gauntlet. "And you know what losers do." Losers ran the gauntlet, of course.

Jaldane re-gripped his wooden sword, all but salivating with anticipation, as he prepared to land a perfect swing. How I wished I hadn't joined their silly game to begin with. There came the chant as I took a runner's stance: "gauntlet, gauntlet, gauntlet!"

True, none of them were allowed to move from their spots as they swung and thrust those practice swords. Yet, if they managed to trip me, I would never escape without getting bruised and bloodied head to toe. How could I show Father such a face on the very day he meant to return? Then again, who wanted a coward for a son?

I needed to do it. I just had to…

I felt myself turn tail and run for the schoolyard, fast as legs could carry. The rough cobblestone made it easy to fall, yet farther and farther across the courtyard I went.

The young nobles cried, "Coward!" and "Weakling!" One glance over the shoulder revealed a dozen lord and ladylings in pursuit, waving weapons overhead. I ran faster still, widening the gap between us.

Before the hallway to the schoolyard, the palace had a veritable forest of pillars shrouding a whole entryway in shadows. The hallway connecting to the schoolyard lay to the right, while a servers' entrance was nestled back at the far side. I weaved between the shadowy columns as if heading for the schoolyard, then slipped in the servers' entrance and bolted it shut behind me.

Pressing an ear to the crack between doors, I listened to the pattering of feet going through to the schoolyard. As that chorus faded away down the connecting corridor, I caught my breath at last.

With no telling whether one of them stayed behind to snoop around, I slid to a seat on the grimy floor. Soon, the palace bell would ring ten, ushering in the head bard and safety to the schoolyard.

A server boy approached, struggling to hold a tub of laundry and wearing the same expression as if someone had just hopped into the family bed unannounced. He spoke with that upriver accent that turned words like "part" into "pot," and "loud" into "load."

"Beg pardon, master. These doors are having to remain unlocked all the day long," he said.

"Sorry," I said. "I was just... exploring."

"Begging it again, but these service halls are being very narrow, aye? Our orders are strict to keep them clear and that."

At that, something outside crashed into the bolted doors, raining dust all over. Was it the lordlings with a battering ram? Instead, a middle-aged maid shouted, "Open up in there, now." Fast as I could, I slid back the bolt and pulled the door open, concealing myself behind it.

"By thunder," the maid roared as she shoved her fruit cart through the gap. "Who's left the doors locked the dashing day before the Full Moons?"

"I'm sorry, Mother," the young server said.

"That'll be making one of you's. Who's hiding back there? Show yourself."

I silently obeyed, and the server woman immediately assumed an air of deference.

"Master Mattian? What's bringing you here?"

As I grasped for a better answer than exploring, she hissed at the server boy, "How many times have I told you not to go bothering masters and all that? You've got work to do." She smiled at me apologetically, but there was no affection in her eyes.

"But it wasn't my fault," he said.

"It's always our fault. Let me find you doing this again and see what happens."

Seeing the coast had cleared, I squeezed past the fruit cart and headed for the schoolyard. As I rounded the corner into the connecting hallway, someone latched onto my collar. Next thing I knew, my skull was throbbing, and Jaldane had me pinned up against the brick wall.

"Do you think you're clever, you cheat?" he said, digging his broad thumbnails into my collarbone.

"It was just a game," I mumbled, fighting to keep the pain out of my voice.

"Until you wriggled off into the shadows like a little worm. Do you know what I do to worms, Shranny?"

As I imagined some combination of dangling from a fishing line and tasting a fresh boot-sole, the high tower bell mercifully began to ring for the tenth hour. Jaldane dropped me like laundry down the chute and scampered into the schoolyard. I followed on

3

his heels, the two of us stepping into rank not a second after the last bell toll died out.

* * *

The palace's schoolyard housed dozens and dozens of unique statues. Each was polished and shimmering in the late morning sun, collectively depicting the endless figures from Newmund History. While most of those sculpted had died long ago, their feats sat there in stone for all time. Each one had been so finely crafted it perfectly captured the people and events in question. So, why did we have to memorize a song for every single one of them? Of course, as Falen reminded us last time, countless bards could recite all the songs for every sculpture in a whole statuary on cue. How all those words could fit in one man's head remained a mystery.

I shook the stray thoughts away as Falen wrapped up the month's final review. The colossus he stood beneath depicted all the young nobles' own great-grandfather. There he was, President Dessidon Stohvan the First, locked in combat with his treacherous brother, Sarlinor the First.

Gradually, my eyes wandered still higher, tracing the marble carvings that wrapped all around the upper rim of the schoolyard. I supposed many of them got along fine without a hint of noble blood.

"Shran," Falen called, and I tried not to jump. He leaned on the bulbous handle of his standing stick, gripping with those bony fingers of his and increasingly blending in with the statuary for stillness. The thoroughly aged man made my skin crawl the way he moved—or didn't move.

"Yes sir?" I sputtered as Jaldane and some of the other students leered my direction for a moment.

"Would you kindly summarize today's lesson for us before we disperse?"

I hadn't caught probably the last ten minutes, but prayed memory would serve for once. "We learned about the Great President's legacy, how he was very important."

Falen tugged at his peppery gray goatee. "Do elaborate."

"We learned more about how he united the whole continent, then, his two sons there—"

"In verse, please," the bard directed.

In schoolyard fashion, I gazed at the sculpture of the presidential brothers from feet to heads, hurriedly ushering the words into my own head. I sang what came out:

O the mighty President

All Othark he united.

He got his Mayors aplenty

To his presidency indicted—

"Invited," the young nobles corrected, like they knew everything.

"...his presidency invited," I mumbled.

And out from him did

The Starlight Monad

Dessidon and Sarlinor the Firsts

Rule peacefully, the east and west'ly halves

From their due births.

"Your rhythm needs a little work," Falen said, "and why does our palace house a monument of two Stohvans from Frandesia?"

"Um…"

"Audible pauses are not part of the English language," the bard said, followed by giggles from the lordlings.

"Sorry, sir. Because Dessidon the Second married Clenhilda, the last of the Pelterns."

"Thus," he said without stopping for a breath, "giving her eldest the mandate to rule Newmund mayorship. Mayor Guilen may have a Stohvan for a father, but the purest Peltern blood flows through his veins." He cocked an eyebrow at the warring brothers behind him. "We also ought to honor his father's father with this sculpture and its songs. Word-perfect recitations are due Monday. You may disperse."

The palace bell rang twelve noon. Falen took up his standing-stick and disappeared down an adjoining hallway. I sighed in the relief that we had not one thing left to hear out, recite, or otherwise learn all weekend long. The young nobles broke ranks and left, while I delayed leaving as long as possible. Who knew what they might have in store for me the moment I exited?

When it appeared they really had gone off to their own business, I hightailed it through the main courtyard, dodging between the many booths already being set up for the weekend's festivities. I went straight out the gate and through Newmund city, soon reaching sweet fields in the open sunlight. An under-trafficked cart path brought me near the jagged, branching network of crevasses that made up the forbidden zone. Even from there, it hurt my neck to look up at the single structure in the center of it all: the Great Tower.

After checking my flanks, I hiked down the crevasse's gentle incline. It soon became deep enough to conceal me from view on either side. It felt almost cozy, knowing no stray eye could catch me.

I rarely dared to break actual rules in the palace, but exploring those barren tracts of land felt different. If anything, wandering through the forbidden zone meant the nobility didn't have to waste energy turning their noses up at me. Everybody won.

After hiking far enough into the crevasses to avoid being spotted, I climbed one of the less treacherous patches of wall back to ground level. From there I dusted off my palms and headed to one of the sunny faces of the Great Tower.

The stability of this structure beggared belief, no matter how many times I'd seen it. About a hundred meters in front of me stood the south side of its northern foundation. It spread wide enough to house the better part of the mayor's palace and rose many times higher than any human structure I'd ever heard of. The whole thing was built from some kind of metal no one could identify.

The four foundations resembled pillars, one placed in each of the cardinal directions, with nothing but empty fields between them. Way up at their tops is where they actually joined, like the spokes of a cart's wheel. From that central point, a spire pierced through clouds and sky until disappearing out of view. Some actually claimed the spire had no top, but either way it was simply too tall and too narrow to ever work. Why hadn't the whole thing toppled or snapped in half at the first gust of wind?

I lay out in the field, grabbing a mouthful of some dry snacks from my side pouch as I pondered the impossible Tower. No words ever came. If anything, the Tower seemed to steal the words from me, though in a good way. As I lay there, simply watching it stand firm brought the strangest sense of comfort.

"Looking for something?" came a man's voice from nearby.

I sprang to my feet, half expecting one of the mayor's men. Instead, there to my right stood a man with smooth white hair that almost seemed to glow and a clean-shaven chin with no beard or even a mustache. He looked about forty, yet couldn't have been, with that hair. His stance gave the strange impression as if he'd been there since time immemorial, watching me with those piercing hazel eyes.

Of course, my first instinct was to flee for my life and never return. Yet his warmly commanding presence overshadowed even that fear. He had asked a question of me, after all. So, I kept my feet planted where they were, gave a deep courtly bow and answered, "I don't know sir. It's just amazing such a building is here, in Newmund."

"Ah. And who might you be, young man?"

"Shran Mattian, my father's one of the mayor's generals."

"A Mattian, you say?"

I nodded, and he seemed surprisingly interested from there on.

"As for the Tower," the man said, "where else would it be?"

"Maybe down in Frandesia, or somewhere more influential."

"And why is that?"

"No one in our whole mayorship could build something like this, could they?"

The man chuckled. "Son, no one on Tew could build it in ten centuries."

8

"What is it, sir? The Tower I mean." I bit my tongue. Why waste such a man's time with silly questions like that? Yet he took no offense.

"What do the bards sing about it?" he asked.

"That it's from before the Storm, I think."

"Why should that matter?"

"All I know is, well, I remember part of a song about it. It's due Monday."

"Excellent. Sing away then."

I nodded, straining to make the song come without its statue present:

The man of arcane

Made of metal his brain.

When the Storm came and reigned

All man's knowledge was drained

Till he learned once again

And made song his strong cane.

In reality, I stumbled over a few words, but the mysterious man smiled. "Your song holds true enough, son. Gradually, gradually before the Storm, almost everyone offloaded their knowledge, their intelligence, their ingenuity into various machines made of metal as well as other materials."

"But why would they do that? Wouldn't it hurt?"

"It hurt in more ways than they could imagine. Still, they desired to transcend the flesh that way. And as the flesh between their ears atrophied from disuse, they heaped on more and more machine enhancements to make up for the difference."

"And all their machines got destroyed by the Storm," I said, proud of myself for remembering that.

"Yes," he said. "It pretty well erased all they 'knew' in the times before. If you knew all man's knowledge was drained, why would you ask me what this tower is?"

"I'm sorry, sir." It really was a dumb question.

"No need to apologize. I'd just like to hear your answer."

"Oh. I asked because you seemed like someone who ought to know."

"Well enough, I should say. Better than that, I'll *show you* what this tower is, if you come back tomorrow."

"Inside the Great Tower?" I marveled.

The man nodded. "Make sure to bring your mother along too, of course."

"How do we break in? And my mother, what if she's busy?"

He just said, "I'll see you tomorrow," and made his way towards the Tower.

I called after him, "Sir, who should I say sent me?"

"A relative of sorts," he said, not slowing.

"A relative? What do I call you? I've never seen you on holidays."

"Steve's my name," he said, already some distance away, and chuckled. "Don't wear it out."

At the base of the Tower, "Steve" genuflected, and a guillotine door slid open before him. He stepped inside, and it slid shut behind him fast enough to slice a foot off.

I sprinted after him. Many glowing lines woven into mysterious patterns covered the silvery surface of the Tower, but I found no hint of a door. Though I took a knee like he had, nothing happened. I couldn't even say for sure if I'd found the same spot as Steve had. Clearly no use without him.

At last I turned homeward, not dejected but bursting with excitement. The man had given his word, and so I'd make the greatest discovery in all of Newmund, all of Tew itself. As easily as that, we Mattians would enter legends.

Chapter Two

Liza

It was breakfast, Friday morning, and Zieglon should have already been home again. Of course, if I knew my husband, he was off answering the mayor's call before setting a toe inside the palace. So, once again, Shran and I sat breaking our fast on the lonely edge of the mayor's high table.

The whole court chorused with chatter of the silver stag hunt. Mayor Guilen, his noblemen and my husband had all gone on the hunt. And at his request, half of the northern Newmund villagers had abandoned their work mid-harvest if only just to catch a glimpse of the legendary silver stag.

"Whoever catches it receives a great blessing," one woman said.

"We'll just have to ask my Thordin when he returns," said Thordin's wife… Virna, was it?

"Do you really believe his fur heals ailments?" another said.

I gave Shran a little smile as he ate sausage and porridge in silence. "Are you excited to see your father, back with that stag leashed behind him?"

Shran swallowed a mouthful excitedly. "I want to ride it first if he does!"

"That's way too dangerous, even for a thirteen-year-old."

"I was kidding," Shran said with a hint of irritation.

"Sorry. Yeah, that's funny," I said, and he went back to his breakfast. "How are lessons going?"

"The head bard's coming today, for the monthly reviews."

"That'll be great. Falen knows practically everything."

He chuckled to himself. "He sniffs out the tiniest mistake and makes sure everyone else hears about it."

"It just takes practice, right? You'll learn all of it soon enough."

"Our recitations are Monday. I barely know the difference between a Stohvan and a Peltern."

"Maybe your father can sing them with you tomorrow?"

He nodded with an expression that said he'd heard that one before.

"What about the other students?"

"They're all little Stohvans, though."

"Ha! So, you do know the difference," I said.

He shrugged and lowered his voice. "You know how they are."

"Sometimes you have to be the first to make a move before you find a friendship."

"What if I don't want to be friends with them either?"

"Sometimes you have to," I said.

"How many have you made here, since we left home?"

I hadn't really, quite exactly made any. If the nobility treated my husband as an outsider, they treated me more like a slug: hardly worth squishing for the mess it would make. They granted me the basic rights of ladyhood with none of the respect. Of course I couldn't let on about that with my son. "This is our home now Shran. And we're here for good reason. Even if we're not of the nobility, we have lands to our name. We own them. Do you know what that means?"

"It's not that simple, Mother."

"Because we need to act like it. You know what I'm saying. Right? What does that make us?"

He rolled his eyes. "It's supposed to make you a lady and me a lord-to-be."

"Well, you *are* a lordling, I *am* a lady. We need to act like it, act like we belong. Right?"

Shran sighed, "Okay."

Soon enough he went off to the courtyard where the noble lord and ladylings had gone. Perhaps they'd let him join one of their games before schoolyard. That left me with a span of empty seats to my left. I was alone and set on display for everyone in the court below to see. Would that be my life, always apart from and never a part *of* anything? No. I had to bite down and put my own advice into practice.

A ways to my left sat Haldra, the youngest of the mayor's siblings and the worst of the bunch. Today, she had her dark braided hair spiraled up around the back of her head, her perfectly albescent cheeks tense just shy of a smirk. As I pondered whether they'd been like that since before she was widowed, Lady Haldra cocked an eyebrow my direction.

I instinctively turned away and stared blankly at the lower court. No. I resolved to get over myself. I picked up my dish and sat right next to her and her elder sister, Gilda. The three of them fell quite silent from whatever they'd been speaking about.

"Well, isn't this a surprise," Haldra said.

I internally screamed at myself. Why hadn't I thought of one thing to say beforehand? "Placed any bets on whose party will catch the stag?" I blurted.

Haldra smiled. "Honestly, Gilda and I were just debating whether brushing that silver pelt could heal your Zieglon after he gets gored by those crystal antlers."

"Idle chatter, really," Gilda said.

I nodded: idle indeed. "He'd sooner drag the creature here with his own two hands," I said.

That got a giggle out of them, for better or worse. "And anyway, your brother's fortunate to have a general as fine as him."

"You don't worry about him, then?" Haldra asked.

"Not if I can help it." Not every day at least.

"Hmm," Haldra said. "It's just, where would you go without him, I wonder?"

Sometimes my tongue would not allow itself to be held back. I *had to* respond. "Where would you be if your brother weren't the mayor?"

Lady Haldra just sighed, letting my rash talk hang in the air.

Gilda daintily swallowed the mouthful she'd been chewing. "No more talk like that at *his* table, please. Our sons would only be a step closer to the office. May All Father forbid it."

Deciding I'd had enough embarrassment for one morning, the screech of my heavy chair scooting back echoed across the entire court.

"Going so soon?" Haldra said.

I let a breath out and answered in the most courtly tone I could fake. "I've got to be moving along at the moment."

Haldra smiled again. "Smart girl," she said. And she was, in fact, my junior by a year. "You could hardly show up this afternoon in," she eyed the rough gown I'd thrown over my chemise for breakfast. "With the president arriving and everything..."

"The President? Today?" I asked.

"Pay the silly rumor no mind," Haldra said. "Chances are he'll miss the Full Moons banquet this afternoon."

I nodded, pretending I knew all about it. "It's not this evening?"

"You know how it is. With the Full Moons, the president en route, and the silver stag to boot, the festivities had to commence sooner. Otherwise, we'd hardly have time left to sleep before Monday. You don't mean to show up—I'm sorry but—dressed like that."

I supposed I'd made a habit of dressing down on the mornings when most of the important people were gone. Suddenly, I felt filthy in such common wear. "I wouldn't dream of it," I said with a curtsy.

Back up in the Mattian family chambers, I flung open my wardrobe. It had been bared to the boards. "What in three graves?" I cursed. Hurriedly, I checked under the bed, checked Zieglon's things and even hopped over to Shran's chamber. Not a scrap of my formal wear remained.

A service bell with a purrium handle hung next to our bed. I lightly flicked its handle, and it softly purred, awakening the link to its sister half downstairs. I rang on my end and waited. And then I waited some more before I flicked and rang it again. Where was the server?

Then the bell did ring back, as by an invisible hand, and I sat tight for whoever was coming.

Several agonizing minutes later, a maid found her way up to our chambers, a thick-limbed young woman with brown eyes and a cherry red nose. I'd rarely seen her upstairs, and she spoke through a hard upriver accent.

"Grave apologies and that for the delay, Mistress Mattian. We caught your ring, but with all these preparations…"

"It's fine. Just… I have no dresses, no ball gowns, no other clothes at all, nothing. What happened to them?"

"Great Father beyond," she gasped. "Please pardon a poor server girl, Mistress."

17

"You're pardoned. I just want to know what happened to my things."

"The Lady Haldra, be she haled, told me you needed everything washed for the banquet tonight."

"Tonight? No. It starts this afternoon."

"Afternoon, my lady? We don't have time for that."

"Could you please just go fetch my clothes before it's too late?"

"As you please. I'll be up again directly, my lady." She curtsied out, perhaps more politely than usual.

I dropped into an armchair by our fireplace. How could that woman Haldra be so rude? Why would she go out of her way to make things difficult for me? True, Mayor Guilen gave us some lands originally allotted to her, but they had to come from somewhere. How could I help that?

The maid took so long I heard the tenth hour bell chime from the high tower, and still, no maid. I rang for service again, and finally she rolled a cart up to our door. "Begging your pardon, Mistress. There were a lot of these to grab. You've no idea how hard it is fishing through wash water betwixt everything else."

Then I noticed all the clothes on the cart were soaking wet and covered in suds. "What happened to them?" I asked.

"We meant to wash them, of course. They dunked them in soon as they got them from the laundry chute."

"It's past ten already. I can't go in this," I said, pulling at the rough gown I wore. "I might as well visit the president wrapped in a burlap sack."

"These are powerful thick ball gowns you've got here," she said, picking through them. "It could take beyond five hours to get them washed and rinsed and dried. That's not to mention the fittin' them on and everything."

"That just won't do. I have to have these by noon. Try fire and fanning and that," I said, slipping into an upriver vernacular.

"Ooh. You don't want this fabric anywhere near a flame, and it'd soak up a pungent smoky odor to boot."

"Then I'm stuck. Haldra will have me dressed in rags at table with the President himself, not to mention Zieglon. I'll be the laughing stock of the entire Mayorship." I said, collapsing onto the bed in frustration.

"Is there really nothing that can be done? Could you borrow someone else's, perhaps?"

"Who would I ask?" I said into the mound of pillows.

"Lady Haldra wanted your laundry done. Maybe she'd lend you something of hers?"

"No, no. Please just get this stuff dried as fast as you can."

"It'll be hours, mistress Mattian, but as you please," she said and rolled away with the dripping cart.

Suddenly I had an idea. What if I did "borrow" one of Haldra's dresses for the afternoon? She probably had so many she wouldn't notice one missing. It was only fair.

I crept my way to Haldra's chambers. What kind of plan had I gotten myself into? I pondered as I neared the destination. Now I'd thought about it, surely she'd show up any minute if she wasn't already inside preparing.

I rang the hall's service bell. Mere seconds later, a maid emerged from an adjoining server hallway. Apparently some sections of the palace got significantly better response times. "Oh, it's you, Mistress Mattian," the maid said, in well-practiced Presidential English. "I half expected Lady Haldra."

"Oh, I was just walking by," I said. "Have you checked her room?"

"Pardon." The maid curtsied and scampered over to the chamber door.

I hid behind some of the curtains that lined the hall. I wouldn't win any prizes for hide-and-go-seek, but this was practically the first plot I had ever done. I heard the maid knock several times, getting no response, then I peeked as she opened the door in desperation and stepped inside. Relieved, I hopped out from my hiding spot and made a slow promenade towards the chamber, admiring the gilded wall carvings and marble sculptures on the way. By the time I arrived, the maid re-emerged from the chamber, clearly having failed her search.

"Don't worry," I said. "She had to be somewhere else, and didn't need service after all." It was technically true, I suppose.

"Thank All Father," the maid said, and hustled back into the server hallway.

I cautiously checked over both shoulders and slipped inside. Whereas the Mattian family chambers had a nice cozy feel to them, this one, with its bright color palette and tall vaulted ceiling felt more like a ballroom than a bedroom.

Her walk-in closet wasn't nearly as packed full of garments as I'd expected. Besides that, each ball gown was so unique I'd have to find a way to modify one, disguising it. I grabbed a nice blue-themed gown that appeared vaguely similar to some others. Hopefully she wouldn't notice.

As I pondered how to get such a huge thing all the way back to the Mattian chambers without raising eyebrows, a hinge creaked somewhere outside. It had to be the front door, of course. In a terrified flurry, I pulled the closet door shut and froze. There was no way out. Would she go straight for the gowns?

Voices carried through the very thin closet door, Haldra speaking with one of the maids. "So, what's become of our friend now?" she asked.

"I put every scrap of her clothing out of commission for a good minute and kept her waiting a dreadful long time for service in the interim," the maid said.

"Splendid," Haldra said, "and she didn't suspect anything?"

"Oh, she thinks you did it, but who would ever expect a lowly maid to be up for a bit of fun as well?"

"Absolutely. Even farmer folk like her—especially farmer folk like her—never see *you* coming."

Indeed I could hardly believe what I was hearing. Why on Tew would two women of such opposite walks of life team up against me? Where was my team?

"Oh, and I nearly forgot to tell you," Haldra said. "the meeting this evening is going to be very important. Big plans for this weekend."

"Falling off my seat to know what about, Mistress."

"Ah-ah-ah. I can't say a word of it until we're all there."

"Begging your pardon, Mistress."

"Oh, stop, Penna. It's time for my bath."

So, Penna was the self-same maid who came to my room earlier. One part of me hated her for helping that woman, while the other envied her. How I wanted to be part of something. Beyond that, I wanted to know what this meeting could be about. But they didn't say another word about it.

I remained trapped in that closet for at least half an hour before the bath was drawn. A whole assembly line of maids had brought bucket after bucket of hot water, until the presumably massive tub was filled and the connected bathroom door closed. Finally, amidst the sound of scrubbing and idle chatter, I ever so quietly opened the closet door and tiptoed out to the hall with the borrowed gown in my arms.

The eleventh bell rang from the high tower as I slammed our chamber door behind me. Only an hour left. In that time, I needed to make the gown unrecognizable. Unlike those palace nobles, my grandmother taught me the art of mending from my youth. I got right to it.

The frills and ruffles made it easier for a clever woman to hide where she'd stitched something else on or cut something off. I used any fabric I could find—curtains, bedding, table cloths—to make it significantly different. I even lengthened the train considerably, hastily sewing on some heavier fabric to the back. Finally, punching a few new holes for the side buckles made it a perfect fit.

In no time, I wore the modified ball gown and styled my hair and makeup. The woman in the mirror could have been mistaken for the Third Lady herself. I'd never seen a statue of the First or Second Lady, but presumed they would've been jealous too.

The twelfth bell rang out from the high tower: I was already late. The banquet would be starting. I flew down to the mayor's court. The doorman looked on me in amazement as he opened the doors.

Inside, there at the mayor's table sat Haldra, Gilda, and Virna, quite casually. In fact, the court was practically empty—like no banquet was happening at all. Now I looked completely out of place, but maybe I could play it off somehow?

As I briskly walked inside, a bit of my lengthened train must have caught in the door jam. Before I registered half of what was going on, it ripped a large section off the skirt. I whipped around to grab the fallen fabric, only making the gigantic tear more obvious to everyone at the Mayor's Table. They burst out laughing.

I scrambled to cover myself with the fallen fabric, cursing under my breath. They'd made an absolute fool of me. On and on they cackled until I couldn't take any more. I screamed at Haldra, "You liar!" It echoed across the court and out into the hall.

Their laughter died out abruptly. "Me?" Haldra said, swiftly making her way my direction. "When did I ever lie to you, Liza?"

I didn't want to give that the dignity of an answer. "You did lie to me," was all I could say.

"No, no, no. That was just a bit of fun," she said, condescending to one knee as she looked down on my puffy red eyes. "I didn't lie to you, farm girl."

"I am Lady Mattian. A Lady of Newmund."

"But you don't act like one. Here you are, screaming in the halls, crying in your… where did you get this? Oh no." She felt at my collar and sleeves, then whispered. "And you stole it. I may just have to tell Guilen about this."

I scurried out of the court without another word, the tears escaping between my fingers as I prayed no one would recognize me. On and on I went, up the grand stairs and through the halls till collapsing face first onto my bed.

Haldra's words kept repeating in my head. The lies I could handle. The truth hurt far worse.

Chapter Three

Zieglon

We advanced step by careful step through the heart of Ohha Forest. Each bird's chirp, each swishing branch, and every crunching leaf sent us its own special message. The only thing I wanted to know, where was the silver stag?

The very morning I meant to return, villagers had spotted him: the first of his kind in over a decade, though some claimed there was only one. By mid-morning, Mayor Guilen recruited villagers who covered a twenty-kilometer parameter of forest near the sighting.

I jumped at the chance to catch the silver stag myself, and predictably, so did Guilen's brother, Thordin. So, no less than three hunting parties had set out, scouring the forest. One of us would catch this legendary creature. If I had any breath left in my body, I wouldn't let Thordin Stohvan take credit this time.

Something broke a few twigs in the foliage ahead. A common buck could have made the noise, but I held my breath all the same, counting each quickened heartbeat. Nearer and nearer we approached the source of the sound. I couldn't afford to let any bards tag along with my hunting party. Those singers could make a good hunt sound like a great one after the fact, but to track clever game like this, I needed men who knew how to keep silent. I trained them to select each step as precisely as an artist with his chisel. One false move and the creature would undoubtedly escape. The only songs people would hear of this hunt would come directly from me and my men. Finally, there on the forest floor lay the freshly broken twigs. Had he slipped our grasp?

A bird call came from the right flank. It sounded like Hothen, my second-in-command. His call translated to "target sighted."

Taking one deep breath to quiet that racing heart, I gave the hand signal, "horseshoe formation." The signal propagated from man to man, out of view. It would travel all the way back to Hothen on the right and to the farthest reach of the left flank. Slowly, steadily, my men closed in around the target, leaving him but one direction to travel.

With his keen senses and nimble limbs, completely encircling the silver stag risked losing him for good. As the songs had it, he could jump clear over a man's head. Only if we pushed him just right, could we cut off his path of escape. As we advanced the horseshoe formation, the distant creature casually meandered onward.

The faint rushing of a small waterfall faded into earshot. I recalled that this landmark curved in on itself, so there was only one narrow entrance, and it reached a few meters in height. Praying the stag couldn't jump that, I signaled again, directing towards the falls.

We had to make him notice our presence just enough to saunter off in the right direction without being spooked. So, gradually, gradually we crept forward. The odd "target sighted" bird call from one of my men gave an updated bearing on the stag's whereabouts.

Whether he banked left or banked right, hidden in the distant foliage, we gently nudged him back towards the trap. Louder and louder the crash of water grew. Soon the falls drowned out the sounds of the forest.

At last, I caught sight of the falls through the brush, sheer rocky walls stretching all around it. The stag had no escape but through our tightly formed ranks. There, by the pool at the base of the falls stood the creature, its silvery coat glistening in stray rays of sunlight, its twelve-pointed antlers clear as crystal. The silver stag walked as if gravity held no claim on him, as if each step he took were a gift he freely gave Tew's surface. With the same grace, he lapped up a drink from the pool.

Witnessing the beauty of this creature, I almost wanted to call off the hunt. Almost. Instead, I resolved only to trip and bind him. Still hidden in the bushes, I felt for the bolas on my hip.

An awful clattering of hooves and shouting men cut through the sound of crashing water. These riders galloped right on past us, into open air. Thordin, the mayor's younger brother, sat astride his ebony horse. He wore over-decorated iron armor, his favorite bards on their mounts beside him.

That dashed oaf. How could he bring those whinnying nags on such a delicate hunt? I still gripped the bolas at my hip, furious. Thordin's rank of horses completely obscured any hope of a shot at the stag.

The stag immediately charged the two dozen riders like a child chasing a flock of birds.

"Loose," Thordin commanded.

They loosed a volley from their wrist-mounted crossbows. The stag only swerved slightly, swatting several missiles out of the air with a flick of his antlers.

"Ready harpoons," Thordin shouted. Before his men could even draw, the stag jumped, soaring over their heads like nothing. This feat spooked Thordin's horses so badly a few of them bucked their riders headlong into the pool. Even *I* froze by the grace of this jump, till he landed behind us. The rest of Thordin's men raced into the woods after it.

Wasting no time, I hopped onto a newly riderless horse and whipped it into action. What it lacked in courage, this horse made up for with speed. Soon, I caught up to Thordin, riding right next to him. He shot me a glare but couldn't take his eyes off the path for long.

We crashed through branches and twigs to stay on the stag's tail. I hacked and slashed with the family sword, just enough to keep branches from striking my unarmored face. No time to slow down.

The stag raced on ahead of us, skipping and bobbing through brush and bramble, his head appearing one moment, and disappearing the next. There was no way of lining up a clear shot with the bolas. The silver stag was faster, but he didn't know these woods like I did.

Finally, the creature came to a large clearing. We trailed so closely behind him, he had no other escape. The full sunlight struck his skin, and he shone more beautifully than before. When we too emerged into the clearing, I swung bolas overhead, studying his every movement, half enamored and half planning my one shot.

Thordin shouted for his men to loose another volley. They had a better shot this time. Somehow the creature anticipated it, skipping two meters in the air, easily avoiding the volley. But then came my turn. I cast my bolas at his hind legs. They twirled across the clearing and entangled round and round his airborne hooves. At high speed, he struck ground, tumbling in the midst of the clearing with legs bound. The stag gave a loud mournful cry that carried out into the woods. The bolas immobilized him, without serious injury.

Thordin halted his men, taking a moment to steady himself. "Again," he commanded. Each man flicked the Purrium platelet on his crossbow. The metal platelets' high metallic hum summoned the loosed bolts back again, each to its respective crossbow as if reeled in by an invisible line.

"It's already tripped and bound, Thordin."

"Nonsense," Thordin said, looking to the bards beside him. "They shall sing that Thordin's bolts pierced the elusive creature of legend."

The men cocked their crossbows.

"Aim…"

I lightly snapped my finger, striking a purrium platelet on the palm of my glove. The purrium sustained a low hum, invisibly linking it to the other half on the tossed bolas.

"Loose."

With my glove linked, the weight of the ensnared hooves rested in the palm of my hand. Clasping both hands, I pushed my glove against thin air, and the bolas mimicked the movement, rolling the stag out of the way. As the bolts missed, I silenced the platelet with my fingers, dismissing the link. My hand moved freely again.

"Dash you on the rocks, Zieglon. I nearly hit the thing," Thordin said.

"The catch is mine," I said.

"Spoken from the back of a stolen mount. Nevertheless," he said, spurring his horse forward, "it was my horses and my men that chased him down."

Just before I kicked off after him, my mount's ears perked up. I froze as I too detected something and scanned the tree line for its source.

Thordin reached the stag, fresh bridle at the ready. The silver stag made another mournful cry as it thrashed against Thordin's bridling.

The birds stopped singing. In the stark silence, I heard it clearly: something sprinting towards us in the distance. This was big, much bigger than any animal I'd ever heard of, with a gait that sent a chill down my spine. What approached us ran on two legs, not four.

Thordin finally secured the harness to my catch. The hidden animal sprinted now, almost to the clearing. Then Thordin and his men heard it too. They scanned the brush, cocking their crossbows uneasily. Branches broke. Trees swayed violently. Thordin scrambled over to his mount, drawing a one-meter harpoon to guard the prize from the ground.

I kicked my horse into action, Thordin's men coming after me. I would not let him defend my catch for me.

It burst into the clearing. This hideous thing stood almost five meters tall. Though its face appeared almost human, its mouth and nose protruded far beyond the chin, like a rude snout. He had huge cat-like ears poking out the sides of his head, and thick oily fur covered his muscular body. The monster roared as he charged, revealing many jagged teeth.

I galloped forward as Thordin stood his ground.

The monster raised his arm to strike the noble. The men loosed a volley. Unfortunately, their wrist crossbows weren't designed for infernal monsters. Several bolts poked through its fur but barely enough to startle him.

Thordin took the split-second opening, jabbing at its leg with the harpoon. The monster swatted it into the grass. He grabbed Thordin in one hand and the silver stag with the other.

Finally I reached them. I'd just drawn the family sword when the giant kicked my mount. The horse and I hurdled through the air in a sickening arc. I landed with a thud, rolling out of the way as the screaming horse nearly landed on top of me.

I stumbled to my feet, the world spinning around me, too dizzied to catch the fleeing horse. I shook my head, desperately regaining my bearings. I just caught the last glimpse of the monster, retreating whence he'd come with Thordin in one hand and the stag in the other. The riders went off, who knows where, either fleeing or seeking some route to cut him off. Thordin, though hardly a friend, would surely be killed if I did nothing. I couldn't possibly catch up to the monster on foot, but I had one fool idea.

Behind, the family sword stuck into the ground in the middle of the clearing, but I sprinted straight ahead for Thordin's fallen harpoon. I planted its barbed tip deep into the grass, unsheathed my hunting knife, and sliced away the insulation at the butt of the weapon. Finally, I uncovered the harpoon's Purrium core. I gave this a solid clank with the knife. Like a fishing pole with an invisible line, the harpoon yanked towards the monster, somewhere in the surrounding forest. Clearly, Thordin still had the sister-half of the harpoon core attached to his person. The purr grew so shrill, it made my ears ring. Still, I dug heels into the dirt as I pulled and pulled against thin air.

The monster had a strong grip but perhaps not stronger than a purrium summons. Indeed, it felt like the harpoon pulled Thordin a bit closer, then a little closer, then... slack? Had Thordin's sister-half detached? Had the purrium bond broken? But no. Some tension remained, pulling skyward. I looked up,

31

seeing Thordin plummeting towards me. The closer it was, the stronger purrium pulled. So, dropping faster than gravity, he'd be skewered on his own harpoon, not to mention crushed by the fall. I and my family would surely be held to blame.

In the moment, I only had one more insane idea how to save him. I silenced the core, deactivating the summons. Ears still ringing, I cast the harpoon way up into the nearest tree trunk. He'd strike the ground any second now, leaving no time to waste.

"All Father guide my blade," I prayed, then threw my hunting knife at the tree-planted harpoon. It struck the exposed core with a nice solid clank. This summoned Thordin mid-drop, yanking him by the arm until his glove touched the core. The halves silenced as they reunited, dropping the nobleman to land with a clatter somewhere inside the tree line.

I wondered, how had Thordin ended up hurdling so high through the air? Unless that thing threw him.

The monster broke through the tree line. Ignoring Thordin, it ripped the harpoon from the tree and snapped it in two. Out of habit, I swapped glove platelets, attaching the platelet for my hunting knife to the palm. With a solid snap, I summoned the knife back. Unfortunately, the hairy monster seemed to hear everything quite well. Its beady eyes squinted my direction as those cat-like ears angrily twitched.

How could I be so stupid?

He charged furiously.

In that moment, I felt worse than naked: not a weapon on me, standing right out in the open. About fifty meters away, in the middle of the clearing lay my family sword where it fell. I must've dropped its platelet when I lost that cowardly horse. And about the same distance to the left was the tree line, with the charging monster only seconds away.

The knife I'd summoned kept flying towards me, leaving precious few options. I could test my fortune battling the monster armed only with a knife, or perhaps I could buy myself a few more seconds to escape. I yanked out the still-ringing purrium platelet, chucked it high, and sprinted for the tree line. The knife and platelet clinked together, silencing each other and dropping like so much rubble.

Forty meters left. It did indeed buy me a few extra seconds, as the monster chipped a tooth biting down on the stray knife.

Thirty meters now. Flailing for absolutely anything in that open field, I lightly snapped the platelet for my bolas, linking to them without summoning. I felt their limpness in my palm. Clearly, they no longer held the stag. I snapped my finger to the platelet as hard as I could, the high-pitched purr making my ears ring once more. It yanked my hand right towards the charging monster, who roared angrily at the shrill sound.

Twenty meters. I opened my hand, and the glove simply pulled itself free. It sailed back to my pursuer. He chomped down on it, but the platelet continued to ring out from between his teeth.

Ten meters, the chance of escape right there. A gigantic muscular hand swiped for me. I dove, tucked and rolled, but he stayed right on top of me.

Five meters and another hand came swinging in. It forced me to dive away from the tree line, that rock-dashed monster. Behind us a bugle sounded. Thordin's men had returned, but too late.

As I landed the roll, two hands grabbed ahold of me, pinning my arms to my sides. I wriggled and thrashed as the fiend lifted me to his filthy grinning maw, his teeth still clamped down on the ringing glove. He slowly opened his jaws, with what passed for a sly smile, preparing to devour. The glove sprang free, pulling itself to the back of his throat.

The cavalry continued their charge, and the monster coughed on the ringing glove. It pressed further out of reach. Then, my lost bolas swooshed in, wrapping themselves tightly around his throat. He dropped me, clapping hands to his neck.

The cavalry arrived, throwing a hail of harpoons at close range. That sent the choking monster retreating into the woods. But for the moment, no one dared try to reel the thing in.

Hothen and the rest of my men caught up with us after the monster's groans faded out of earshot. I led them in the same direction the bolas had returned from. There we located the silver stag. No self-respecting butcher would accept the carcass that remained.

Chapter Four

Shran

I finally stopped to catch my breath at the palace gate. Some of the young nobles stared down at me from way up on the battlements. For probably the first time, I felt glad to see them, to tell anyone what I'd found.

I called up to them, ready with the whole account of the strange man who'd entered the impregnable tower. "You'll never guess what I just saw!"

"Oh no. Who could that fellow be?" Jaldane said to his cousins.

"It's an invader," one of the girls said.

"No. I'm serious," I said, to deaf ears.

"Quickly, the hot tar," Jaldane said. Then he and his cousin Amer dumped out several bucketfuls of mud. I jumped out of the way, but some splashed onto me all the same. Then the lordlings burst into laughter as I sputtered and spat mud.

"Wait. You don't understand."

"Archers, loose," Jaldane commanded, and they all chucked volley after volley of pebbles. At that point, I accepted none of them would ever listen. When several pebbles smacked my skull, I ran for the safety of the inner palace. By design, the gatehouse offered no cover for anyone entering the gate, so the lordlings easily continued their rain of missiles as I scrambled up the broad stairs to the main courtyard.

I went straight into the inner palace and up to the Mattian family chambers. At least my own family would listen. I pounded on the door, expecting to see the young ladies and lordlings over my shoulder any second.

A groggy voice asked, "Who is it?"

"It's me," I said.

Soon enough, the door opened and I rushed inside, finding the place in shambles. Scraps of clothes littered the floor, with curtains and tablecloths slashed to ribbons, and a large ball gown flung over the wardrobe door. Before I could ask what happened to the place, Mother appeared from behind the door, bolting it fast behind us. Half her hair remained mostly well braided while the other half hung loose and unkempt. Eyeliner streaked down her cheeks, though she didn't seem to notice, and I couldn't bring myself to tell her. Despite half the day gone, she still only wore bedclothes and a rough gown. I hated ever seeing her like that but was too embarrassed to say anything.

"Shran, what happened to you?" she said, looking at the mud streaked down my face and coat.

"I was coming home when they... dumped this stuff on me." Suddenly I had to fight back tears that I was too old for. Why was I so weak?

"The Stohvans again?" she asked.

"It's nothing. It's..." That old knot welled up in my throat as I tried to keep a steady voice. I had incredible news for once, yet what did it change? "They were playing a game like I was the invader, is all."

She pulled me into a hug, my arms pinned tight to my sides. I just wanted to leave, but I couldn't. "I'm so sorry," she said, not loosening her grip a millimeter. I didn't want to be some boy who goes crying to his mother, but then she started sniffing and crying, herself.

The whole thing had become so awkward I got the sudden urge to bite my own fingers clean off. Here I'd met some incredible figure, who was able to enter the Great Tower that no one else had as much as scratched in a millennium, and still it got muddled up in three buckets of slop. The lordlings effortlessly spoiled it.

In all her gushing about what the Newmund ladies had done— I could barely make out most of it—she at least spoke one pearl of wisdom: "Some people are just evil, Shran."

Whether from real sadness or raw tooth-grinding frustration, tears welled up in my eyes too. I couldn't seem to get a word in. Soon a cheerful chorus of bells chimed from the high tower: The mayor's hunting parties were nearing the palace.

In a sudden flurry, Mother said, "they're nearly here! Come on Shran. We need to get presentable for Father's return.

Then I blurted, "I met a man named Steve! He went straight into the Great Tower!"

"Shran, please don't tell me you've been exploring the forbidden zone again. Not today."

"But Steve said we've both got to be there tomorrow, and then he'll bring us in there with him."

She gave a curious look, as if waiting for the punchline. "No one's been in that thing in Newmund history. 'Steve' isn't even a name. Shran, what are you talking about?"

"It's true! He had hair whiter than milk, and he knew all about times before the Storm. You can see for yourself."

"After *today*?" she said. "I can't. All Father be thanked I'm not awaiting trial in a holding cell."

"Why won't you believe me?" I asked.

"Today, it doesn't matter if I believe it or not. We Mattians can't afford to go committing any kind of offense, if we want to keep our heads attached."

"But—" A knock came at the door. Was it more of the lordlings with a bag of rocks to throw?

"Laundry's here," came a chipper elderly maid's voice.

"Finally!" Mother said, and let the woman push in a cart stacked high with freshly folded dresses. "Shran, please. We'll have to talk about it later, or else we're going to miss the grand entrance."

I went to my own chamber, resigned to save the news for a better time. Perhaps for her sake, I could wait a bit longer to tell the whole story. In my chamber, I tossed my side pouch on my bed, threw on a decorative knee-length gambeson, and buckled on a pair of polished leather shoes.

Soon enough, Mother exited her chamber. Now she looked as much like one of the noble ladies as anyone, in a red dress with sharp sleeves that nearly reached the floor. Her hair was finely tied up, bright as an oil lamp, with a curl hanging by each ear.

"Shran, you look great," she said.

"Thanks."

"And make sure to be on your best behavior tonight. We've got to keep up appearances."

"Okay," I said, fighting like a champion not to roll my eyes.

The atmosphere as we went down to the main courtyard helped raised my spirits again. Garland in the presidential crimson and white had been strung around every single lamp post and hung over every door and window, adding a royal gravitas to the weekend's Full Moons festival. All sorts of vendors and traveling performers had set up booths inside the courtyard, with excited Newmundians crowding every inch of the makeshift aisles and stages. The aromas of the many pastries and roasting meats renewed my appetite. Above all, my father was only minutes away. Surely he would listen.

Villagers who weren't helping themselves to delicious confections, sang and danced to the tune of flutes, mandolins, and banjos. Unlike palace music, the village stuff bounded forward like a wild stallion: it was all you could do just to keep up with it.

While I wasn't much for singing in public, I clapped along to "Fleeting like the Breeze," performed by musicians at the bottom of the steps. Each verse sang of the many types of men who tried to catch the silver stag, usually meeting some hilariously gruesome fate.

Soon enough, the trumpeters sounded the mayoral anthem from the gatehouse. Almost immediately, the crowds formed into orderly ranks on either side of the courtyard's middle aisle. Mother and I swiftly found a spot atop the palace steps, next to where the nobles stood. Dominating the whole stage was the monument of Clenhilda, the late Third Lady, smiling with arms outstretched to her people.

The anthem played as Mayor Guilen's procession entered the gate. First came many ranks of young men, mayoral standards raised on high iron poles. They marched to the beat of several ranks of drummers following behind.

Next came the mayor's own hunting party, mounted on horses dressed in the presidential colors, followed by Mayor Guilen Stohvan himself. He wore a sharp military uniform, with large golden buckles up the front, and golden fringe at the shoulders.

On his head sat a ceremonial golden helmet that came to a point at the top, gold chain mail hanging down to his shoulders. The two braids of his beard fell on either side of his stiff collar.

The riders trotted a large circuit around the fountain, Mayor Guilen waving to the cheering crowds as they went. Finally, they passed between the columns of youths, who stood at attention with sculpted standards raised. The mayor gracefully ascended the staircase, taking his place right below the Third Lady's statue.

Next came Thordin and his horsemen, all in brightly colored plate armor, sporting the finest weapons and gadgets. They victoriously shook fists in the air as they passed through the courtyard.

At the foot of the stairs, Thordin motioned his riders to a halt. They all shouted, raising spears towards the mayor. He saluted them, and climbed the stairs to join his brother.

Then came Father's hunting party, in rugged forest green with brown accents, carrying well-crafted, functional gear. They marched slowly but surely. Not a hoof seemed to be out of step. At the front I saw Hothen, Father's second in command, but I didn't see Father anywhere.

They reached the foot of the stairs and halted as one perfect unit. The mayor cocked an eyebrow, echoing my own confusion. Where had his best general gone?

Then came the rapid chorus of four galloping hooves, singing across the courtyard. Father raced straight up the center aisle on his trusted gray stallion. The horse rounded the fountain at such a sharp angle they leaned in practically sideways.

His riders still completely blocked the way to the base of the stairs, yet Father spurred his horse faster. In a second, he'd definitely crash, yet not a man moved. I almost shrieked, and a few of the folk in the audience actually did. At the very last moment a pair of riders parted ways, barely enough for Father to pass between. A pair in the next rank parted after that, and then the next rank, each one returning to position again directly. The whole maneuver looked smooth as a fish through clear water, leaving less than a ripple behind.

About as soon as the horse skidded to a halt, Father's boots were already on the ground. He nodded respectfully at the mayor's salute, then looked at me and Mother. His dark beard had grown longer than last we saw him, his blue eyes radiant as ever.

Something came over Mother at that moment. She grabbed up her skirts and bolted down the stairs, practically skiing. So much for keeping up appearances, I thought. She leapt into his waiting arms, and I flushed with humiliation when they kissed for all to see.

I tore my eyes away, unintentionally looking straight at Nella— Thordin's daughter. She stuck her tongue out like she'd caught me or something, the little... As if I hadn't already been embarrassed enough. I decided to stare at my feet for a while. At least *they* couldn't stare back.

Mother and Father ascended the steps, arm-in-arm, while all the horsemen dismounted and found their places. It looked like Father truly had come back straight from the hunt, a few fresh scratches on his cheeks and a hint of earth still on his leggings.

"Hi son," he said with a smile.

"Hi Father," I said, hugging tightly as I tried to forget what had just happened. He patted my back, one hand in a tough leather hunting glove, the other bare. "What happened to your other glove?" I asked.

He just winked and held a finger to his lips.

"So, what happened on the hunt?" I asked excitedly.

He answered in a hushed tone. "I'm sworn to secrecy. Mayor's orders."

"Secrecy?" I asked. "But everyone knows you were hunting the silver stag."

"Well, you know," he said with a laugh, "I've really come to enjoy having my head attached to my neck. Just feels right. So, I can say no more."

"Did you catch it though, Father?"

He indicated Thordin with a nod. "Some may disagree, but..."

"I knew it," I said. Before I could get a better answer out of him, the trumpeters blasted the theme for an announcement. Everyone fell silent at a hand wave from Mayor Guilen.

"Fine people of Newmund," the mayor said, "it is with great gratitude to all my generals, huntsmen, hired village folk, and all of you that I make this announcement: today we have caught the legendary silver stag." Everyone clapped and cheered. The minstrels contributed a few popular bars before quieting down again.

The mayor continued, "However, and I say this with a heavy heart, I cannot show this legendary prize to you tonight." The people were not nearly as pleased with that. "Nevertheless, pray continue in all the Full Moons festivities, and when the time is right, the stag shall be revealed."

He signaled the trumpeters, and they blasted a victorious anthem. The marching drummers joined in with a hearty beat, gradually spreading singing and laughter across the crowd once more.

Father, Mother, and I all went down to mingle with the common folk. It felt great being with the family and away from the Stohvan clan. We stomped and clapped along to the songs we knew, and sampled some of the tastiest pastries.

After licking his fingers clean, Father turned to me. "I just remembered, this is for you son." He handed me a pair of rectangular metal platelets, about the width of my thumb. One had a strap of leather strung through one corner, making it resemble a rudimentary necklace. "Better not use these in public," he said.

"What are they for?" I asked, feeling the thick platelets between my fingers.

"Those are military-grade purrium platelets."

Now, anyone in the palace would be familiar with this mysterious metal, though the presidency owned most of the high-purity stuff. True to its name, when you lightly flicked or tapped purrium, it emitted a low metallic purr that lasted for longer than you'd expect.

They say that purr reawakens a memory in the metal—anybody's guess why or how. Skillfully split some purrium clean in half and then, whenever one half is purring, both halves reorient themselves and move just as if they were still connected. I guess you could just as easily say, while they're making that sound, they actually forget they were ever split apart.

Purrium also has as second function, when struck harder. I'd rarely got to see in action. For that you need as high of purity as you can get.

"Awesome," I said. "So, I can summon these back together too?"

"Yep," he said. "A nice solid clank on one of these platelets could pull about a kilogram from a couple hundred yards."

"Zieglon," Mother said, "he could get into trouble, or hurt himself."

"I'll be fine, Mother. I won't use them inside the palace anyway."

"See that, dearest? He knows," Father said.

She had just sighed with a resigned shake of the head when someone cried out, "Thief!" We all turned to see an angry vendor pointing after a scrawny young man making off with an armload of silver wares.

"Clear the dashed way," he cursed, shoving through the crowd.

Father bolted off after him, tackling the would-be thief and sending silver clattering in all directions. A few common folk quickly gathered up the wears and returned them to the owner. Then the mayor appeared on the scene, demanding an explanation.

The thief fell to his knees, gripping the mayor's heels. "Begging your pardon, my dear Mister Mayor, sir. It was just a game I was playing, y'see? A couple of my pals bet I couldn't make off with an armload of silver, and well, looks like I lost."

The mayor's face glowed red with rage as his voice reverberated across the courtyard. "Who can attest to this man's honor? Tell me, who." Those words hung heavily in the empty air, and no one dared defend the thief. Finally, the mayor said, "It looks like your friends don't agree."

The man kept groveling, knees digging into the cobblestone, but the mayor seemed to be in a particularly ill mood. He commanded a chopping block be brought then and there. When it was set up, the mayor himself chopped off the thief's left hand as swiftly as you'd kill a chicken for dinner.

Mother gasped from beside me, stumbled and caught herself as if she'd half fainted. It made me shiver horribly too. And that was the first time I'd ever witnessed a de-handing.

Village elders, the sheriffs, and a few of the poor chosen by lottery, filled in the tables in the lower court. The adult nobles and my parents sat at the mayor's high table, overlooking the whole court, with their lordlings, ladylings, and I at his lower table.

I ate at the last seat on one side of the table, then went straight up to my father where he sat. "You'll never guess what I found today, Father."

"Right you are. What've you got?"

"I was out hiking by the Great Tower—"

"Shran," Mother cut in, "I don't think you'd better talk about that at the mayor's table."

"But—"

"Listen to Lady Mattian. I'm sure she knows what she's talking about," Father said, putting a hand on my shoulder.

"He abhors anything to do with that," she lowered her voice "that tower. That's the reason."

Father nodded agreement. "We don't go ratting ourselves out with minor infractions in public, do we?"

I shook my head.

" 'At a boy, young man. Until we're in a secure locale, you'll be sworn to secrecy, aye?"

"It's important though. I've got to tell you," I said.

Just then, someone shoved his way past me from behind. "Sorry Shranny," Jaldane said.

A torrent of frothy ale poured down the back of my gambeson. He must have spilled half his stein, as if you could do that by accident. I turned straight onto him and said, "Some people are just evil."

Mother almost fell out of her chair at that, laughing sheepishly as she sprang to her feet. "Happy New Moons, Lord Jaldane," she said, tugging at my wrist. "We were just heading out. Good evening."

I followed her out to a secluded corner of the hall outside, the ale now soaking clear down to my shoe soles.

"That's no way to talk to anyone," she said, "especially not Haldra's son."

"I only said what you told me earlier," I muttered.

"I'm sorry. I shouldn't have. But still, you can't talk to the lordlings like that." She rested her forehead in her palm. "Sometimes you just have to forgive."

What could she mean by that? "Until you can get revenge later?" I asked.

"No."

"Well, why does All Father let evil people rule over everybody?"

"I wish I knew," she sighed. "And sometimes I wonder, who else does he have to choose from?"

And that sad note was the final one of my momentous day.

Chapter Five

Zieglon

I dropped a hand on the overgrown lordling's shoulder, readying to give him one warning for such foolish behavior.

He spun around, flailing a punch. Young though he was, Jaldane's fist would have a lot of weight behind it. With the effort it took to block the blow, I ended up whacking his eye. In a stunned silence, he clapped hands to the extremely minor wound, as if he'd lost a limb.

"*Do not* try that again," I said, looking him in his good eye, "any of it."

The lordling scurried away, his pride clearly hurt more than anything else.

Guilen waved me over, seemingly unaware of the little scuffle with his nephew. "Zieglon, I can't sit on this another minute," he said. "You, me, and Thordin in the war room, right now."

"Yes sir."

He nodded, coned his hands, and announced, "This banquet is adjourned." So abrupt was this untimely command that everyone stared in confusion. "Go on. Out with you!" he repeated.

The whole place cleared out, abandoning the long tables set with many half-eaten dishes and still steaming platters.

I found Liza and Shran as the last few people filed out, and gave the news.

"What's this one about?" Liza asked.

"More secrets, I'm afraid."

She nodded. "I just wish I knew what you were doing again."

"Soon," I said.

* * *

The mayor stood with his back to us, gazing at the war room's main diorama. Spread across a large portion of the floor, this diorama modeled all of Newmund, its borders with the mountainous Motland mayorship, and the coastal region of Frandesia. Tiny shadows of miniature hills and oversized outposts danced in the golden glow of a few sparce oil lamps. Each little outpost had a purrium bell next to it, part of a Frandesian technique for signaling across any distance. The diorama was sunken a few steps below floor level, giving a bird's-eye view of the mayorship.

The room felt rather vacant, with the doors bolted shut, and not a soul inside but the three of us, and of course, head bard Ergester Falen.

Guilen set a monstrous figurine in the northern forests, marking the giant's last known location. He stopped short of placing a silver stag figurine in the ravines where we three had hidden it. Satisfied the diorama was up to date, he turned to me and Thordin.

"I must admit, today's hunt was an utter disgrace," Guilen said. "The silver stag was supposed to be a ray of sunlight: the proof All Father's favor rests with us."

"I got you your prize, brother," Thordin said. "A catch is a catch."

I stopped just shy of scoffing out loud. "His" catch indeed.

"You're both at fault," Guilen said. "You were to capture him: *alive,* not dead and maimed beyond recognition."

"In all fairness Mister Mayor, even Thordin wouldn't have fumbled a catch as badly as that."

Thordin shook his head bemusedly as I continued, "It was that giant thing that attacked us. It—he—wanted more than a simple bite to eat. He intended to harm. I assure you, he'll be back again."

The mayor paced round the diorama, drumming fingers on the pummel of the sword on his belt. "None of your men have broken their oaths of silence on the matter, I trust?"

I shook my head resolutely, and Thordin gave a bewildered expression that said they would sooner drown themselves.

Mayor Guilen continued. "I want to know, has anyone else spotted that abomination? And what in Tew is it?"

Falen answered in his dry wizened voice, "No such reports have reached my ears." The palace bard had a reputation for making people jump whenever he spoke. This undoubtedly resulted from his habit of becoming so like-a-statue as he leaned on his standing stick, that people forgot he was even present. So much the better for him as he silently observed and silently remembered practically everything in the palace.

"As for the giant himself," Falen said, "the description your men gave sounds like a common form that existed around the time of the Storm."

"So, what is the rock-dashed thing?" Thordin asked.

"It's human," the bard said. "Or rather, it should have been. Though man scarcely had the brain power left to sing or pass down

49

skills at that time, the songs bear out that before the Storm, man had attained the power to modify his own biology."

"Are you saying they made that monster on purpose?" I asked.

"No one can say for certain."

"What we do know," Guilen said, pointing to the monstrous figurine where he'd set it, "is that that thing is out there, right now." He walked into the center of the diorama, squashing several model trees as he did so. At his feet stood a comically truncated model of the Great Tower.

"I can smell it," he said, scooping up and clinching the tiny tower in his fist. "We've discovered a curse on this land today. Somehow, it's this thing—this undashable Tower that drags its shadow over this palace every day the sun shines." He squeezed the figurine harder, but it held firm. "It's an artifact of, by, and for evil. We've got to solve this curse now, before it affects our harvest, or worse."

What could be worse than Newmund villagers starving, one might ask? Unlike the original Peltern dynasty, Guilen had to worry about losing his mayorship while he yet lived. Ever since the Frandesians turned all of Othark into a presidency, Newmundian mayors could be declared "incompetent" by the Frandesian president, despite being the true eldest of the Peltern line.

Guilen's situation was hardly helped by the fact the one Peltern to survive the siege of Newmund became the reigning president's third wife. Though, as I heard it, the Third Lady declared that she married for the love of her people.

When Clenhilda died birthing her fourth child, the last of the pure Peltern line was replaced by an estranged half-Stohvan half-Peltern generation. It of course fell on Guilen to build up from the ashes, and I saw the task weighed on him more heavily than ever that night.

Thordin made to reassure the mayor. "Don't worry brother. I'll hunt down that giant for you."

"Not on your own you won't," I said. "Last time, you were the very first one he captured."

"Balderdash. I had nothing but a short harpoon on me."

"Enough," Guilen said. "Yes. I've got quite enough in my cup without my top generals bickering."

I tried another tact. "I was just going to say, scaring him off isn't good enough. We've got to attract him, get the thing close enough to kill it on our terms."

"Exactly what a well-placed harpoon does," Thordin said.

"He absolutely hated the sound of purrium. So, we could use that to draw him right up to a well-armed hunting party."

"Very well," Guilen said. "Have your parties ready to leave tomorrow morning."

"Yes sir," I said.

Then Falen cleared his throat, and all eyes fell on him. "Pardon an old man."

"Please, Ergester. Speak freely," Guilen said.

"I only wonder, my mayor, how would that look: announcing we caught the silver stag without displaying it, only to send off another hunting party the very next morning?"

Guilen sighed. "A gravely true point. That wouldn't do at all."

Had the mayor gone mad? "Guilen," I said, "we've got to stop that thing."

"You said it yourself, Zieglon: it's no mere predator. He tried to steal the stag, did he not? It's well hidden for now. We'll foil his plan, give the folk an excellent omen, and then we'll kill him."

"And keep this secret from everyone in the meantime?" I said.

"Finding someone up to the job could take a mighty minute," Thordin said. "My taxidermist does fine work, but I'd never trust him with a secret like this. By graves, he'd wax artistic with it and never finish."

Suddenly, an idea came to me. "Liza's mended things since her youth. Let's have her do it."

"Her, fix that sloppy mess?" Guilen said.

"Why not? We need it done fast by someone we can trust."

Guilen sighed. "But when she's sworn in, we'll tell her as little as possible."

I nodded.

"Alright, Zieglon, I'm counting on you."

Chapter Six

Liza

"See you soon," I said as Zieglon left for his secret meeting. As long as those things took, I might have to fall asleep alone, even on the night of my husband's return.

As Shran and I headed up the main staircase for our family chambers, the day's worries came right back again, swirling round and round my head. It all came down to the fact I'd truly stolen that gown, and Haldra knew it. Had she told her eldest brother already?

The image of that poor young man in the courtyard hung in the background of it all, the thief gripping a handless arm, frozen in shock. So, that was how the mayor treated thieves. My wrist ached and throbbed in response, as if crying out, "Not me too." I could almost see everyone every day staring down their noses in disgust at the stub where my hand ought to live.

When we reached the Mattian family chambers, I made up my mind. I could not and would not be next.

To his credit, Shran calmed down about whatever he'd seen at the Great Tower. We wished each other a good night, and he went to his chamber without complaint. I entered our chamber, and it greeted me with the infernal state in which I'd left it. No way I could let Zieglon find it like that.

Having cut half the curtains to strips earlier, I merely cut the other half to match. Zieglon might believe it some burgeoning fashion. The tablecloths were an intricate lace. No way to fix those, so out the window they went. I scooped the dry laundry off the floor and stuffed it into my wardrobe. In a short time, our space looked clean again, though not so clean as to raise suspicion.

Last of all, I looked to the pilfered ball gown. If it took an hour to modify that afternoon, it would take far longer to change back, and Zieglon could return any minute.

"Where did you get that dress, my dearest?" he would surely ask.

"Glad you asked," I would say. "I came up with this plan of how to humiliate myself. Welcome home. You're married to a bumbling idiot."

No. He could never know about any of that. Besides, he had enough to worry about already. Yes. Zieglon had his occupational secrets, yet they never made me love him less, did they? So, as long as no one got hurt, I would have mine too.

I tightly folded the gown and clung to it like a life raft in the middle of the Great Sea. I turned to the door, but my feet wouldn't move.

"Come on Liza, one step. I only need to take one little step," I silently lied to myself. My feet didn't fall for it.

"Okay, I admit it. We've got to walk a bit farther than a step, but I'm in charge here. Get to it already."

Still, nothing budged.

"And yes, there's a terrible, horrible woman at the end of the walk and a dismal chance of success. But it is the right thing to do, returning what I took." Nothing.

"And if you cooperate, at least maybe we'll still be awake when our very own man finally comes to bed." That one worked.

I crept my way through the halls, in a sort of daze, forcing myself only to think of his loving embrace. To my surprise, I quickly arrived outside Haldra's chamber door, the very one I had snuck into that morning. Two low voices came from inside. I held my ear to the door, hoping to get a bearing on what I might meet therein.

"It's infuriating," Haldra said. "We can't do a thing until we get hold of that stag."

"But Mistress," came Penna's voice, "the meeting—"

"Thank you, my good Lady of the Obvious," Haldra jeered. "We had to cancel until my wretched brother brings it out of hiding."

"What about one of their men?" Penna asked.

"No good. Guilen has this one wrapped up tighter than ever. I gather only three in the whole mayorship know where it is."

"Pity, and that."

They fell silent long enough that it seemed safe to knock. It reverberated all over the dim hallway. A few seconds later, Penna cracked open the door. "Oh. It's Lady Mattian."

"The Mattian girl?" Haldra repeated. She came to the doorway, waving Penna off somewhere, and eyed me with a flat expression. "Well? Explain yourself."

"Lady Haldra," I said in the most deferential tone I could manage, "I've been a sneak... and a thief." I barely kept my voice from trembling. "This morning, I must've misheard your reminder about tonight's banquet and had nothing of my own to wear in the afternoon. Because of that, I stupidly broke into your room and took the most beautiful ball gown I've ever seen. I defaced it, so you wouldn't recognize it, but severely underestimated your... your keen eye. I'm so sorry for all of it."

I held out my peace offering, eyes to the floor. "I hoped bringing this back could be the beginning of repairing the damage I've done to our… friendship."

Haldra took the bundle, puzzled. "That whole speech for this old thing?" she said, carelessly tossing the gown aside. "Did you know Guilen has the right to pardon almost any offense?"

"You mean I should ask him myself?"

"Oh. Except that, I'm afraid even he couldn't deny justice to his own little sister. You strike one of us, you've struck each of us." She sucked air between her teeth in mock frustration. "I suppose he does prefer a proper confession before a de-handing. That's not even to speak about what just happened to my only son. Perhaps, with all the feasting, the crowds missed it. But you're right. I really don't miss a thing."

Before I knew what I was doing, I found myself sobbing at her feet. "Please! I know I haven't fixed it yet, but give me time."

"Don't you see? The gown's had its entrance, a horrible one at that. No sane woman would be caught dead in it now."

"Then let me help you," I sputtered. "Just give me a chance."

"Help me? What could you possibly—" She fell silent.

When I looked up, her lips curled into an almost maternal smile. "Do get up from there, Liza." Haldra actually used my name for once? No insults attached? In fact, she helped me to my feet.

"Do you think I would let a silly misunderstanding like that come between *friends*?" she said.

I shook my head cautiously, having no clue where she could be going.

"Of course not, Liza. See? Here you've brought back what you borrowed without me even needing to ask it of you. That's what friends do, isn't it?"

I nodded slowly.

"What's that now, Liza?"

"Yes," I said. "That's what friends do."

"Exactly. We share things, even precious things. Now you mention it, there's one little thing I hope I might ask of you, as a friend. See?"

What kind of demand had she come up with right on the spot? Repossessing all of our lands, or some bizarre fresh humiliation? Yet what did I have to bargain with? I fought tooth and nail to keep the terror out of my voice as I replied, "What do you want?"

"Oh, I was just hoping you could find that pretty silver stag my brother's hoarding away somewhere. I'd very much like to get a peek before everybody else."

"But I don't know where he put—"

"Don't worry about the nitty gritty details. I only want one little peek before the big reveal. That's not too much for a lady to ask of her friend, is it?"

"No, but—"

"Now this is all between friends so," holding a finger to her lips, she shushed quietly, "friends don't give away a secret, do they?"

"No, Lady Haldra."

"And you would never let me down with such a *simple* little thing as this, would you?"

"I wouldn't."

She clapped excitedly. "Splendid. Then we have an understanding. Good night, Lady Mattian." The door slammed in my face before I could return the pleasantry.

I started back for the Mattian chambers. The favor couldn't be that hard at all, could it? Zieglon caught the stag after all, so he ought to know where the mayor put it. Then it hit me: he also swore himself to secrecy. That was the confounded catch! What if the mayor found out? But no. He had always had his secrets—he needed to. This one little time, I needed to have mine.

Quietly as possible, I opened our chamber door. All the lamps had gone out. I stepped across the threshold, wondering how they could have burned out so quickly.

Someone yanked me inside, slamming the door behind me. A strong hand muffled my yelp. I struggled and kicked, but the attacker wouldn't let me as much as turn to face him before pushing my back to the wall. "Zieglon, you scared me senseless," I said, slapping at that joker. He caught my hand in his and kissed it with a special tenderness that melted worries away. I could never predict that man, but oh, how I loved having him home again.

Chapter Seven

Shran

Saturday morning, I waited alone in a secluded spot in the gardens. The palace gardens extended all the way to the edge of the cliff that Newmund Palace stood upon, overlooking the countryside with the Motland peaks visible in the background. Back at breakfast, Father had promised he'd join me, to help me practice recitations. I was sure he'd also permit me to go back to the forbidden zone, if I had a minute to explain. Instead, some quick-footed little messenger stole him away for more mayor's business right after breakfast. Even when he wasn't off at war, I barely ever got to spend real time with him.

So, there I sat, bored out of my mind as I dangled my feet over the cliffside. I watched a villager, tiny in the distance, pulling a load of something down one of the cart paths. Probably hundreds of those paths wound through the yellow fields, curving around every hillock and thicket as they passed from one boring village to another.

Something started to gnaw at my very insides—a longing after a sort of unknown, untouchable purpose. The time rolled on by, till I concluded Father wasn't coming.

Unable to take any more, I wandered back the way I came, through the hedge maze. Just moving somewhere often helped. Better yet, I closed my eyes, spun around, and headed in an unknown direction. It created the strangest feeling of being truly lost in a familiar place. The hedges curved around a whole side of the palace, hiding many small gardens and gazebos within.

As I went through the maze like that, I grabbed the purrium platelets from my side pouch. One, I threw in the air. The other, I pinched between my fingers and lightly flicked it. The thrown half reoriented mid-air and began to mimic the pinched platelet's every movement.

I came to a certain walnut tree, destroying my sense of disorientation instantly. It had a few ripe walnuts growing well out of my reach. With a toss and a light flick, I'd created a little purrium "nut-knocker" floating a few meters overhead. It only took one well-aimed swipe to send the nuts careening down to my waiting hand. Success. I cracked them on a rock and sampled the harvest in solitude.

A few turns later, I thought, what better time to try out summoning? I threw one half at random, and it landed way out of sight in the hedges. Any normal present would be hard to find again, but not mine. I gave the other half a solid flick. It yanked itself straight out of my hand, singing a distinct high-pitched hum as it shot through the hedges. I heard the two halves clink together, killing the sound immediately.

I jogged around several turns, pawing through brush for several minutes before finally finding them again. They lay separately beneath the hedge. Unlike magnets, all purrium platelets fell apart again as soon as they touched each other.

This time, I tossed one platelet within eyesight and gripped the other after wrapping its leather strap around my palm a few times. I flicked my half, nice and hard. It rang sharply, yanking away, but I held on with the help of the strap. Its sister-half soared through the air. Then it clipped my fingertip.

"Ouch," I yelped, shooting the offended finger into my mouth. That military grade purrium worked a bit *too well*.

Once again, as they clinked together, they silenced and released. It reminded me of my family. We made a big display when we came together again but fell apart just as quickly. Where was the meaning in that?

In the silence, there came the faint sound of a girl singing. Most songs I knew of were either festive, heroic, or academic in nature. The schoolyard stuff I had to learn mostly used melody as a kind of grammar. The lyrics came straight from the school song about seasons and the red moon eclipsing the blue one. Yet this singer's melody was a whole 'nother animal. It mixed deep longing and tragedy with the tiniest glimmer of hope. Then that glimmer grew, weaving itself into every earlier part of the song, transforming the tragedy into a special kind of beauty.

I found myself chasing after it. I had to see this singer before she stopped. The melody rose towards a crescendo—as much as one voice would allow—as I sprinted for the area it seemed to originate from.

I rounded the corner, right into one of the little rose gardens within the maze. The singer stood there in the center of the square, facing the other way. The morning sunlight shimmered across those golden-brown braids that draped between her smooth white shoulders. There was something about the majestic way she stood there that drew me in all the more. I just had to see who this singer was.

She must have heard my footsteps and turned right to me. It was Nella, the girl who'd tried to embarrass me the night before. She finished the song and fell silent, returning a chilling stare. I froze, terrified. When I looked away and back again, she was still staring at me.

She was the same girl as ever, but for the first time, I noticed Nella was more than another one of the ladylings: she was so pretty. Every freckle on her face, everything about her suddenly fascinated me. And I almost wanted to pop out of existence at the thought she could see all of this in my eyes.

A dozen other useless thoughts raced through my head with my pounding pulse. In the end, I blurted, "What were you singing just now?"

"Practicing for Monday," she said with a shrug.

"But," I said, feeling slightly less terrified, "where did you learn to sing it like that?"

"I made that up to make it more interesting."

"Well, it sounded really... nice." I couldn't say the word beautiful out loud.

She nodded.

Then came an idea. "I was also trying to get some practice in for recitals today. Maybe... maybe we both could?"

"Do you have a group?"

"Only me so far."

"You should go get one together, Shran."

What's that? Then she had all but agreed to join. "Yeah. I could do that. Oh, and about yesterday, I just wanted to say that I forgive you."

"For what?"

What did she mean, "for what?" Wasn't she with the ladylings crying "invader" from the gatehouse? Now I couldn't remember for certain. And had she been making fun of me last night on the steps, or what? Or maybe she just felt no guilt for what she and her kin did to me. Instead of asking all that at once, I said something even worse, which I immediately regretted, and then fled around a corner.

If only fleeing far enough could cause that whole scene to never have happened in the first place, to "unhappen" itself. She'd seen me, caught me in a moment of awe and wonder—all at her. I cringed at the thought of her seeing me looking at her, and yet longed to be back there with her still.

My mother's advice the night before had only made things worse, but off I went, searching for anyone willing to join me.

Chapter Eight

Zieglon

Saturday morning, a sharp ray of orange sunlight poked at my eye. I silently thanked the Father for yet another day among the living but wondered why He'd woken me up so abruptly. My bones had become accustomed to sleeping in cots to the point that waking up in my own bed felt disorienting. A moment later, finding my beautiful Liza, serene and asleep in my arms, I knew exactly where I was.

Then, I noticed the odd pattern of sunrays that had woken me up: many narrow vertical bands of sunlight all across our window. Someone had gone and shredded up our curtains! If I was going to get back to sleep, I'd have to drag a wardrobe or something in front of that window. I shifted ever so slightly, and Liza woke up instantly.

"Don't get up now," Liza said. "I'm too cozy."

"In a minute that giant fireball'll be in your little eyes too."

"A minute sounds nice," she giggled.

I resigned to slap a stray throw pillow over my eyes. "Good thing for you I'm no sun-sneezer."

"Thank you," she whispered, and I must have dozed off for a bit after that.

Soon enough, I got up and donned a pair of jodhpurs for the day's ride, and Liza was up, happily humming to herself as she got ready for the day.

"So, you're still into mending things," I said.

"Why would you say that?"

I nodded towards the window.

"Well, Zieglon, it was a new fashion, rapidly going out of style, so…"

"Right," I said. "Not my point. The mayor's got a job that needs doing. I told him you're exactly who we need."

She perked right up at that. "Something with the silver stag?"

I nodded. "I can't say any more until you're sworn in, but yes. Good guess."

"So, will I get to see it before anyone else, then?"

"Yes ma'am. Though, don't get too excited about what it looks like today."

"I'll do it, Zieglon, whatever it is."

"Now understand, this one's very important to the mayor. We can't tell you anything you don't need to know, and you can't tell a soul about this once you're sworn in."

"Oh," she said, looking a bit more surprised than I'd expected.

"Don't worry about it, Liza. I've taken dozens of oaths like this by now. Limited-time things. It'll be over before you know it."

"Okay," she said, stifling a distant look as she did.

"What's the matter?"

"Oh, nothing." She hurriedly started braiding her hair. "It's too bad Shran doesn't get to know. He's almost a man already, and I hate leaving him out of things while you're here."

"Me too," I said. How many of those formative years had I already missed? "I'll make time for him today. That's a promise."

As I stepped inside Guilen's chambers, it appeared he hadn't left them all morning. It was past the tenth bell, and still bags drooped from his eyes as he motioned to a seat across from him. I sank into the odd armchair, a trophy in its own right, framed with polished antlers and upholstered with the same animal's hide.

"Have you told her about the job?" Guilen asked.

"She's happy to do it," I said.

"Good. We'll still have to swear her in on pain of death or banishment."

"Guilen, we're not even telling her all the details."

"It doesn't matter," he said, the bottle still on his breath. "I need this to go off without a peep, you hear me?"

"She's already agreed, Mayor. What's got you so on edge?"

He fell back in his chair. "It's Father. Every year, he marches up here with a cart-full of questions and criticisms. He didn't show up last night, thank All Father, but exactly where is he? No envoy, no messengers. He could be here any day to catch us with our belts untied, or worse."

"Worse?"

"Yes. Don't you see? Up till now, he's always given fair warning before he shows up. Now I suspect he's put away such courtesies. He could have his spies anywhere. We've got to tie this whole thing up fast, and with as precious few confidants as possible. Whenever he does arrive, we've got to have something spectacular to show him."

"Of course," I said.

"Good. We'll swear her in, then get that stag prettied up."

"About that. I only just got home last night. If we're not hunting that giant today, for your sake, I have a promise to keep to my son this morning."

The mayor groaned under his breath. "Very well. Get to it by the twelfth bell then, no later."

After that, I brought Liza up to Guilen's chambers. Thankfully, Guilen wore more mayoral attire now, standing with his brother Thordin and the bard Falen. The five of us circled up, each of us placing our right hand in the center and the left hand on the shoulder of someone else.

The mayor briefed Liza on the barest details of the matter: an "event" had compromised the condition of the silver stag, I would bring her to its secret hiding place in the forbidden zone, and she would mend it to the point of presentability.

Falen led the oath, Liza repeating after him, "I, the Lady Liza Mattian, will uphold the secrecy of this circle. No hint of this task shall I share in body or mind, until permitted by the mayor of Newmund, Guilen Stohvan, first son of the Third Lady Clenhilda Stohvan. On pain of death, I swear it."

Liza shook like a leaf the entire time, more than I expected, as she spoke the routine oath. Down in the stables, I brought it up, as we packed our saddlebags. "You seemed a bit on edge back there."

"I did?" Liza said. "Sorry. I've never done something like this before. I don't want to mess it all up."

"We need you on this. They'll all see it soon enough."

She nodded agreement, though her eyes said otherwise.

"You'll be fine, better than fine. It just takes…" Then I remembered my promise. "I don't have long. We've got to go find Shran."

The two of us headed straight to the palace gardens. We wove our way through the hedge maze, all the way out to the cliffside, finding it empty. The sun was fast approaching its zenith, so the two of us started wandering back through the maze.

I called for him several times. No one answered.

"Where could he be?" I asked, and Liza shrugged.

I did hear the pattering of someone's feet fast approaching through the maze. Not quite a young man's gait.

"Shran?" Liza called when the steps got closer.

Instead, Thordin's daughter Nella rounded a corner and jogged up to us. "I saw him here earlier, but he left in a hurry."

"You don't know where, Nella?" Liza asked.

The young woman shook her head.

"We'll just have to check in the palace," I said.

"Oh, and he left this." The ladyling produced what looked like one of Shran's purrium platelets, dangling from its leather strap.

"How could he lose just one half?" I wondered aloud, as she held out the piece. Surely he knew how to summon the two back together.

"Before he ran off, he said this was for me to remember him by," Nella said.

I must have misheard. "To remember him by?"

She just blushed and held out the platelet more stiffly. Finally, I took the platelet.

"How could you give such a sweet gift back?" Liza demanded.

The ladyling hesitated. "I've got a pretty good memory. And it's purrium, right? One half isn't much good on its own." Then she pranced off for her next escapade, stopping just before rounding a corner. "And tell him I am sorry."

"For what? Breaking his heart?" Liza said.

"No. For throwing the rocks and things. I'm sorry." Then the ladyling scurried off out of sight.

"We've just *got to* find him Zieglon," Liza said.

"And we don't have long." I let the purrium platelet hang free from its leather strap. "If Shran gave this to her, then he'll have the other half on him. So..." I flicked the platelet hard enough to activate a summons. It purred at a relatively low volume without pulling in any particular direction.

"What are you doing with that thing?" Liza asked.

"Trying to get a bearing on him without yanking a hole in his pocket." I flicked the platelet a bit harder.

"Why isn't it doing anything, Zieglon?"

"Must still be too far away."

"Doesn't it work the same from any distance?"

"Linking does. A summons weakens with distance."

"Then why not just link?"

"Good thought. But that wouldn't tell us where to go and could get him hurt if he's not expecting it. The first rule of military-grade purrium: don't link before you think."

"Oh," she said.

"Now where was I?" I clanked the platelet with my new hunting knife.

It still hung there, limp as a fish as Liza protested, "That's hurting my ears!"

We searched around our family chambers, the mayor's court, and way over in the schoolyard, finding no sign of the young man.

As we crossed the main courtyard, I simply couldn't give up yet. I grabbed my knife and took one last swing at the platelet. Liza and some passersby clapped hands over their ears at the shrill ring.

Watching as it remained completely limp, I silenced the platelet. I sighed, upset I hadn't gone ahead and made some noise earlier. "At that volume, the entire palace ought to be in range."

"So, where's Shran?" Liza said.

"What was he trying to tell us about last night?"

"The Great Tower," Liza said, then covered her mouth and checked her corners for who might've overheard.

Not a moment later, the twelfth bell began to ring from the high tower.

"Then we may just have time," I said.

Chapter Nine

Shran

In the palace courtyard, I caught sight of Jaldane with some other young nobles. Amer pointed me out, looking rather surprised. Jaldane turned on me, revealing a black eye swollen to the size of an orange. "Looks like your papa's not here to help you today, Shranny."

"About that, Jaldane. I'm sorry for what I said, and—"

"Too late for apologies now, boy." He tapped a finger to his black eye.

"What? I didn't do that."

"Ah, but you see, that hack you call a father thinks he can strike a man of nobility"–and I could only assume Jaldane was referring to himself. "It comes down to me to teach him differently."

He took a swing at me. I ducked, feeling the wind of his massive arm passing over my face. Before I knew what happened, he jabbed, sending me tumbling backward, seeing nothing but stars.

I shook my spinning head, fighting to move again. The blurred figure of Jaldane marched closer and closer, and I was still sprawled out on the ground. "Come on," I told myself. "Get up!"

I ran for my life, the angry lordling chasing me, as Amer and others laughed at the spectacle. My legs carried me, even as my cheek throbbed and my head spun. Jaldane huffed and he puffed and he wore himself out. The other lordling only jeered at his failed hunt as I kept running right straight out the palace gate. Maybe I wasn't the biggest or strongest or good at making friends, but at least I could run.

Mother had definitely said not to go back to the Tower, but I had only gotten into this mess from following her advice, twice.

I had just climbed up the crevasse near the Great Tower when I spied a familiar figure.

"You're back," Steve declared, shaking my hand vigorously.

"Yes sir."

Steve gave a strong handshake, then furrowed his brow. "You alright, son?"

I pushed for my most masculine tone. "I'm fine."

He pursed his lips, eyeing my probably swollen cheek, but let it slide. "And when can I expect your mother here?"

"I'm sorry, sir. She said she can't be anywhere near the Great Tower."

"That's unfortunate, but I suspect she'll change her mind soon enough. But, Shran my boy, what brought you here today?"

"Well, I was hoping to get away from the palace for a while."

"In that case, it's time you come see inside."

The sheer size of the Great Tower always made it look closer than it was. Our approach took minutes when it seemed a mere stone-toss away. The northern base of the Tower already rose beyond what I could see without hurting my neck. The borders of this sunless side of the foundation gradually encompassed more and more of my field of view, blocking out the surrounding landscape. The closer we got, the more it felt like we had walked into a little pocket of night.

The shadow stretched so far in all directions that it became hard to see my own feet. That tough, dry ground that grew cooler and cooler, as if a chill radiated from the sunless walls. Then came a sharp echo, each step bouncing back at us till we arrived.

At the very darkest, chilliest point, we stood before the outer wall, with no sign of an entrance. I looked to Steve, a figure dimly visible in the pocket of night, more excited than ever to see what he'd do. Steve took a knee. He remained silent for a surprisingly long time, then with a voice that trembled, spoke the words, "I'm sorry."

A hidden door slid open.

Soon as our feet crossed the threshold, the door slid down again behind us. After our trek through the shadow, the light pricked my eyeballs, making me squint. A hall stretched out before us, taller than it was wide. I also wondered at the lack of a doorman, and any mechanism for the guillotine doors was hidden behind the wall.

"Who mans these doors?" I asked Steve.

"No one."

"Does it use purrium or something then?" I asked, scanning his hands for metal pendants.

"Or something," he said, already several paces ahead.

I jogged up after him. "So, how does it move without anyone touching it?"

"Man forgot many things since the Storm. Many of them were worth forgetting."

"So, they built it before the Storm?"

"Not that I know of."

Regularly spaced sconces bathed the hallway in a cozy amber light. Despite the silvery outer wall, inside, the Towar had carved wood paneling and fine carpets. Beautiful art pieces like I'd never seen before lined the wood panels. Unlike regular art, all of these were squished flat, not carved or sculpted. Instead, the mixture of many different pigments gave the illusion of depth and detail. Landscapes, animals, and people were all represented, but the chief subject of the art was the human face. They lacked the grandeur of Otharkian sculptures, but impressed me, nonetheless.

"Who are all those people?" I asked.

"Old friends and family."

"Are they in here?"

"I'm afraid not. Most of them are dead now."

"Oh."

"Come on now, plenty of time to worry about them later."

At the end of the hall, another guillotine door slid open at our presence, revealing what looked like a well-tended forest. Stone walkways wound to-and-fro between art pieces and small wooden buildings. Some of the plants looked like art in their own right, with even large branches curved or woven into impossible forms.

Birds chirped above us, and only when I looked up to see them did I remember we were still indoors. There, some ways above the treetops, was the ceiling.

Steve coned his hands and called out, "Bill."

"A bill for what?" I asked, genuinely confused. But before he could answer, a large chestnut stag galloped right up to him. The animal happily received a pat between his antlers.

"Sorry. That's this fine stag's name," Steve said, "but to answer your question, he's for riding, if you'd like."

"You think he can hold me?"

"Only one way to find out." He held Bill still as I climbed on. Before I'd even settled myself, Steve smacked the stag into action, commanding him to take me to "the elevator," whatever that was.

The abrupt start whipped my head back. I grasped wildly for the swaying rack of antlers, my legs flailing behind me. Even so, I didn't dare bail out, for fear of slamming headfirst into a passing tree.

The mad buck galloped on through the forest about as recklessly as possible. Bill rocked back and forth every pace, slamming me with his back end each time. It took all the strength my arms could manage to inch forward and cling round his neck.

At long last, Bill halted next to a pair of doors. I shakily dismounted, aching all over. The doors led inside a large pillar, a couple of meters in diameter. As I started wondering why in Tew I'd been dropped off here, Steve arrived on a buck of his own.

"You're a natural," he said, hopping off. "It took me weeks to figure out how not to fall off one of these critters."

"Thanks," I said, pretending not to notice my aches and bruises, and praying I'd never have to touch such a thing again. "So, what is this place? A giant stage for game hunts?"

"It's a bit more than that. For instance, you might've noticed, it's a bit on the tall side. That's extremely important."

I chuckled at that. "And how tall is it, Steve? Or does it go up forever?"

"No no no. Only about a hundred kilometers," he said, pressing a small circle next to the door. They chimed and slid open. "But why not see for yourself?"

Wondering whether I'd ever traveled that far from home my entire life, I answered, "Yes sir."

We stepped into the empty room in the pillar with nothing but another patch of those little circles on one wall. I had expected a staircase or ladder or something and looked to Steve in confusion. He chuckled and tapped one of the circles. The doors closed again, and the whole room shot straight up, like a dumbwaiter on hard alcohol. I would've collapsed but for the handrailings.

The elevator had a couple windows, which I peered through in amazement. We quickly surpassed the first ceiling, emerging into a completely new garden with completely different plants and structures. Faster and faster we climbed, passing too many indoor vistas to count. It would have taken an army decades to carefully cultivate all of it, and this was only one of the four foundations.

"Who planted all this?" I asked.

"Too many long-dead men and women to name, but I helped with a lot of it."

The thought of spending every day tending plants wasn't exactly what I'd had in mind when I fled to the Great Tower. "So, is that why you brought me here? High-level gardening?"

"No. I've got a much more important job for you."

Finally, we reached the top of the Tower's foundation. I released the breath I didn't realize I'd been holding. Steve led the way through to a metallic hall. I stopped dead, eyes glued to the windows. We'd reached a truly breathtaking height. You can't even describe how much higher heights appear when you're looking down from them. There I gazed at all Newmund spread out below us, far richer than any diorama could depict, though a tad flatter than expected.

"Come on son," Steve said. "We've got a long way left to go."

Chapter Ten

Liza

"Beautiful, isn't it?" Haldra remarked.

Just after breakfast, on Saturday morning, she had practically dragged me off to the gallery, where we now stood, in front of the World Eater. This limbless obsidian sculpture twisted and tangled around itself, barely recognizable as one distinct creature except for the snarling reptilian head. The whole thing was a work of pure fantasy: a thousand children's nightmares chiseled into one block of stone.

"It's really something," I finally said, definitely making that nervous grin I hated seeing in the mirror.

She burst out laughing, gripping my arm as a mock support. "I'm kidding, silly. It's terrifying."

"Oh. That's more what I was thinking." I could certainly try wriggling free and escape but where could I hide? No. I would persevere long enough to guarantee Haldra's protection. All said and done, I might even gain some respect from the palace Ladyship if I stuck this out.

"Lady Liza, do you know any of the songs for the World Eater?"

"Only children's ones. I never had a classical education."

"No matter. You wouldn't learn them there anyway. I was just going to ask if you slept well last night."

"Very well, thanks. And yourself?"

"To be honest, I turned and tossed," she said, "worrying whether someone could truly keep a very small but very precious promise. Forgive me, but I had to know a woman's word won't be broken."

"Well, I'm halfway to keeping it already, and then maybe tomorrow morning—"

"Mmm, I'd very much like to see it sooner."

"But Lady Haldra—"

Her overlong nails dug into my bicep. "Tonight, I think," she said cheerfully.

"That hurts," I said, flatly as I could manage.

She smiled and slowly released her grip. "Tonight," she repeated, and I felt myself nod along.

Zieglon and I galloped onward for the Great Tower. Shran had certainly run straight there, based on everything he'd said the night before. I should've paid more attention when he pleaded for someone to listen. I knew how it felt to be rejected and should have been there for him before he got himself into real trouble. By All Father, I'd find a way to help him now.

I spurred Nippy, my poor horse, forward so fervently she just managed to keep up with Zieglon on his steed. Near the Tower's northern foundation, we tried the purrium platelet again. It still hung limp as a sheet. Zieglon suggested splitting up, to search the whole circumference in half the time. He rode one way around the base while I went the other.

Soon as we'd ridden some distance apart, I saw a man like Shran described. He looked about forty, with hair like bleached linen, and piercing hazel eyes that... *knew*. I reined Nippy to a stop right in front of him.

"Excuse me, sir. I've lost my son. Shran is his name. Have you seen anyone by any chance?"

"That I have," the man said, "and in fact I was just looking for you."

I cheered and called after Zieglon, loud as I could. He seemed to be out of earshot. I knew he'd circle the foundation soon enough.

"So, where is he, sir? I don't mean to rush, but we're in a bit of a hurry."

"Shran's in the Tower. I can take you to him right now," he said, ushering me towards it.

"Thank the Father," I said, trotting right behind him, "and are you this 'Steve' he told me about?"

"Yes ma'am."

"That's such a strange name, though."

"I'm a touch strange myself these days. You can call me Steven, if you must."

I'd never heard of that name either, but at least "Steven" had the ring of a man's name to it. "Well, do you realize we're about to run straight into a giant wall?"

He laughed as he took a knee and apologized.

"It's alright, Steven or 'Steve' or whichever." As I spoke, a tall door slid open for us—slid so rapidly it scared Nippy. What manner of man was this, that the Great Tower opened for him? "How did you do that, Steve?"

"I'm not entirely sure I did anything. You're in a bit of a rush, aren't you?"

81

"Well, yes. I've got to get Shran as fast as possible."

"He's way up in the Tower. Better follow me, before this door closes again," Steve said, sprinting inside.

I looked off in the direction Zieglon had disappeared, then looked the other way, wondering which could get me to him faster. By the time I caught up with Zieglon and returned, surely that mysterious door would be shut tight, our only child sealed within.

Steve had already gone some distance up the hallway, and in one moment I made the decision that would change my life forever.

I kicked Nippy on after him, and the door sealed behind us immediately. We'll be out again before Zieglon even circles the foundation, I told myself. Yet it took even longer than I'd thought to get to Shran.

We rode an "elevator"—a large dumbwaiter that climbed so high and so quickly it could make a hawk sick—until we reached the top of the foundation. By that point, I was properly concerned about Zieglon getting worried down below. It was too late to turn back, and after all, his tracking skills would lead him right to the hidden entrance, would they not? Steve led me up through one of four spokes, beneath which was a whole lot of nothing between us and the ground. Then we boarded another elevator.

It had cushioned chairs whose backs were oddly sunk into the floor, one of which Steve climbed into. I wasn't keen at all to lie on the floor in a small room next to some self-proclaimed strange man, but felt more at ease after he securely strapped himself in. He kicked that elevator into action. It shot up the central spire like a crossbow bolt and didn't let up for a second.

Steve and I emerged from the final elevator at the very top of that topless spire. This uppermost portion was circular, the starry array visible all around us through giant panes of glass. The view stole my breath in the most peaceful way. Through those panes, I spied what must've been all of Othark and the Great Sea stretched out to the south. We were truly on top of the world.

I gasped, for the first time, considering the night sky full of twinkling stars. "Steve, how is it night already?"

"No no no. We're above Tew's atmosphere. See that?" Steve pointed out the sun, shining high above us. "It's still mid-afternoon."

I sighed with relief. "So, where is Shran?"

"He must be around here somewhere. A born explorer, that young man."

"Shran," I called.

"Over here," he answered.

The place had multiple catwalks at several different levels, blocking some of the areas from view. I followed his voice down a short flight of stairs, coming to a floor with several dozen clear glass pits, almost like extra-large baths. There sat Shran, in the middle of one of the "baths," transfixed as he stared at the view below.

"There you are," I said, hugging him tightly. "Are you alright?"

"Yeah," Shran said. "Thanks for coming, Mother. Steve said you would."

"I had to come find you after what happened with Nella."

He went red. "What do you mean?"

"She told us about it. And did you know she wanted to say she's sorry."

He sighed, discontented. "I don't know what I was thinking. She's just like the rest of them."

"What if, maybe she didn't mean to be? Maybe she wants to do the right thing. If you love her..."

"I never said that."

Why had I gone and thrown a word like "love" around? And by all accounts, I ought to have been dragging Shran by the wrist back to Zieglon, who must have been worried sick down below. That place atop the Great Tower had a certain unfathomable weight to it, making me feel as light as a lily in a brook. The urge to get on with all those schemes below had drifted to the least important part of my mind. Something in the air itself—not the part I breathed—made me want to stay, to know more.

After a while of silence, I spoke again. "Everything looks so beautiful from here."

"Up here," Shran said, "it sort of feels special, like no one can hurt me."

It filled me with joy to hear him open up like that at last. "I know," I said, truly humbled. "You were right about this place, right about Steve. Sorry, I didn't listen to you."

He smiled at that.

"So, now I'm here, why is it so important that I came too?"

Steve walked over to us. "Yes, sorry to be so vague. You two will be granted very special gifts."

"What are we getting?" Shran asked excitedly.

"It's not going to be easy at first," Steve said, "but I can teach you along the way."

"Steve, what are you talking about?" I asked.

He beckoned us after him. "Right this way, Liza. See for yourself," Steve said.

I followed him onto a round balcony completely surrounded by glass. There, I quickly walked to the railing, taking in the fullness of the surface so far below. "I love the views up here."

Steve grunted agreement, still back by the door. I turned to see him slam it shut, blocking Shran from entering the balcony with us. Shran looked very confused too.

"Hang on to something," Steve said, motioning to the iron railing.

"But Steve, why would I need to..."

He threw a lever and clung to the nearest railing himself. The entire glass barrier separated at the far side of the balcony, sliding wide open to the black space beyond. Winds raged with the escaping air, and I slammed into the railing, nearly plunging off the side.

I gripped the cold railing white-knuckle tight as the pressure dropped and dropped. My ears popped painfully, as if they would burst. I heard nothing at all. My eyes nearly popped out of their sockets, and I couldn't breathe even a little. Gasping only shrank my lungs further.

I looked to Steve in desperation, tapping a hand to my throat, unable to make any sound. He had pain in his eyes, yet no sign of physical harm as he walked over.

No. By All Father, please no. Everything had gone according to Steve's plan. He meant to hurt me, then do who knows what to Shran. Coming here was my mistake but wouldn't be my last one. I rushed for the lever Steve had thrown. Standing only made me more lightheaded.

Steve grabbed me before I'd taken two steps. No! I kicked and tried to scream. No sound came out, and he held me quite firmly. At that, the last of my strength evaporated. It was all I could do merely to hold onto consciousness.

When the last draft of air left us, something very hot struck my hand, followed by more and more all over. Each one seemed to originate from a different star, uncountable sparkling particles shooting through the emptiness, bathing everything in an otherworldly light. Each one sparked as it touched me, each like an exhilarating and terrible heartbeat. It was the same feeling that made me wish to stay earlier but now amplified beyond what any heart could bear.

I looked for Shran, seeing without hearing as he pulled and heaved at the door. He couldn't open it, couldn't save me. Cold steam rushed from my eyes, obscuring everything in a flickering haze.

The sparks burst into something like flames, both on me and on Steve. My skin flaked like glass, and the light kept pushing deeper, beyond my flesh.

I felt utterly naked, wholly exposed within that raging starlight river. It kept peeling, peeling apart my very soul, wordlessly declaring back to me all I'd ever done or thought or intended. The intentions above all, ruined me. All had been deeply examined, thoroughly known.

I knew death hovered somewhere nearby, ready to snatch me for itself. I only prayed that light would break me apart before I was swallowed alive.

Then all was darkness.

Chapter Eleven

Shran

I tugged and tugged at the door's wheel-like handle. The pressure held it so tightly it simply wouldn't budge. I watched helplessly as Steve threw up the lever again. The glass bubble resealed itself around the trap balcony, cutting off the otherworldly light as a hiss reverberated through the window. Steve gradually started to breathe again, but Mother lay unresponsive. Her hair had turned so white it almost glowed, and her skin was hideously crackled and glassy. What in Tew had he done to my mother?

Steve knelt beside her and blew in her mouth a few times until her bosom rose. She sprang to life, and in a few moments, her skin healed as good as new. Steve held out a hand. She frantically crawled back to the wall and slid quivering hands over her face.

That almost glowing white hair didn't change back. Somehow, I knew, whatever Steve was, she was like him now.

When I pulled at the door one more time, it hissed and then burst open. I ran straight to Mother, amazed she had survived without a scratch.

Pure horror filled her eyes. Before I could say anything, she grabbed my collar, and looked stunned when she did it. "Shran—" Something caught in her throat. She coughed like I had never seen her do. Suddenly, out from her mouth came some otherworldly object, a translucent orb, amber in color and weightless as air.

The orb had a dim, opaque core, surrounded by a substance that rippled outwards in a sphere. The outer sphere got fainter and fainter the farther it was from the center, making the orb appear to float at about waist-height.

Was this her soul? Was it her memories? Or was it some mysterious new creation? Whatever it was, I knew it was very special, that it had to be saved like a special part of me or part of us. I didn't know. No one could have described what the orb felt like as my fingers pushed into its clear outer sphere. It seemed to buzz ever so slightly—not with sound—and the amber-colored mid-layer almost felt like warm water, rippling without wetness.

Steve answered a question I was not ready to ask. "It's a monad, well, a demi-monad. When an Eldenvolk is born—"

"Shran, hurry," Mother said as if waking from a nightmare. "We need to get back to Zieglon."

That gave me a start as well. What did I have down there to return to and why so soon? I had to figure out... to understand. What was the meaning of it all?

Steve answered. "But Liza, my lady, I haven't even begun to teach you two about vibrance or monadology—"

Mother had already gotten to her feet. "Now," she said only to me, "Steve got us up here. He can get us back out."

Steve sighed resignedly. "As you wish."

Didn't she understand? We were supposed to get special gifts. How could we leave without knowing? The look on her face and tears flowing down her cheeks told me I had no chance to protest. None of it made any sense. She'd gone through all that for me, and now what?

Mother ushered me out the door, and I knew under no circumstances could I leave the "monad" behind. Was that my gift? It shrank even as I grabbed it, keeping its shape and feeling more solid the smaller it was. I threw it into my side pouch, buckled it tight, and dejectedly went with her to the elevator.

What is a demi-monad for, I wanted to ask, but couldn't make myself speak a word. Everything had gone all wrong. What kind of man would put my mother through blazing starlight without any warning? Who knew what to believe?

The three of us strapped into the elevator, tears drizzling down Mother's face and mine. It made sense to cry after pain and terror from being hurt by something. What I felt made no sense. I only had a sinking feeling, growing emptiness. I feared all of it had amounted to nothing, to no real change in the world below. It had been false hope all along.

Steve prepared to press the circle that would send us back to Tew. "All you have to do is touch it," he said, winking at me as he began counting down from five.

What could that mean? I'd seen him operate elevators already. I could only assume he was trying to tell me something about the demi-monad. Yet I'd already touched that, had I not?

On "one," Steve hit the circle. We dropped and dropped, faster and faster.

After another elevator and a stark walk through the inside-outside area, we reached the same entrance hall. The door shut as soon as we set foot on the soil of the forbidden zone. Right there before us stood Father, flanked by a pair of men wearing stern expressions: Lord Thordin and Mayor Guilen Stohvan himself.

Section Two

Into Shadow

Chapter Twelve

Liza

I felt nothing at all like normal. All had gone black as the grave until air filled my lungs once more. Before I even opened my eyes, I sensed a person touching me, his face right above mine, someone full of a vibrant living power. Somehow, I sensed that living power as clear as day. And immediately, I sensed it was Steve—sensed it through that living power more vividly than by hearing or seeing him.

I got as far away as I could manage in that small balcony, and then the tears came. What had happened to me? Pain! Pain everywhere came to the front of my mind, as did another bizarre realization. I sensed more of that vibrant power invisibly clinging onto me from somewhere outside, most of it focused towards my scalp. I recognized the sensation as it brushed against me: starlight. So much of it clung to me, I felt almost full to bursting.

By a sort of new instinct, I imbibed the starlight until the sensation of holding too much subsided. My arms and legs, and everywhere sucked it in. They all surged with activity, each member repairing whatever was damaged, and then I felt as healthy as a hatchling.

When Shran came to rescue me, I had to warn him to get away before Steve hurt him too. No sooner had I touched him than I sensed more of that living power in him, much like Steve. The sensation felt so strange. It was similar to a taste, though not on my tongue and similar to a rhythmic melody, though not a sound. Shran's very being seemed to pulsate with a certain identifying essence, as clearly distinguishable as his own face. And lots of the stuff filled him.

All of it was too bizarre, too much to think about. I had to get back to Zieglon. He would make it alright again.

When we arrived back in the indoor forest, I untied Nippy where I'd left her and found she had a unique, distinctly animal variety of that vibrant living power. By merely touching her, I perceived her whole form from head to hooves. Was this power I sensed the "vibrance" Steve mentioned? I could make up a word as good as him, like... Well perhaps it was an okay name.

Each plant that brushed my shoe I sensed completely, from the leaves on every shoot to the ends of each root. They had a noticeably floral rhythm and flavor to them. Of course I didn't want to say a word about it—to let on to Steve that he'd changed something about me. It would surely all wear off once we left that strange tower. Yes, I was still quite myself, with important things to tend to.

I led Nippy by the reins as Steve showed the way back through the indoor forest. As we went, a bit of the sparsely trimmed foliage caught one of my braids. At first it seemed like a trick of the light, but once I got the braid free and examined it up close, it really had turned as white as Steve's.

I quickly threw on my riding cloak and hood.

The mayor and his brother stared in disapproval as Zieglon pulled me and Shran into a tight embrace. I kept my hood fastened tight, concealing the bizarre look of my hair. None of the weirdness had worn off yet, and I dared not tell him until it did.

"Alright, you've had your reunion," the mayor said. "Thordin, would you escort Lady Mattian, and I'll deal with the rest."

"As you wish, brother," Thordin said.

"What?" I gasped. "I don't want to go with him. I came here with Zieglon."

"Yes, and look where that got you," the mayor said. "Got you into the very heart of the forbidden zone. Fraternizing with this tower dweller." He eyed the white-haired Steve darkly. "Consider this your last pardon."

"Liza, it'll be alright," Zieglon said. "I need to spend some time with Shran anyway. Then I'll come help when he's home safe."

"Now hurry up, my lady," Thordin said, taking Nippy's reins as I mounted.

Zieglon stepped up to him. "And if she so much stubs a toe before I get back, I know exactly who to blame."

Thordin groaned. "Because baby-watching this one isn't punishment enough." And he gave me the most dismissive look I'd ever seen. I glared back as menacingly as I could muster.

Thordin rode down into the crevasses, with me following close behind. We took several odd turns before arriving at the mouth of a cave. I grabbed my saddlebag, and Thordin led the way through the cave by lantern.

We reached a nice, cool chamber where I caught the faint scent of decaying flesh. Thordin worked his way around the room, lighting some spare oil lamps. They illuminated a hack job, a dead creature with parts torn to shreds and peppered with strange wounds.

I was still staring in shock when Thordin broke the silence. "Hop to it, Lady Mattian."

"You mean, *that's* the silver stag?" I sputtered. "What happened? How do you expect me to fix that thing?"

Thordin walked up next to me, baring his teeth in a grin I wished I could smack clean off his face. "I figured it out. Your husband, he idolizes you. He has this crazy idea you can do whatever he can't. Sad, I know."

"How could anyone fix that mess? I didn't bring supplies for something like this."

He tossed me a pair of oversized leather gloves and a tanner's apron, then headed for the exit. "Just don't hurt yourself."

"Thordin, you can't leave me here. I need help."

"Do I look like a seamstress to you?"

"I need," surely there was something someone else he could do, "stuffing."

Thordin's laugh echoed across the cave. "The manikin is over there," he said, gesturing to a deer-shaped wire frame in the corner. "You're welcome."

"Oh," was all I could think to say.

Then he left, chuckling.

"Thordin, don't you care if this gets mended?"

"My bards saw me catch the thing while he was still pretty. And it appears that's the only story we'll ever get."

"But the mayor needs this, and Zieglon promised him—"

"I'm not convinced that's my problem."

He left me all alone in that dim cave with nothing but my bag of mending supplies to help me. Gripped with dread, I approached the tattered carcass. Only its crystal antlers retained a hint of beauty now.

Then I noticed the stab wounds were bite marks, gigantic human-like bite marks. So, that was the mayor's big secret. Giants exist now, and they destroy the most beautiful creatures in Othark. That's two foul omens in one.

I hung up my riding cloak, donning the gloves and apron instead. Grabbing a meaty flap of skin, I almost jumped in fright. By my new sense that still hadn't worn off, the flesh still seemed to sizzle and sing with life. It was a kind of animal life quite different than what I'd sensed in Nippy. It was all localized, only vaguely unified. I could sense the nearby tissue wherever I touched but not the body as a whole.

I spent some time pinning everything in its place, and it still looked a mess. Working with hide proved very difficult due to the lack of excess material and soon-to-turn meat clinging onto it.

On the one hand, I needed to sew everything back together, and on the other, I had to strip it all off and mount it on that manikin. If I stitched the torn bits into place first, I could hardly scrape them free for mounting. And scraping them free first would make it that much harder to piece back together correctly.

The most important part would be the head, so I moved there. Uncertain where to begin, I sliced down the back of the skull to the nape of its neck, then around its chin. I tried pulling it off like a sock from a foot, but plenty of fascia kept it glued down tight. After a lot of scraping, I got up to the eyes and had no idea how to cut around them without making it look freakish. And looking at the fleshy nose and lips, I was at a complete loss how to deal with them.

As I compared eye sockets from one to the other, it occurred to me the manikin had no antlers at all, just a flat section sliced out at the back of the skull. I knew regular deer shed antlers every year, so I tried my hand at pulling the crystal antlers free. Light wiggling did nothing. I ended up pressing my foot on the skull and yanking with all my might. Part of the skull cracked.

I leapt—almost fell—back. "You're impossible," I told the dead animal. "Even a real taxidermist couldn't fix you." The whole thing only looked worse for my effort.

Sulking on the dirt floor, I racked my brain for answers. What could possibly fix the mess I was in? And where was Zieglon when I needed him? Nix on mounting. If I could only keep the mayor's secret another way. The bite marks and the worst of the tear damage needed fixing. Yes. Let them worry about prettying the thing up later.

That all sounded good in my head. Actually doing it fared little better than my first attempts. No matter how I went about stitching up the gigantic gashes left by human-like teeth, the creature simply didn't have enough material there. Everything kept bunching up and looking horrible. There was simply nothing I could do.

I prayed desperately, "All Father, help me. I don't know what to do. I can't do this," and let the prayer rise as I knelt there in the dim lamplight.

As I waited, a thought came to me, how I'd apparently been brought up from the grave itself mere hours earlier—and *that* after being promised a special gift. So, what exactly was this gift? I'd already healed myself before by pure instinct. If I could sense others with this gift, could I heal them too?

I removed some stitches from one of the silver stag's smaller cuts and carefully focused on the life power or vibrance or whatever with one hand. Plenty of that starlight still invisibly clung to me, so I simply released some of it through my gloved finger into the area of the cut. The skin and muscle set to work, healing themselves back together in seconds.

I squealed with delight. Who on Tew had ever gotten such a gift? I moved on to one of the bite marks, fed it a little more starlight, and again it healed the missing bits. The flesh seemed to know how it was supposed to grow back, each wound merely needing a nudge in the right direction.

Within a matter of minutes, it looked like a silver stag ought to. It was still dead, of course, but as far as animal corpses go, it became beautiful.

Chapter Thirteen

Zieglon

At last, I gained the opportunity to spend some time with my fast-growing son. Though as Thordin and Liza rode off into the distance, Mayor Guilen continued to cast a less than hospitable mood over everything.

"By all counts, I ought to have all of your feet chopped off for straying out here," Guilen said. "I cannot keep making exceptions for you, Zieglon. That's not even to mention the rumor you struck my nephew."

"My apologies for the delay, Mayor. However, I had to find Shran."

Guilen grunted angrily. "Then help me get his kidnapper to the palace," gesturing to the white-haired man who called himself "Steve."

"Kidnapper?" I said in surprise. "He brought Shran *to* us, did he not?"

Shran shook his head in silence. It was not like him.

"We'll sort it all out at the palace," Guilen said, grabbing cord from his saddlebag. "Come here man," he ordered Steve. "Hands together now."

Steve had every appearance of a respectable elder, though his years were hard to place. Treating him like a runaway pack mule simply wasn't right. "Guilen," I said, "he doesn't deserve this."

"It's a precaution," Guilen said. "I'll even let you be the first to put him to the question at the palace."

"It's fine," Steve said with a sigh, allowing Guilen to bind his wrists. Guilen took the lead on his mount, Steve leashed behind him. Shran rode with me, still in stark silence.

"Keep your eyes and ears on him, Zieglon," Guilen said, kicking his horse to a trot.

Steve kept up at a pace just brisk enough to slacken the leash. "Though he's right," Steve said. "You really don't need these."

Guilen laughed. "You managed to break into that rock-dashed tower. I've had men batter that eyesore with everything you could imagine, yet none of it seemed to make a dent."

"Did you ever try knocking?" Steve said.

"Don't be coy with your mayor," Guilen said. "Answer me. How did you break in there?"

"The truth is, the Tower chooses who enters."

"Poppycock," Guilen chuckled. "And how exactly does it go about the selection process?"

"It chooses."

It astounded me to think the Great Tower had chosen my own son and wife from everyone else on Tew. They must have done something right. The mayor didn't share that disposition at all, unfortunately.

"Fear not Steve, we'll get the truth out of you eventually."

"Certainly," Steve said, "and do you treat all visitors to your mayorship this way?"

"Visitor? I wager you've been in there all along."

"Ah. The Tower is under no man's command." Steve said, matter-of-factly.

Guilen yanked at Steve's leash, nearly sending the man face-first into the dirt. "In that case, you best hope it's prepared you a handsome ransom."

"Indeed," Steve said.

Soon enough, we left the forbidden zone and the chill of the Great Tower's shadow. Guilen steered us on an out-of-the-way route back, so that we passed through some of the villages as we went. Each one had its own unique clustering of thatched roof houses and shops, usually kept a tasteful distance from the animal pens.

Near the center of one village, aromas of thyme, sage, and rosemary wafted through the air. Some of the women looked up from spice patches and whispered to one another. Guilen remained quiet as the rumors spread.

A group of playing children parted ways, allowing us to pass through. A young girl ran right up to Steve, pointing excitedly. "His hair's white as a cloud," she said, and Steve smiled with amusement.

"I wouldn't do that if I were you, little girl," Guilen warned, then turned to look straight at her. "This is a dangerous man, captured from the Great Tower."

The girl retreated like she'd just seen a spider. Whispers of the Great Tower floated in the air.

Outside the village, I hung back a bit so Shran and I could speak privately. "I for one am impressed you managed to get inside the Great Tower," I said.

"Yeah," Shran said. A tad terse of a response, though perhaps he still worried about his vow of secrecy.

"Right. I officially announce your oath of secrecy complete. I've just got to know, what was it like in there?"

Shran proceeded to tell a series of incredible things I barely would've believed a day prior, but he grew increasingly troubled as

103

he went on. He described everything he'd seen on the lower levels of the Tower, all the way up to the big room at the top. Then he trailed off.

"And is that where your mother found you?"

"Uh-huh," he said, cautiously.

"And why was she covering her head in her hood like that?"

"The starlight's way stronger up there."

"Starlight? What does that have to do with it?"

"Nothing. It wasn't my fault."

"Son, I'm not angry, just interested in what you've been up to."

"Why now?"

"We may not have a better chance for a while."

"But I can't go back to the palace. Jaldane's worse than ever lately."

"Well, I took care of him last night, didn't I?"

"I think that just made him worse."

We had just topped a mound, bringing into view all of Newmund city, the palace overlooking the many tall shops and houses from atop its hill.

"I'm sorry Shran. But one way or another, we've got to get back now. Come on, tell me more about this man, Steve. Seems like a fair chap to me, whatever Guilen says."

"He seemed very good and wise. Then when Mother got there, he..."

"Well?"

"He hurt her, really bad."

I reined my horse to a halt and took a breath. "What happened? What was she hiding earlier?"

"I can't. I can't go back," he said.

"Shran—" It seemed like Shran got yanked right off the horse in one swish of wind. "Son?" I called out, but he was nowhere to be seen. Only a strange floating orb remained.

Chapter Fourteen

Shran

At that moment, I knew only one thing in the world: I had to get out of there. No way I'd let Father take me back to that place. I couldn't trust anyone anymore.

Escape. Escape! I needed to escape.

My hand had shot into my side pouch. I anxiously squeezed the mysterious orb, at which point it seemed to pop open. With that pop, it yanked violently, everything rushing up around me in an instant.

Dizzied, I found myself standing on a beach, with ripples lapping at my feet. The dim sun beat down on me—except there *was no sun*. Instead, I saw a hazy red dome overhead, full of stars. But these lights in the sky couldn't have been stars. Each one of these odd skylights was shooting a tiny beam of light directly onto me. Even with the place generally dim, my own body and everything I looked at stood out, clear as a deer in a green meadow. I wished they would let up a bit, leaving me so exposed like that.

I had just strapped my side pouch shut again when a guttural chirping from an approaching breaker made me jump. I saw nobody there, but when I sidestepped the wave, it followed. I jogged for dry land, and then the chirp became more like a maniacal laugh. Water ramped up at my feet until I could barely trudge forward at all. The wave arched right over my head and powerfully crashed. I spun through its watery vortex and smacked onto the sand, sputtering, as salty water burned my sinuses.

Even as the water receded, I heard more sounds, like laughing, from within other breakers. I noticed each one had a bright spot inside. The source of the chirping? Then two merged into one, doubling their height.

I scrambled to my feet, running for my life, which only seemed to excite them more. Before I'd gotten three paces, the water level reached knee-height, sucking me in once more. The wave arched over me, then crashed. I got another mouthful of brine before face-planting.

Then came a torrent of breakers in a frenzy, crashing down and around me again and again. The best I could do was pop my head out for a breath before getting pulled under for more punishment.

Then the waves withdrew, leaving me to cough my lungs out on stable ground. Brushing the hair from my eyes, I spied a wild-eyed bare-footed boy running at me. He too stood out bright as daylight, struck by light beams made visible in the ocean mist. It seemed he meant to stomp my head in, so I naturally shielded it with both arms.

Instead, he leapt over me, yelling, "Come on you puny puddle ripples. Just try and splash me." They only withdrew further, until the briny sea sat quite still. "Cowards," the boy muttered, kicking up sand as he stomped back up the beach.

I shakily rose to my feet, absolutely drenched. How I hated wet clothes, not to mention itchy salt water. So, I hurried after the young savior before the waves returned.

The wild-eyed boy wore plain yet well-fitted hide garments, cut just short of his knees and elbows. He had a wiry head of hair that stuck out in every direction, as if he'd never heard of a comb.

Other than that, he didn't look much different from anyone else in Newmund.

We crested the drop-off and got a nice view of the landscape. We stood on a small island, the plain before us dominated by scraggly grasses and a scattering of plump trees, each tree bearing several large triangular leaves at its top. Small groups of fluffy critters with snouts reaching down to their toes scampered through the grass, snorting and grunting cheerfully. Everything that lived seemed to shine bright as daylight, but anything else remained dim until I looked at it directly.

The trees thickened into a forest towards the middle of the island, which itself grew into a mountain. The mountain rose steeper and steeper until it actually pierced into the hazy dome where the skylights sat. The whole area, sea-included, couldn't have been more than a few square kilometers.

"Excuse me, um, boy?" I said.

"What gives, yellow head?" he said, glaring at my still-dripping hair. "Why you gotta' hog all the fun when I'm trying to catch a wave?"

"How is that fun? I'm all soaked now."

"Quit bragging," he said, stomping onward. Despite several clear paths, he went straight through the scraggly grass. Blades hissed and squawked angrily as he did so. Despite the weirdness, the boy had saved me once already, and I worried, what else might come my way without him? I didn't want to squish that poor grass, but he walked so quickly, I stomped down a bunch of it anyway.

"Sorry to bother you again, but where are we? What is this place?"

He shrugged. "You mean outside?"

Then I remembered how I'd gotten there. Reaching into my side pouch, I felt the purrium platelet and a handful of snacks still there but no monad. At that moment, I realized somehow I'd ended up inside of that mysterious orb. That must have been what Steve meant when he said all I had to do was touch it.

"So, who's your mayor here?" I asked.

"Mayor?" the boy asked.

"Well, the guy who tells everybody what to do."

"Oh. You mean Funnela and Siever."

"Who are they?"

"Oh, just a couple of adults. Say, you want to go roll down a hill?"

I didn't know what else to do but stick with him, so I went along.

"I'm Shran, by the way. Do you mind if I ask your name?"

"Oh, you'd like that wouldn't you."

So, I guess for the moment, he'd just remain "Scraggle-head."

We passed through a bit of the forest, swarming with pale bat-like creatures squeaking happily as they passed over us. I expected the plump trees to give a bit of shade, but every living thing remained in daylight even under the thicker parts of the canopy. I glanced at the skylights, and they appeared brighter, as if adjusting to keep warm daylight on me. I supposed it helped dry my garments, but I still ought to have the option to cool down when I wanted. "How do you get cool around here?" I asked.

"Funnela likes it hot," Scraggle-head said.

That co-regent sounded like a lovely woman. But how could anyone possibly control such a vast array of things all at once? "How?" I finally asked.

Again he shrugged.

We hiked a little ways up a rocky slope till the boy stopped. "You ready to roll, Shran?"

"Here?" I gasped. While it teemed with soft and quiet grasses, many jagged rocks and thorny bushes also jutted up all across the slope below.

"Wouldn't we get hurt?" I asked, increasingly confused how anything worked in the monad.

"Not that I know of. I heard falling never hurts anyone. It's only when you stop falling you can get hurt."

It was nonsense, but he seemed so sure of himself, I didn't know what to do. "Could I just watch first, then?"

"You said you wanted to do this. Now we're all the way up here."

I didn't want to upset him, but I couldn't believe tumbling down that rocky slope would be better. Instead, I agreed to run down with him as he rolled.

"Okay. Watch this." He ran and jumped, tucking into a ball mid-air. He slammed backside-first into the ground, breaking the hold around his knees as he belted out a loud "oof."

The slope was so steep, he couldn't stop as he rolled right into a prickly bush. He flailed like mad, grabbing at tufts of grass, but nothing would slow him until he crashed into a dirt mound. I caught up as he lay there nursing his wounds and crying openly. "Why didn't you tell me this would hurt?" he whimpered.

"I'm sorry. I did warn you, though."

"No you didn't. You just asked if it would hurt. I said I didn't know."

"I thought it was obvious, or else you knew something I didn't."

"Well you thought wrong. I only said what I heard. Just get away from me, yellow-head. You're no fun anymore."

I obediently retreated down the slope, leaving him to lick his wounds. That wasn't how I'd remembered our conversation at all. Hadn't I warned him? Then again, he was correct I'd framed it as a question, and hadn't insisted on what I knew to be true. Was some of it my fault after all?

I wandered around alone for a while, watching the bat-like creatures flap around and whip bugs out of the air with their elongated tongues.

Soon, a petite girl strolled out the mouth of a nearby cave. She wore a bejeweled hairnet, holding her ebony hair just above her shoulders and dark lipstick that made her face almost pasty by contrast. To my surprise, she turned my direction. I looked over my left then my right shoulder: there was no one else around. She wore long, black velvet gloves on each hand, one of which she was pointing at me. "You!" she said, curtly.

"Yes, ma'am?" Why was I calling her ma'am? She had to be younger than me.

Her finger came dangerously close to my nose as she continued, "I hate you," she pronounced it matter-of-factly.

"What? Why?"

"I suspect it is either because of your soggy clothes or because of your ugly face."

For some reason, I just ignored that blatant insult and tried to plead my case. "It's not my fault. A bunch of waves—or whatever they were—were coming after me earlier."

"Humph," she exclaimed. "And a braggart to boot. I should have known."

"I'll be dry soon, though, with all this heat." Talking about the weather. Great idea...

"Then I will just have to stick around until then. Perhaps it would fix your face."

Was that a good sign or a terrible one? In any case, something in me couldn't resist the attention of such a pretty girl. "I'm Shran, by the way, Shran Mattian."

"Introducing yourself to an unaccompanied lady, I see. That's positively scandalous. Someone must teach you the courtly manner of a gentleman."

"I'm sorry."

"Lady Courtlya," she announced with a curtsy, free hand lightly extended, palm down. I looked on dumbly, as she held her stiff pose. The longer she stayed there, motionless, the more furious her expression grew. Finally, she spoke through gritted teeth, "The hand... you're supposed to kiss it."

I bent towards it, but she protested again.

"No. You must hold it first."

Despite the rudeness, I was still thrilled at the opportunity.

"Not the left one, you savage."

So, I grabbed with my right, and the instant my lips touched one knuckle, she ripped it free, leaving me stooped there.

"See how easy it is to give a lady her courtly due?"

"Uh, yes. And..." I had to keep the conversation going somehow, "May I ask how you gained the title, Lady Courtlya?"

"I've always had it."

"Oh. So, which lands do you own?"

"I do not have any. Why would I?"

"Well, where I come from, ladies or lords are people who own lands."

"This simply will not do," she said, disgusted. "Go on then, Shran Mattian."

"Go what?"

"You must go explain that to Funnela and Siever, of course. A lady must not be without her Siever-granted lands."

"But I don't even know where they are."

"Up there, man," she said, pointing down the tunnel she'd emerged from.

If I knew anything for sure, it was that down is down and up is up. Withholding basic observations like that already made things worse with Scraggle-head, so I took a deep breath and carefully said, "That's down, not up."

She clapped a hand to her breast, gasping in offense. "It is not gentlemanly to contradict a lady."

"I'm sorry but—"

"You will be, if you do not march up there and get me my lands."

She ended up following me into the cave, saying she still hoped to see what I looked like dry.

Despite the natural darkness inside there, everything we looked at became bright as day, thanks to the innumerable skylights that seemed to watch everything. Past the mouth of the cave, no skylight could strike me from the front, but the heat on my back got twice as hot. Apparently, all the skylights conspired to make sure the same total amount of light hit me, no matter what.

I hadn't seen a single shadow cast on the island, until we were deep into the tunnel. At one point, Courtlya once stepped between me and the distant cave mouth. Suddenly, a full body's worth of daylight got focused onto my ankles and the head.

I instinctively ducked out of the heat, expecting a shady respite. Instead, my shoes started sizzling like an egg on a hot iron. Those skylights meant to boil my two feet alive. I yelped and jumped back into the light.

Courtlya frowned. "Shran Mattian, what are you doing?"

114

"You nearly burned my feet off."

"That serves you right when you ought to be escorting me properly. Come here then." She held out an arm. I cautiously reached for it. "No, no. Absolutely not."

"You just said—" I groaned.

"Lend an *elbow*, please, sir."

Thus, we walked side by side, her hanging off my right elbow. She gripped so tightly that my arm fell asleep until she took a moment to "fix" my posture out of a more comfortable slouch. Strangely enough, I didn't really mind.

The cave's mouth shrank and shrank in the distance behind us into such a tiny speck that I wondered when we'd lose sight of it all together. Surely some curve would eventually hide it, plunging us into absolute darkness. We should've brought a lantern. Though come to think of it, I hadn't seen any artifacts of civilization since arriving.

Eventually, the cave mouth did disappear around a bend, but the skylights were smarter than I'd given them credit. Rather than everything plunging into darkness, the ceiling around the corner met us with countless tiny holes, as if the skylights burned holes clear through the mountain. From those, we and anything we looked at shone as bright as in full sunlight.

"Why do they do that?" I asked.

"I am sure I do not know what you mean."

"Why do those skylights track us like that? How do they even see us?"

"You have it exactly backwards. Life sees, therefore the light complies."

"But wouldn't that mean when I blink, all the light would turn off?" I closed my eyes to test.

"Not if I see you, silly."

"Well, you should close your eyes too then."

"And be found alone in the dark with a strange young man of unknown origin? Humph."

I wondered if she'd closed her eyes when she made that last utterance. In any case, nothing changed, so I doubted her strange theory.

Finally, entered a larger cavern. To our right, something like a giant funnel made of what looked like bone drooped down from the ceiling. Directly beneath that structure lay a massive pile of bones, so tall it nearly reached the funnel. A little ways ahead of us, a natural rock bridge stretched across a dark lake far below, and the small landing at the far side of the bridge had a narrow corridor that glowed crimson.

Just like the tunnel we'd followed to get there, light peeked through pinholes stretching all across the cavern ceiling. As it did so, it illuminated two darkly clad figures by the nearside of the rock bridge.

Courtlya nudged me cautiously. "There's Funnela and Siever. Hop to it, Shran Mattian."

Chapter Fifteen

Zieglon

I searched all over the vicinity, calling out for him till my voice went sore. No one answered. Grabbing the regifted purrium platelet by the leather strap, I clanked it once again. It rang out loud and clear, hanging as limp as ever. What on Tew happened to Shran?

"He's gone, Zieglon," Guilen said.

It could only be that cursed orb. First, a giant took my catch out of nowhere, then Steve came for my very family with sinister magics.

"This is it," I said, proffering the floating amber orb. "It must have done something to him. I know it."

Guilen gazed in bewilderment, twirling one of the braided tips of his beard. Then he tugged at Steve's cord. "Out with it, Tower-dweller. Where is the lordling?"

"Shran could only have left of his own accord," Steve said. "Now all we can hope is that he'll find his own way back."

"Bah! That's enough from you," Guilen said.

I eyed the man. He had to be lying. Shran had seen what really happened at the top of the Tower and disappeared just before he could tell me. I pushed back the torrent of images of what could have happened to Liza, of what might be happening to Shran that very minute.

Did I go back to Liza to comfort her with the news our son had truly disappeared? Dash the thought. I had to get him back now. "Like you said, Guilen, I'll handle this man."

"What about the orb?" Guilen asked.

I shrugged. "Do what you can."

Once at the palace, Guilen brought the mysterious orb to his bards and corps of engineers, while I escorted Steve to the dungeon tower. He remained silent, calmly biding his time.

Steve stood calmly in the corner of the small cell as the jailer locked him in. A few rays of daylight shone through the barred window, overlooking a small courtyard. I hung back until we were alone. Yet Steve had taken to grinning incessantly and piped up right away. "Good to see you, Zieglon my boy."

Was the man loony, or simply didn't care what happened to him? " 'Boy,' you say?"

"My apologies. When you reach my age… I mean no offense by it."

"You're not past forty."

"Then how do you explain the hair?"

Even in that dim setting, it almost glowed white. My interest in cordialities waned thinner by the second, but if it could help get my son back, it was worth it. "I would've assumed that was hereditary. But you're right. Sometimes appearances can be deceiving."

"True," Steve said glibly.

Had he only stood a few centimeters closer, I thought I would've reached through those iron bars and slammed his head into them. Probably for the best, he kept just out of reach.

"Tell me, Steve, what did you do to her?"

The man sighed resignedly. "If you believe me, I simply did my duty and brought her back to you directly."

"'Duty?' Is that what you call it?"

"Call it whatever you wish. With the coming of the silver stag, I was to bring the last of the line and his mother to receive the old gifts."

"You understand I'm the only reason Guilen's men aren't torturing you for answers this minute?"

"Torture? I think you're more intelligent than that. Besides, why take my word for it when you can go ask her yourself?"

"Intelligence has its limits. Where is my son? What did you do to him?"

"The fact is, he left purely by his own hand. He should be fine."

"He should be here in the palace with me. Great job with whatever trick you pulled. I applaud you, but it's time to bring him home."

"I am sorry. I should have explained it all to him, gone in with him, but we had to get back to you so soon... He's your only child, is he not?"

"Yes," I grunted.

"I thought he was. I thought he was. You see, only Shran can touch it."

"Touch what? Speak sense, won't you Steve?"

"The monad, Zieglon. He's not necessarily far from us. It's just that only he can break through the buffer layer."

" 'Monads?' Buffer layers? Care to put that in English?"

"It's bare basic monadology… though it's technically more of a demi-monad—spurious connections to the rest of the world except through your offspring. The offspring, that's the whole key."

"How about you explain one thing before going off on a dozen more rabbit trails. What is this monad you're talking about?"

"Yes, yes. For much of history, people kept forgetting the nature of substance, of what it means to exist. Time and again, many believed all that existed was merely a conglomeration of tiny balls mindlessly bumping into each other in various ways. They obscured that foolishness through levels of complexity and sophisticated nomenclature, but fundamentally, that was their claim all along.

"So popular was this idea at one point—I can't imagine why— that most forgot the far grander view once described by a man named Leibniz. He reasoned that active will, comprehension, and relationships were the fundamentals of all substance, of all that exists. He tried to communicate the endlessly vast web of relationships that hold the entire world together, beings—not mindless balls—are the basic stuff of existence. And because of that, each being must fundamentally contain the completeness of the world within its own essence.

"According to monadology, every being is a monad, regardless of its shape or size. Each one contains the fullness of the world from exactly one perspective. Leibniz theorized that an entire extra world or a million extra worlds could fit quite comfortably in the palm of your hand. That orb you found: your son is both here in the palace, and from our perspective, quite far from us."

"That would explain why his purrium platelet was out of range," I said.

"Exactly. There's bound to be plenty of extra space for him to roam around in there."

"Great," I said. "So, how do I get him out?"

"He alone can find his way back out again."

"You haven't been much help then, have you."

Steve removed a simple necklace. The pendant was made up of three nested iron rings. The center of it, maybe two centimeters in diameter, was hollow, bearing no ornament where it looked like it ought to have one. He pulled a spring-loaded pin at the bottom of the pendant, and the rings swiveled shut, something like a spherical bear-trap.

The innermost and outermost rings also had a golden eyepiece, one overlaying the other so you could see through both at once.

"True monads are windowless," Steve said, "but seeing as it's a sort of demi-monad, who says you can't add a window?" He passed it through the bars. "Do me a favor, and don't give *this* to your mayor too."

"So, if I put that orb in here, I'll be able to see my son?" I asked.

"Couldn't hurt," Steve said.

Grabbing the necklace, I pulled the pin, clicked the rings down into their open position, and concealed it under my collar.

I found the bard Falen in a palace workshop, studying the strange little orb with some of his trusted bards and engineers. All I had to do was trap the thing inside the necklace and see what I could see.

They had it set out on an anvil, and one of them pounded it with a hammer right as I entered. The anvil clanked as the hammer came down upon it, but the little thing shot right at me. I caught it, instinctively, surprised again by how lightly it flew.

"Falen, exactly what are you doing?" I demanded.

"I consulted with the other bards," Falen said, "and we agreed no reputable songs have a word about such a thing. So, we're having the corps of engineers break it open."

"What?"

"We've tried saws, swords, axes, nails, and now hammers. The pesky thing's as resilient as ever. It even ended up in the fireplace once, to no avail."

"But," an engineer said, "that's why we need to throw it into the forge, to get some real heat into it."

"My son might well be in this," I said. "You'll do no such thing."

Falen scoffed. "Even if someone managed to squeeze a young man inside such a tiny space, that orb still weighs almost nothing. Beyond that, any engineer can tell you bodies resist changes of momentum. The more massive the body, the more it resists. It's simply impossible any human could be inside there. It's too light."

"Supposedly, it's a 'demi-monad.' That's what I got out of Steve. There might be a whole other world packed into there."

At that moment, Guilen entered, followed by a small throng of palace guards. "You believe that tower dweller?" he scoffed.

"I believe my son was there one moment, and the next moment there was only this."

"Enough of this foolishness, Zieglon. Can't you see? Your son's gone."

"He must be alive. I just need to—" I reached for the concealed necklace but never would've expected what happened next.

"Guards," Guilen said, "arrest him."

The men with him grabbed at the orb before I'd even fished the pendant from my collar.

"Guilen, what are you doing?" I asked.

They grabbed my arms, but I wouldn't let them pry the orb from my hands while I had breath in my lungs. Unfortunately, the tighter I grasped it, the smoother the thing became and the more it pressed back. It shot out of my hand like a loosed arrow as more guards latched onto me limb by limb.

"I'm sorry, Zieglon," Guilen said, "laws are laws."

Snug-fitted irons chafed at my wrists and ankles as I stood before the mayor's court, a guard to my left and another to my right. Guilen, his sister Gilda, and a few palace bards made little comment as Jaldane laid out his accusation from the mayor's lower table. Haldra served as Jaldane's counselor. The eye where I'd struck him bulged to match the rest of him.

"General Zieglon Mattian, you stand accused of knowingly striking and injuring Jaldane Stohvan, a noble six heartbeats from the Mayorship. Such a crime confers the right of satisfaction to the offended party, or a minimum of ten lashes for you. How do you plead?" Guilen asked.

"First, I would need to know specifically what punishment I stand to receive, Mister Mayor."

"Of course," Guilen said. "Mister Jaldane Stohvan, what manner of satisfaction are you seeking for this offense?"

Haldra whispered something in her son's ear before he stood once again. "Mister Mayor, I request that the general give me a sincere apology for what he did."

"That's all?" Guilen asked.

"And he has to beg for it on his knees."

"These terms are acceptable," Guilen said. "Lord Mattian, how do you plead?"

I chuckled to myself at the thought. If I ever got within kneeling distance of that boy again, I might well strike him with a real blow. I made my decision. "The boot of no man will I kiss. Nor at the knees of any boy will I kneel."

Guilen sighed angrily. "You've had two chances to answer the charges, General. Don't make me hold you in contempt of the mayor's court. Have you no further plea, no further case to offer?"

"I am most definitely not guilty, Mister Mayor. Your nephew here—Mister Jaldane Stohvan—went looking for a fight, and he got one."

"Be that as it may," Guilen said, "the law is clear. To strike a noble, in line for the mayorship, is to strike the mayor himself. Is that very clear, General?"

"It's clear he was asking for it, clear he was abusing our laws to boost a sorely swollen ego. So, yes, I struck him and now begin to wish he demands a rematch."

Guilen slammed down the gavel. "Guilty as charged. General Zieglon Mattian, you will kneel and apologize to him, or else suffer ten lashes."

Jaldane grinned from ear to hear, running right up in front of me. "Hurry up, General," he said.

"Down you get, then," one of the palace guards barked. He and his mate made to shove me to the ground.

I head-butted one and elbowed another, sending him toppling to the floor before a few more swooped in. "All Father's sake!" I shouted. "Just give me the lashes, Guilen."

Of course, the rest of the guards seized my cuffed hands and feet. To my surprise, Lady Haldra pleaded with the mayor as they dragged me away. "No, brother. Don't do this," she said.

"I gave exactly what you asked for, little sister. There's no reversing it now."

She kept pleading with him as the guards dragged me out of the court. A bit odd.

In short order, they led me to a whipping post outside the palace gate. They stripped my shirt off and bound my hands around the post, polished smooth by the many hands that had grabbed it. I noted Jaldane in attendance, cheering gleefully.

Soon enough, Falen arrived and restated the charges and Guilen's final judgment for all to hear. At last he addressed the whip-man. "Proceed."

I'd never received a proper lashing in my life. The first blow struck like lightning. Nothing could've prepared me for it. Unlike taking wounds in the heat of battle, I felt all the pain immediately. I gasped, truly shocked how much it hurt, how deep and wide it sliced. To my credit, I stopped short of screaming out in pain but just barely. I gripped hard as I could around that cursed post, preparing for the next lash.

"One," Falen counted.

By the final lash, I felt myself shaking involuntarily, and it took two men to pry my fingers from the whipping post. My ears still rang from the blows, I only half caught Falen proclaim, "...is now complete... hereby forgiven."

Ston Mevrin, the head physician, slapped on a bit of ointment, wrapped my torso with a roll of gauze, and left without a word.

Where did I go from there? Back to the workshop in my weakened condition? Perhaps the whipping put some sense into me after all: how could such a tiny, weightless object contain anything? There was only one other person I could ask.

I headed for the stables, just inside the palace gates, throwing a saddle over my gray stallion. I'd make sure Liza was getting along alright with the mending and finally hear what happened in that tower. In the meantime, why had the stable hands taken it off in the first place? As I was cinching the saddle tight, a woman strolled into the stall, kicking aside loose straw as she entered.

"General Mattian?" Haldra gasped. "Where are you off to in such a hurry?"

"Mayor's business," I replied.

She laughed in surprise. "Right after he had you whipped?"

I tugged the latigo tight. "Don't you have another show trial to see to?"

"I'll have you know, I was helping you. I begged Guilen not to leave a mark on you. Now you've ruined all of it."

"Good day, my lady," I said, and galloped out of there despite her protestations. Whatever game the mayor's little sister was playing at, I wouldn't be roped into it.

To my surprise, a short way down the city streets, who else did I run into but Liza, back already. The woman never ceased to impress.

Chapter Sixteen

Liza

On the ride home, the stark reality hit me all over again. In a moment of weakness, I had made a deal with Haldra that I *just couldn't* keep. And whatever happened in that tower did not seem to be wearing off.

Riding up the main drag of Newmund city, surrounded by multi-story shops and houses, who else did I run into but Zieglon! Yes. He would fix it all somehow.

"I've done it," I said.

"Spectacular," he said, not as cheerful as I would've expected, as he dismounted. "I was just headed there."

"Well, took you long enough," I said, now dismounted and walking with him.

"Sorry about that. I had a few delays."

I stood on my tiptoes for a kiss. The second our lips touched, with that strange new sense, I became aware of very large, very fresh wounds slashed all over his back. "What happened, Zieglon?"

He stifled a look of surprise. "I'm fine, just… I've been better."

"But you're bleeding," I said, trying not to immediately reveal how I'd noticed.

He let out a breath and nodded. "Alright, I took a few lashes for a silly mistake."

"Lashes?" I gasped. "How could they?"

"I defended Shran's honor last night, and then Haldra coached her son to lay an accusation against me. That's over with. I want to know how you are now."

I wanted to tell him everything, to throw myself in his arms and let him convince me all of it would work itself out. Instead, I froze up. How could I tell him what I'd become when I didn't know my very self? What would he do if he knew?

"I'm fine," I said. It was no lie, talking about my bodily health.

"Shran said things, said that man Steve hurt you."

I resisted the sudden urge to tighten my hood further. "Yes. He brought us up in this elevator contraption that had to be climbing at a hundred kilometers an hour. It almost made me faint."

"And what else?" he asked me.

What else? I told him what I wanted to tell him, hadn't I? He had no business taking every one of my worries on his shoulders along with his own. Yes. He would not be forced to bear this burden of mine on top of all his.

"Then, we brought Shran back down to the gardens. He was very upset to leave, but I said we had to get him back to you. I knew you'd be worried sick about us."

"Why are you hiding from me? You're about the only person left in this mayorship I can trust."

If he thought he knew so much about what I'd been through, how could he demand I relive it right there? Forcing down the instinct to say something mean, my tears found their way out instead.

"There, there, dearest, I won't force you," Zieglon said, wrapping arms around me. "Still, something has happened that you ought to know about."

Fear jumped up in a heartbeat. Had he discovered what I said I'd do? Of course I didn't mean to if I could avoid it. Exactly how was a matter of time, though.

Zieglon continued. "On the way here, Shran disappeared."

He wasn't joking. "What do you mean, Zieglon?"

"He was sitting behind me one moment, and a moment later, all I saw was some sort of weightless little orb."

"That 'monad' Shran took?"

"That's what that man Steve called it. He said there's a whole world in there that Shran disappeared into, that only he can find his way back out again. It all sounds impossible, but I'm not sure I know what to believe. Would you trust Steve?"

"I did," I said glibly. How could Shran just disappear, and why hadn't Steve warned us earlier? What kind of gift was that anyway, a little ball that makes your son disappear? "I don't really know either."

"Then what are we going to do?" Zieglon asked.

"You lost him while I was off doing mayor's work for you." Why had I said that? Why couldn't I apologize immediately?

"I thought you wanted to be more involved. And you've been invaluable."

"It's more than that," I continued. "You put me up to doing the impossible. You didn't tell me half of what I'd have to do. Only by some good fortune did I manage to save it at all."

"And I believed you could," Zieglon said, eyes undaunted.

How did he do that? How did he just not let anything affect him, whether wars or giants or angry wives? I only knew that too much was going wrong for me to handle. And whenever I tried to fix one problem, two more kept sprouting up elsewhere. "I can't though. I wouldn't even know where to begin."

"Well, you could start by explaining what happened at the top of the Tower."

"It wouldn't help."

"It might. And clearly, you need to talk about it too."

"I was wrong. Okay? I shouldn't have gone up there, shouldn't have trusted Steve, shouldn't have let Shran take that, that thing."

The conversation didn't improve after that. I blamed him, and he was also clearly hurt.

We left our horses in the stables and went our own ways from there. I wandered through the main courtyard until I came to the fountain. It was a nice, wide-open zone amidst the sea of New Moons booths. There I sat, staring at the rippling water. My mind yanked me in a dozen directions at once, leaving me at a complete loss what to do or where to begin.

"Lady Mattian, why are you wearing your riding hood like that?" a woman asked. I looked up with a start to see Lady Haldra standing there.

Perhaps dying my hair was the best thing I could do next. In any case, "I don't feel very well," I truthfully said.

Haldra nodded sympathetically. "I'll have some mint tea brought for you right away, with lots of honey."

I was about to refuse, but actually, that did sound nice right about then. The lady gave a happy nod to Penna, who was walking with her, and the maid hurried off for some hot tea.

"I could do with a nice sit-down myself," Haldra said, taking a spot next to me.

One of the dozen thoughts swirling around in my head flew out of my mouth a few moments later. "Why did you do it?"

"What's that, Lady Mattian?"

"I already gave my word to help you," I said, "and still you had my husband beaten. Why would you do that?"

She looked taken aback. "He struck my son last night. Didn't he tell you that?"

"Well, not exactly."

"And you don't give me credit for the plea bargain I tried to make. We couldn't deny my son justice as a true-born of the Peltern line, but I simply wanted an official apology. You can understand that, can't you?"

Perhaps any mother would want that, but this was Haldra talking. "Then why didn't Zieglon take the deal instead of the lashes?"

"It shocked me too. As a formality, we asked that he kneel for a moment while he apologized. He wouldn't have it. Ask Ergester Falen too, if you like, but your husband preferred to take the lashes. At that point it was too late for me to do anything, no matter how I begged."

Penna returned, holding a large silver tray set with a steaming teapot and hot buttery cookies. She poured tea into three finely decorated little cups, stirring in a healthy dose of honey. "There you are, Mistress," she said, passing me one of the cookies as well.

When all three of us had our cups, Lady Haldra raised hers high. "To the Lady Mattian and hers."

I hesitated, in the off chance they had slipped poison into that teapot. When the two of them had sipped a good mouthful, I joined in. It warmed my throat without a hint of bitterness.

"So, did you find it?" Haldra asked once we had eaten and drunk our fill.

"Huh?" I asked.

"The you-know-what."

"Oh," I said. "Yes. But I took a solemn oath to tell no one."

Penna chimed in at that. "Mistress Mattian, haven't you already as much as told Lady Haldra? She knows that you know."

"I know nothing, though," Haldra said. "Honestly Liza, I'm quite out of the loop. My brother shares less and less with his little sister these days."

"I still gave him my word," I said.

"And to me too, did you not?"

"You didn't hear this oath."

"Alright. What did my old brother make you promise? That he'd shave your head bare, or even worse?"

"A lot worse. I had to promise to uphold the secrecy of that circle on pain of death."

Lady Haldra looked truly stunned. "That's pure savagery for such a small matter. You poor thing."

"I'm...." I was about to say fine. "I'm holding up."

"It'll be alright, Mistress," Penna said and pushed another cookie into my hand.

"But of course," Haldra said, "a lady's word is worth a lot all on its own. I don't want to see that tarnished. Think about it, Liza. There's got to be a way to keep both. Just tell me what I must do."

The more I thought about it, hadn't I already upheld Guilen's oath? I completely masked the fact that a giant had bitten the silver stag. On Sunday, everyone else would see the creature just as it already was. Who could possibly be harmed simply by letting Haldra look at the final product a day early? I wouldn't *really* be breaking an oath. No. I would be upholding what I'd already promised.

"If I did show you," I finally said, "I'd be putting my life on the line. You can't tell anyone about this. Ever. Especially not Zieglon."

"Done," Haldra said.

I covertly led the way to the silver stag's hiding place, constantly peering over my shoulder and expecting to see someone watching from off in the distance. Haldra and Penna followed close behind me.

"I'm not breaking any oath," I kept telling myself. "No. I'm keeping both."

Finding the same cave again proved trickier than expected in those crevasses. I had to stop and think at a juncture a few times, but to my relief, we made no wrong turns. We arrived at the cave in pretty short order.

Penna held the lantern, a fancy one with a lens that focused all the light into one thick beam. She took the rear while I led the way through the cave.

Haldra grew positively giddy. "What's he like? Is he as perfectly graceful and violent as they say?"

"I don't know," I said. "It was already dead when they brought me here, see?"

Her countenance fell immediately as we entered the chamber. "What?" she burst, voicelessly. The dead creature lay on the floor, right where I left him.

"He was already like this," I said. "It wasn't my fault."

"So," she said, quietly looking it over, and laughing in disbelief. "All was for naught. You brought me out here to gaze at a useless corpse."

"You should've seen it when I got here," I said, cutting just short of giving away the real secret.

133

"I'm sorry, Liza, but this is simply not good enough. We needed to see a real silver stag. Alive."

"Lady Haldra?" Penna asked from the chamber's entrance.

"Yes?" Haldra said.

"Can we let her go, then?"

Haldra thought for a moment, then shook her head. "It's still too big of a risk. Better get it over with before we leave."

They were talking about me.

"Now, Penna," Haldra ordered.

Haldra grabbed my wrist, and I knew they meant to murder me then and there.

The chamber had one small corridor leading deeper into the cave. I didn't trust myself to dodge past Penna quickly enough to get back to Nippy. Haldra might not have much muscle on her, but not so for the maid.

As Penna approached, I yanked free and went for the corridor, praying it came out somewhere above ground. Haldra persisted, catching hold of my riding cloak, so I tore myself free of the thing. Haldra fell backwards with the limp scrap of cloth as I rushed into the far corridor.

Penna lumbered on after me, her heavy lantern creaking pace by pace. Though I had a fair lead, the farther I ran, the darker it got. The tunnel twisted and turned till I couldn't see a thing. Swift footsteps followed behind me, I couldn't see where from.

I veered off down this way and that. Then I smacked into something solid. My head spun, lips tasting of blood, yet I could not stop.

Hands feeling out in front of me, I ran again in the first open direction. My foot caught a rock, nearly tripping me into a heap. I stumbled, still pressing forward, still at top speed.

My outstretched palms slammed into a cold, hard wall. Sharp pain sprang up my wrists. I followed the wall around one way, then the other. Both curved back to the passage I'd come from: a dead end.

A sliver of lantern light faded into view around a corner, and I suppressed a scream. The "creak... creak... creak" of the swinging lantern grew closer and closer. The maid seemed to be stopping to check down every little passage as she went, leaving no corner unsearched.

I pressed my back against the wall, the terror rising and rising as the ray denuded more and more of the little passage.

Penna rounded the corner, the lens-sharpened flame stinging my eyes.

"No," I said, fear freezing me there like ice.

"There you are," Penna said, as if finding a runaway hen. She set down the lantern, with the beam focused directly on me. Penna became a dark silhouette walking closer and closer.

Tears poured down my cheeks as I begged her to stop.

"I'm sorry about this, Mistress. I'll try to be quick." Labor-hardened hands squeezed round my throat as her knee pressed down into my chest. I kicked and scratched, but her grip held immovable. Even in the sharp lantern light, things were fading out to darkness.

I remembered Shran. My son. Despised by his peers without cause and trapped without help. If not me, then who would save him? This couldn't happen, not now.

Like gasping for breath, I absorbed some of the starlight from my reserves. As if spurring a horse, my body rejuvenated itself, feasting amidst the famine. Yet the maid was strong and still had me pinned. It was only a matter of time.

Penna looked surprised and squeezed harder. As things dimmed again, the unique vibrance in the form of my murderer sang her distinct, flavorful melody, as bright as the sun in the sky. I knew what to do.

Penna shrieked rage and anguish at once, but I didn't stop. With what had come over me, I kept right on going, siphoning her vibrance into my reserves. She threw all her weight onto my neck. When my trachea crunched, I went for it all. That unseen force inside me pulled and pulled that song away from her even more rapidly. The scream waned into a fearful whimper, and she dropped, limp as a doll.

I wheezed for breath, too weak to even roll the strange form off me until I absorbed from my reserves. The rhythm, that unique melody sang on from my reserves, like she were still right there. When I did get free, empty eyes fell on me with a blank stare. It very nearly felt like she'd only hidden around the corner somewhere. "Penna?" I called. The woman did absolutely nothing. It was wrong, so wrong.

I tried putting back the life I'd stolen, the same as I'd fixed the silver stag. When I started to pour her vibrance back into the body, it began to stiffen and rot right in front of me. I had done it. Please no. I had killed her.

Haldra emerged from behind the lantern. How long had she been watching back there? My eyes starting to adjust, I vaguely made out the amazement on her face. "Lady Mattian I was terribly wrong about you," she said. "You can help us after all."

Chapter Seventeen

Shran

Courtlya hung back where she was as I approached Funnela and Siever alone. The man had a cylindrical hat with a broad rim on it, shading his darkly ringed eyes. He wore a sharply trimmed beard, with black and brown hide garments. His collar and cuffs had bones sewn into them too.

Next to him stood a woman in a long-sleeved dress also made of dark hide. The dress had a bouquet of rib bones on the shoulder blades, and over that she wore a necklace of many long, sharp teeth. As much as I feared negotiating a deal with this strange, dark duo, I didn't want to risk losing the closest thing to a friend that I had left.

So, I gulped and went for it. "Funnela and Siever?"

"The same. And who are you, young man?" said Siever, his smile revealing a set of sharpened teeth.

"I'm Shran Mattian, Mister Siever, sir. I'm here on behalf of Lady Courtlya."

"Is that so?" Funnela yapped beside him. "On what business?"

"Well, ma'am, to have the title of lady is to have lands. And she doesn't seem to have any yet."

"I should say not," Funnela said. "All lands are mine."

"*Ours*, Funnela dearest," Siever said, then turned to me. "And by whose authority do you dare to speak of depriving us of our lands, Shran Mattian?"

"Well, this is all inside a monad, isn't it?" I got no response. "My mother coughed it up, and I rescued it. So, that is to say—if it's not too bold—that means it belongs to me."

Funnela's jaw nearly struck the floor. Siever's gob-smacked eyebrows rose to disappearing behind his broad-rimmed hat. "Indeed, young man. That is too bold."

"Tell him, Siever darling," she egged him on. "Tell him where he can go, flapping a greedy maw like that."

"Oh, I'll tell him, dearest. He'll rue the day he assayed to rule the Almighty Siever and his lovely Funnela."

"I'm sorry sir. I didn't mean—"

"Silence your insolence," Siever spat. "You, Shran Mattian, are hereby guilty of treason." Funnela gleefully whispered something in his ear. "Make that, high treason," he bellowed.

"For what?"

"For your attempted usurpation," Siever said, "and for appearing before us noticeably damp while the two of us remain bone dry. It's an absolute outrage, and utter *indignance!*"

As I inwardly pondered whether he'd only misused a word or actually made one up, Funnela jittered excitedly. "Tell him, tell him, tell him Siever."

"You shall be sentenced to a fine of… two liters of fresh water, and no less than three fruits."

That didn't sound very bad, except that I had none of either. My clothes dripped with nothing but brine, and I never saw any fruit outside. Not to mention, Courtlya would probably be very cross with me for not securing any lands.

Courtlya appeared beside me, grinning expectantly, as she curtsied. "So, Shran Mattian, what lands have you gotten for me?"

"The instigator," Funnela shrieked.

"That she is, and she merits the same punishment."

"Punishment? Shran Mattian, what have you done to me?"

"I'm sorry Courtlya—"

"*Lady* Courtlya," she corrected. "In all the time I spent to make a gentleman of you, you learned nothing."

"What?"

"I saw you, Shran Mattian. You did not as much as bow or kiss Funnela's hand before presenting your demands, and now I am being punished for it."

Siever cut in, "You two have been fined the sum of four liters of water and six fruits. Now get to it."

"But where do I get the fruit, and how am I going to get all the way down to that lake, and what about a bucket?"

"Our lake?" Funnela exclaimed.

"You'll not be lifting one drop from there," Siever said. "Off to the tunnels with you two. Start with some water."

"But—"

"Insubordination," Siever bellowed. "For that, you, Shran, shall complete your sentence with only one-quarter of your daylight allowance." He motioned us towards the bridge. "Tunnels," he repeated through his sharpened teeth.

The two of us hurried over the bridge and through to the crimson hallway before incurring further penalties. It glowed crimson all on its own, and no other light rays entered. The circular passage, with a flat walkable area barely wide enough for two abreast, spiraled down to the left so that no more than a half-dozen meters was visible forward or back.

We came to a place where more caves branched off from the crimson hall. "Is this where we're supposed to go?" I asked.

"Menial tasks like water collecting are not the business of a lady."

"Then how are we going to find anything?"

"You got me into this. You shall get me out."

"But I don't know what to do."

"Then do something, Shran Mattian."

"Alright… this way." I offered an elbow hopefully, as we crossed into the passage. She just humphed, damaging whatever pride I had left. Somehow, I would fix this.

More ceiling holes lit the new passage once again, only not quite the same as before. I squinted and blinked, but found no matter where I looked, everything was a lot darker.

"What's happening?" I asked.

"You need to be more specific with all these questions," Courtlya said.

"Everything's darker down here."

She looked around a bit, then shook her head. "No. It looks the same as ever."

In fact, the beam of light that followed everywhere she looked kept her gaze just as bright as daylight. And she too, shone as bright as day, whereas my own hands had gone dim. "It's only normal for you, Courtlya. Everything's dim for me now until you're looking at it too."

"Oh. Well, of course it is. How could you forget Siever's punishment so soon? You only get one-quarter light now. Consider yourself fortunate he was so lenient."

"So, he's doing this to me?"

"His word goes. That is all I know."

I quickly started to notice the difference on my body as well. The humid draft that flowed through the place seemed to bite my damp skin. I wondered if I'd ever dry off as I started to shiver.

We kept passing by these glassy smooth holes as we went, each one large enough to swallow a grown man. Pointing with the light beam that followed my gaze, I asked, "What are those things?"

"Funnel holes," Courtlya said.

"And how far down do they go?"

"Not down. Up."

"They're going straight into the floor."

She threw up her hands and groaned as if I were the one speaking nonsense.

Then came the sound of one small drip from the corner. It had to be water. We followed our ears to a fat, woody plant growing on the wall, bright as day. It had a small, shallow impression near the top, filled with water. As I watched, a new drop of water escaped the little puddle and slid down the side of the plant. Not much later, another drop followed that.

A palmful of the water had a hint of a barky taste to it, but seemed potable enough. "This plant's got water," I announced.

Courtlya brushed past me, dabbing a droplet with a handkerchief. She daintily lapped it up, snacking her lips as she did. "Mmm…" she said, contentedly. "This will do. Fetch the rest of it for me, please."

"How?"

"I am the lady. Figure it out. I even said please."

I ought to have been very irritated, the way she ordered me around, so why did I want more than anything to impress her? With no way to collect the water, I would have to take the whole plant and wrench it out when we got back. I pulled with bare fingers, but it hardly budged. Though perhaps something rumbled inside.

"Well?" Courtlya asked.

"I don't know. It's stuck on there pretty good."

"Simple. Make it unstuck."

I yanked at the plant hard as I could. Something definitely rumbled inside this time. I held a sharp rock to the back of it and hammered it in with another. Maybe it was the way I struck the rock, but it sounded like something squeaked. It was wedged in now, lifting the plant slightly off the wall.

Courtlya still watched expectantly, so I gripped my hammer rock, two-handed, and struck the wedge with all my might. A terrible screech rang out like a kettle over flame. Horrified, I held my ears until the screeching died out.

"What is the holdup?" Courtlya asked.

"It's hurting the plant."

"I imagine it will be dead by the end of whatever it is you're doing. What is that to you?"

"I can't just kill it."

"It is a plant."

That had to be right. Right? Plants don't feel pain, do they? It had to be some merely mechanical sound. So, I pounded away, the screech reinvigorated with each strike. I didn't let up until its daylight dimmed out and the sound died completely. The back of the plant looked all gross and soggy where it had been attached to the wall.

"Thank you," Courtlya said, delicately taking the plant with a handkerchief and tossing it into a funnel hole. I stared in disbelief, hearing it tumble down, down, nay irretrievable. After all the painful toil I'd put into it, all at her command, it was all I could do to hold back the anger from my voice. "Why did you do that?" I asked.

"We can check how much water it has later. No use tiring out your arms lugging that thing around."

"I'll be way more tired if I have to climb all the way down there to get it."

"You really must stop ignoring everything I try to teach you. I already said that hole goes up. You know, up top."

"What are you talking about?"

"Oh, come come come. I will just have to show you." She led back the same way we came. I felt a lot better with her squeezing onto my arm as we went.

From the far side of the bridge, I saw a young girl with braidless white hair hanging past her loose shoulders and wearing a simple linen dress. She sat at the foot of the bone pile, wailing and moaning over something. Courtlya and I crossed the bridge and approached the bone pile. The white-haired girl was clinging to a dead plant, one eerily similar to the one I'd just chopped loose.

The girl addressed us, face ruddy with tears. "Who are you? Who could do this?" she asked between whimpers.

Courtlya answered for me. "Yes. Introductions. Glinta, meet my escort, Shran Mattian. He's the aspiring gentlemen who fetched that for me."

"Shran?" she exclaimed, eyeing me in rage. "I hate you Shran. You took an innocent life."

"But it was just a plant, and I had no other choice."

"You had a choice!" she screamed, then buried her face in the dead plant.

Just then, the macabrely clad couple approached the bone pile. "What in the name of Siever is going on here?" Siever demanded.

Jaw quivering, the girl presented the plant.

Funnela gasped, splayed fingers brushing her tooth necklace as she clapped a hand to her breast. "That's one of my waterbuds."

"I'm sorry," I said. "I was only trying to collect water and had no bucket or anything. Courtlya said—"

"That's a sorry excuse to go destroying our crops," Siever said. "For this gross misconduct, I shall hereby withhold all light from you, Shran. And as for you, Lady Courtlya—"

"The instigator," Funnela corrected.

"Yes, the instigator, I hereby revoke your title as lady."

"But, but, you cannot do that," Courtlya stammered

"I am the almighty Siever. My word is law."

As soon as he spoke, I went dark. The beam illuminating my gaze vanished, and the quarter of daylight that had warmed my body ceased to shine.

I looked to Courtlya, who still had full daylight on her. Yet, the life seemed to drain right from her eyes. She sank to the floor in a daze, muttering in denial. I tried to console her, but she didn't seem to notice me. Perhaps she couldn't see me in the dark.

I patted her shoulder, but it didn't register. "Courtlya please. I'm sorry," I said, but she only muttered on, staring at nothing.

I gently shook her shoulder. "Come on Courtlya. It'll be okay. I'll get you your fruit and water. We'll figure it out." Nothing changed. Grabbing with both hands, I tried to shake her. Her head bobbled, limp. "Lady Courtlya, why won't you look at me? Please don't leave me alone." I couldn't get a response from her. She was gone.

She couldn't be gone. She couldn't just leave me alone, surrounded by people who hated me. If not her, there was no one to help and no way to help myself.

I had to run. Where? I had to get out of that awful monad. How?

It came to me in a flash: the mountain, the bony funnel. It had stretched all the way to the top of the dome outside. The mountain was far too steep to climb from outside, but what about inside? Funnella and Siever had picked their place not for no reason. If I climbed the bony funnel, it would lead me straight up top. It had to.

I ran before Siever could even try to stop me and scrambled up the pile. Strange animal skulls, ribs, and who knows what else rattled with each step I took. There was barely a solid foothold to be found. Heaps of bones rolled to the floor as I frantically climbed.

At the peak of the bone pile, I jumped high as I could, narrowly grasping the inside of the funnel's spout. Sharp edges jabbed into my fingertips, but I held fast. After gaining a proper foothold, I climbed for my life up the funnel.

It quickly grew dark as pitch. So, apparently no one was even looking at me as I climbed for freedom. Thank All Father the inside wall had plenty of handholds I could find by touch, as the path grew darker and darker. From the way things echoed, it was clear that many side passages spilled into that main one. I kept to the most vertical path up and up some more.

Not too far above, a dim red light glowed on the mouth of the hole. Freedom was in sight. I kept on climbing towards it.

Finally, I pulled myself up, into a crimson hallway much like one below. Behind me was a dead end, and adult voices echoed around the bend ahead of me. Whoever they were, I'd have to run past them before they could grab me. The speakers appeared. I was stunned to see it was Funnela and Siever, talking to some errand boy. So, they hadn't chased after me because they knew a faster way to climb up there.

"That's enough of that, Shran," Siever said.

145

Hugging the far side of the tunnel, I sprinted past them. Once again, they didn't even try to stop me. I kept running, as fast as I could. Round and round the glowing hallway looped. Then I found myself at the far side of a bridge.

"No," I said, falling to my knees. Across the bridge sat Courtlya and Glinta, by the giant pile of bones. After all that climbing, I'd ended up exactly where I started: there wasn't anywhere to run.

Chapter Eighteen

Zieglon

When Liza and I parted ways, I headed across the courtyard to the workshop where the little orb was kept. Five of the mayor's men guarded the entrance. He even had Berrin, the captain of the palace guard, stationed there. I approached him, a man of about forty, whose decades of combat showed in his face. "What's going on here?"

"Sorry General," Berrin said, "no entry for anyone but Falen and his men."

"And why is that? I already saw what's in there."

"We can hardly have you disappearing on us too."

How hard would it be, forcing my way past the five guards on my own? Not impossible if I managed to swipe a weapon. Berrin's fingers twitched ever so slightly, ready to draw his short sword any second. Could I live with shedding Newmundian blood with less than a hunch to go on?

"Good day, Berrin," I said.

A smile touched only his lips.

I headed straight back for the palace from which I'd recently been dragged in chains. My back still throbbed something terrible, a price I was honored to pay. Perhaps I hadn't meant to strike the lordling, but what sort of man apologizes for defending his family? Another sort altogether.

Climbing the front steps, I looked up at that monument to Clenhilda, ever smiling down on us. I had gone back and forth on the question a dozen times in my life: was she a hero or a traitor? Looking into those sculpted eyes, at least for that day, for that hour, I chose to keep believing she truly had defected for the sake of her people. Right or wrong, we two defended our own.

I veered off from the main hall and went through to the armory, ever my best hope of finding a clear mind. Racks on every wall and row upon row of standing shelves housed all manner of polearms, swords, and bows, each implement offering his own solution to the problem. Yes. What better way to bring things into perspective than preparing for a proper battle?

Grabbing the rake from its stand, I flattened out the sandpit. In a few short minutes of modeling, the pit looked as similar to the shape of the northern forest as necessary. I had raised up or dug out all the forest's notable hills, troughs, and waterways. A scattering of model trees outlined the major clearings, along with markers for where Friday's giant had appeared and fled.

Just where might the abomination have wandered off to in the meantime? I gripped onto that image, that geography in my head, and let the next day's hunt unfold in various ways.

"I'm dog tired of all these secrets," came a familiar voice from the doorway. Hothen came inside, clutching a pair of large green apples. He tossed one my way and took a hearty bite out of the other.

I caught the fruit, hesitating to sample it. "It'll be over tomorrow," I said.

"Will it?"

The tartness made my jaw ache even before taking a bite. "Aren't you supposed to bake these?"

"See that, Zieglon? More rules. 'Do this today,' 'don't do that tomorrow,' 'don't dare share a word of this.' On and on and on lately."

"Hothen, my friend, I don't like it any more than you. Guilen's just worried because the president's due for a visit this very weekend."

"You keep sticking up for him even after taking a dozen lashes over nothing."

"Ten lashes," I corrected.

"Yes. You can count them all by feel alone, I wager."

"And I'd rather not count off ten more while we're at it," I said. "Come on. Help me iron this thing out for tomorrow."

The two of us got to work, strategizing, contemplating the behavior of our enemy. Thordin would have his party as well, doing the Father alone knows what, and somehow we would work it to our advantage. Between the two of us, we arrived at a vision good enough to set us and the men at ease if nothing else.

With a freshly de-cluttered mind, I asked Hothen if his wife ever refused to say what's *really* wrong.

"Only every other day or so," he said. "Why do you ask?"

"If you can believe me, Liza and Shran went into the Great Tower not a few hours ago. Steve, the man everyone's talking about, led them up there. Now Shran has disappeared practically before my eyes, and Liza will hardly say a word of what happened up there."

"Have you asked the tower-dweller, then?"

"I did. He spouted some nonsense about the nature of existence and unfathomable connectedness between everything and impossibly small worlds."

"What's that got to do with anything?"

I told him all about the so-called monad the mayor had under guard, and he nodded his head, intrigued. "It makes me think of one of these." He spit an apple seed into a garbage basket a few paces away.

"A garbage can?" I asked.

"The seed, or an acorn or whatever. It's a tiny speck of wood right now. Then again, when it breaks open in the right conditions, it's got a whole tree in there just waiting to come out."

"That's completely different," I said.

Hothen shrugged. "I say if the young man broke himself in, we can break him out."

In the early evening darkness, Hothen and I scoped out the workshop. The place protruded from one of the inner walls, with a few large windows approximately jumping distance above ground. Most of those posted had congregated near its entrance, probably more interested in the ongoing festivities than watching for some fool to try breaking down the front door. A mere two guards patrolled back and forth across the outer faces of the workshop, and that half-heartedly.

I certainly didn't relish the thought of sneaking around in my own home, hiding from my own countrymen. But my duty as a father demanded more than comfort would allow. We crept up to the side of the workshop, taking a place in the shadows. The noise from the New Moons festivities provided fair auditory cover.

When a gap in the patrollers allowed, we headed for the window, planting a broken bottle where it could be seen on the way. We hopped high enough to catch the ledge and hoisted ourselves onto the windowsill. Of course, they had latched the thing shut. For that, I unsheathed a fine-tipped mercy knife, putting the point in the center of a small pane.

As I held the blade steady with leather-gloved hands, Hothen tapped ever so carefully on the end of the handle. The pane broke into a few shards without falling from its place. Still, the sound was louder than I'd hoped.

We pried the shards free, stuffed them in our pockets, and hid in the rafters just as the next patroller rounded the corner.

From my spot in the shadows, I spied the next patroller. He glanced around, not unexpectantly. If he did catch sight of our decoy bottle, he shrugged it off and returned the same way he'd come.

When he'd disappeared around the corner, we got the window unlatched and slipped into the workshop without another sound.

The full moons had just barely peaked over the horizon, leaving most of the workshop shrouded and dim. Objects gradually began to present themselves as my eyes adjusted.

The monad floated inside an empty bowl on one of the workbenches. All sorts of crushing and pinching implements lay strewn haphazardly around it. Could it really be that the thing was indestructible?

"They tried breaking in with everything already," Hothen spoke in a hushed voice.

"Yet Shran must've done it with his bare hands," I said.

"Does it know the difference then?"

I shrugged and grabbed it. At first it felt softer than cotton. Once again, the more it shrank, the more it hardened until it was solid as iron. I released the pressure, and it bounced back to cotton without a hitch.

Hothen tried as well, with similar results.

I whipped out the necklace with its three nested rings. "We'll try this instead." I stuck the monad in the innermost ring and snapped the little cage shut. At that size, the orb looked hardly distinguishable from polished amber, save for one spot. The oval area under the lensless eyepieces had a discolored look to it.

I peered in to see a hazy image. However I rotated the pendant, the image also rotated as if around some stationary object. And the closer I held it to my eye, the larger the image got. It seemed to be two people walking through a cave, not sculptures but real, moving people.

"What are you doing?" Hothen asked.

"There really are people in here. See?"

Hothen stared straight into the eyepiece like I had, then shook his head.

Was the man blind? I looked in again. One of the people was a light-haired girl I didn't recognize, and when I held the necklace in just the right way, the other was most definitely my son. He was alive and still kicking!

"Look from right here, then."

Again Hothen saw nothing at all, no matter at which angle or distance he held it.

It made no sense, unless… "My word. If I can see it and you can't, then this monad truly is tied to our bloodline. I can see when you can't, and my son alone can break the barrier. The offspring is the whole key."

"Then what now?" Hothen asked.

What now, indeed. If it was as Steve had said—and so far it was—and no one else understood monads—and they clearly didn't—what would a wise man do? I could steal away with the object, only to immediately become the prime suspect. From there,

I might incur further frivolous punishments without actually aiding Shran in any way. Alternatively, I could trust my very eyes.

One more good look gave some assurance, the lad was in there, and somehow I would see him again. I clicked the little necklace wide open. "We're leaving it," I said, returning the monad to the bowl where we'd found it.

"Zieglon, did we come for nothing?"

"No. You made me believe, my friend. He's in the Father's hand now."

Chapter Nineteen

Liza

"**P**lease go away," I cried.

Haldra hesitated to approach. "Or what? You'll kill me like you just killed her?"

"I wasn't trying to..." Then what was I trying to do?

"Don't kid yourself, Liza. You ripped my friend's very life from her."

"No," I said.

"As plain as day, you did. Now I see exactly why you tried to hide your pretty hair from me until now. Don't worry. You've got an incredible gift and one that makes you look eerily similar to that Tower man everyone is talking about."

"Just leave me alone."

"You already are. Don't deny it. Husband always gone. Your birth family long dead. We're in this together for now. If Guilen finds out that you've given his secret away—"

"Then you'll be in as much trouble as I am."

"Perhaps," Haldra said. "Though you broke your oath, not I. That's how he'll see it at least. Even if Guilen tried to kill or banish his own little sister, you don't think I have contingency plans?"

"What do you want?"

"I want you to join us, of course. To spare you and yours from ruin, despite your strange efforts to the contrary."

"How can I believe anything you say, Haldra? Tell me that?"

She unholstered a pair of knives from hidden sheaths and tossed them so they fell my feet. They looked a wicked little set of implements with purple leather grips and stubby double edges sharp as razors.

"There. See?" she said. "I've no interest in hurting you, Liza."

I kicked the knives away. "I already did what you wanted. I showed you the silver stag."

Haldra flicked one and then the other platelet at the mouth of either sheath. Each rang out, summoning its knife, which darted into place more cleanly than if guided by hand. "And now both he and my maid are dead. I need a friend's help tonight: your help."

I said nothing, but felt my resolve weaken by the second.

"Oh, for your own sake, take this chance before it's too late."

I rushed to our chambers as soon as reaching the palace. That distinct "Penna melody" floating around in my reserves had grown more and more discontent, accusing me with each disjointed beat. After being sick in the latrine, I looked in the mirror for the first time since the change. My throat didn't have as much as a bruise, but now that very white hair on my head was spattered with crimson. The implication couldn't be clearer: Penna's stolen life. Yet no blood had been spilled.

I rinsed, shampooed, and repeated till I'd run out of water for the basin. The crimson splotches remained clear as ever. The vibrance itself must have caused the color change, and I had to get it out of me.

That distinctly human life continued bouncing around in my reserves, along with the starlight. Like oil and water, they refused to mix. Though I can't describe exactly how, I mentally grabbed at those droplets of Penna's vibrance floating around in my reserves and moved them to one side. Then I pressed some through my feet into the floor. I stopped when circles of mold started springing up all over, rotting the long-dead planks.

I gave up the endeavor and finally put together what this gift actually did. Rather than truly healing or restoring what was ruined, I could only accelerate living processes. Wherever death took hold, death remained.

Nevertheless, I went back to the mirror for another look. While some of the red disappeared, each dimmed spot left a sharp red outline behind. At a loss for how to explain such a change, I pinned it all up and hid it under a bonnet that tied down around my cheeks. That would have to do for now.

Zieglon smiled kindly when I found him by the mayor's court. After how we'd left off earlier, I at least had the sense not to say something stupid all over again. I smiled back as we went to dinner.

Despite being quite hungry, I barely managed to force a morsel down. I just looked at Shran's empty seat, bringing to mind vague images of him trapped in some dark other world. Was he gone forever?

The rest of the time there, Penna's anguished screams repeated themselves in my head. Those accusations kept pushing their way back up despite every attempt to deny them: It's all your fault Liza, and you enjoyed it.

"I have to go to bed," I whispered to Zieglon.

"Me too," Zieglon said resolutely.

I clung to his arm as we strode through the hall, barely aware of anything else. How could he be so strong amidst all those palace folk? Why and how could he endure those lashes when he had another option?

What if he knew I had as good as broken a solemn oath that very night? If I even started explaining what had happened at the cave, he would know. Would he ever look at me the same after that? If I could at least tell him something, maybe it could help.

"I'm so sorry, Zieglon," I said when we were up in our chambers. "You ought to know about this." I unfastened my bonnet, letting my white and crimson splotched hair fall below my shoulders.

"From what happened in the Tower?" Zieglon said.

I nodded.

"Are you hurt?"

"I was." And I finally told him all of what had happened in the Tower, how I thought I'd died before Steve revived me. "And then my hair looked like this," I said, touching some of it that was white. If he believed that meant the red splotches too, that was his assumption.

"I sense things now that I never could before. Whenever I touch a living thing, I feel this flashing, singing essence. It shows me the entire person or creature or plant. As long as I'm touching it, I can see it all even without looking at it."

Zieglon nodded, impressed but not surprised. "That's how you knew about the lashes."

"Yes, and there's more. Can I show you?"

"Please."

"This might feel a bit odd, but this is how I managed to fix the silver stag." I touched his back and pressed in a little starlight, focusing as much as possible only on the wounded areas and striving to keep any of Penna's essence far removed.

Zieglon let out a yelp as if he'd just dove into a frozen pond. Fully visible through that new sense, the skin and muscle rapidly wove themselves back to normal.

He spun me around in a flurry. "Liza, you're incredible."

"It's the least I could do."

"Now let me show you something." He unlatched a necklace and pulled it out from under his collar. It had a pendant of three iron rings but no stone. "I used this, and it worked."

"Huh?" was all I could say.

"It holds the monad like a little amulet, and you can see right inside. Shran's still in there, in one piece."

"Well, where is it then?" I asked.

"Safe as it'll ever be. There's nothing the mayor or any of us can do for now. So, I want you to have this."

'Thank you," I said, taking the simple little token. Then the tears started to flow. Our troubles were far from over.

He wrapped those strong arms around me and kissed my forehead. "Save your worries," he said. "Now's time for sleep."

We went to bed, but after that agreement with Haldra, I knew no rest would come.

Chapter Twenty

Shran

Stumbling backwards into the side of the crimson corridor, I slid to a seat, stiff. Was this the grave I'd fallen into, nothing but enemies and torture without escape? My stomach churned angrily, my mouth parched dry. I couldn't sate my thirst, much less pay off the fine. All I could do was stare blankly at the wall.

At some point, a dark figure stood over me. Blinking parched eyes, I saw it was Siever. "Funnela asked me to come talk to you," Siever said. "She's got a pair of chapped lips, and her palate is all dry. The lake water is ours, of course, but we have yet to figure out how to get down and harvest it. She's also hungry."

If Siever was almighty here, able to control countless lights at once, then why was he begging some interloper for food?

"What I'm saying is, the faster you pay off this fine, the better." Siever removed his broad-rimmed hat. "My top hat should hold two liters. Don't rip it."

I let the "top hat" fall over my eyes, resting on the bridge of my nose. I couldn't even bring myself to move.

Siever continued. "I can't do anything about the no-light penalty—if word got out, you see."

I heard him, but still just stared, mute.

"Anyway, now you've had a minute to rest your legs," he pulled me to my feet with surprising strength. "It's time you get back to work." He dragged me down the crimson corridor and shoved me into a side passage.

I walked blindly about the passage, not bothering to lift the brim from my eyes. Either way I couldn't see a thing. All was pure, uncut blackness. Only my hands guided me, one in front and one sliding along the wall. I figured I'd come to another waterbud eventually.

After a long way like that, my foot slipped, and I fell. It must have been one of those funnel holes, but I didn't even try to stop myself. I slid down, down, down. If that was how All Father wanted to end me, so be it. This slick tunnel swerved this way and that, further and further down.

Then I fell through open air, crashed onto something crunchy, and tumbled to the base of it. I seemed to be lying on the same old bone pile. The hat landed beside me. To my left was Courtlya, muttering and illuminating some of the area with her blank stare. She still seemed incapable of acknowledging my presence.

"This is hopeless," I sobbed aloud.

Praying was a practice I routinely failed at. I never really understood the canonized ones, or why we ought to recite them over and over again. I knew All Father could hear everything, but it never seemed like he cared enough to do anything about it. Then, the times I tried speaking in my own words, the right ones didn't come. What was the point in that? This time, all I knew was, I couldn't make it on my own. "Please, sir. Help me," I said in the darkness.

Glinta popped her head out from behind the bone pile. She'd definitely heard me, and I flushed in embarrassment.

"What's the matter?" she asked.

I sniffed, working to keep my voice steady. "I fell down a funnel hole."

"Oh no," she said. "Anything else?"

"I'm hungry, and there's no food or water."

"Anything else?"

I'd already told her, but I angrily stated the obvious. "Siever took my light away."

"And?"

Why wouldn't she let up? "And I can't do anything. Everybody hates me, and…"

"Yes?"

"And I can't escape. I can't do anything."

"Who says you have to escape? Where would you escape to?"

"I'm not from here. I'm from the real world."

"This is all real. I'm real."

"Well, my world's bigger. I have to go back."

"Why do you have to?"

"Because everything's too hard here, and everybody hates me."

"Are things easy in your world, where everybody loves you?"

I almost laughed aloud. "No, but mine's big enough that I can go somewhere else."

"What if it's hard there too?"

"I'd go somewhere else."

"What if that doesn't work out either? What if your big world just has more hard places to run to?"

Now there was a scary thought. If all I've ever found was terrible, what's to stop the whole world from being the same? Could life be that bad? How could All Father allow it? "Well that's easy for you to say," I said. "You never had to live through what I have."

"I had to live through this," she held up the dead plant.

I recalled the way I'd hacked away at it, striking that stone against it again and again. I knew that ugly thing was hurting, yet I showed no mercy. All I'd cared about was me, was getting Courtlya to like me. But surely, I'd gone through worse than Glinta had. I had to deal with a clique of nobles who made a game of tormenting me with no way to fight back, and then my only hope in the world turned to pointless suffering.

"At least Funnela and Siever aren't mean to you," I said. "At least your only friend didn't order you around all the time and then ignore you."

"That isn't all true. I love anything the light shines upon. I'm a friend to all life. But that doesn't mean they treat *me* like a friend. Funnela and Siever have been ordering me around since the moment I met them."

"You too?"

She nodded yes.

"No light even shines on me. You said you hated me earlier."

"I was heartbroken. I thought you came here for something wonderful. What you did is still breaking my heart now." And she sobbed openly, not even hiding her face. I felt my own face redden with embarrassment. She kept looking right at me, straight into my eyes as she cried and cried. I wanted to leave but feared where else I might fall in the blackness.

I was trapped. Her tears poured on and on without end. Her ruddy crying face wouldn't leave me, and was all I could see, with no light of my own.

I couldn't hold back anymore. I didn't care if I hurt her feelings. In a sudden rage, I shouted, "Stop it!" She wouldn't, so I kept right on. "You childish little... why do you keep embarrassing yourself like that?"

"Because I'm sad. I have to cry when I'm sad."

164

"Then why don't you go cry by yourself?"

"Because I can't bear my feelings on my own. Why don't you ever share yours with anybody?"

What a dumb question. Of course I had to keep those to myself because… because if people knew, they'd laugh at me, or worse, hate me.

Down there, everybody hated me already. But then again, I still couldn't because if they knew… if they knew…

"Shran, tell me what you feel!" she insisted.

"No."

"Why?"

"I can't do that," I said, but my voice cracked.

"Don't say can't if you mean won't."

"I…"

"Tell me, Shran. Share it with me," she sobbed.

"I'm just not good enough."

"What do you mean?"

"No one cares about me unless they have to!" I blurted and then cringed, hating myself for telling her the pitiful truth. Why would I tell her that?

She wasn't laughing at me though. She only sobbed harder. "I believe you," she said, "but I choose to love you anyway."

"No. You don't even know me."

"I know you're hurting, Shran. I know you need help."

"Nobody can help me."

"Then let me just give you a hug."

I only stared off at the blackness as she knelt there, arms open. Tears rolled down my dull eyes.

"Please, Shran."

I held my tongue.

"Don't leave me. Don't leave me alone," she cried.

And I couldn't do it, couldn't leave her like Courtlya left me. I wrapped shaking arms around this girl I didn't even know, resting my chin on her shoulder. I sobbed, letting the tears flow, still she held onto me without letting go.

Chapter Twenty-One

Zieglon

Sunday morning, I awoke before dawn to find Liza already gone and her wardrobe hanging open. It wasn't like her. Her riding cloak was also gone, along with her favorite pair of boots and the necklace I'd given her. What could she be up to?

I needed to prepare for the battle before long, but was in no mood to lose my wife *and* my son in two days. I grabbed Hothen's signal bell, threw on some clothes, and raced down to the workshop.

"Whoa there, General," Berrin said at the workshop door.

I humored him by keeping a respectable distance instead of shaking him by the collar before I asked, "Did my wife come by here at any point last night?"

He yawned and shook his head. "Not a soul has bothered us until now."

"Have you checked it?"

"It's really none of your business, but yes, as it happens. At the top of every rock-dashed hour."

"Check again," I insisted, and when Berrin did, he found the monad right where I'd left it. Odd.

Down at the stables, I found Liza's mare still in the stall. So, where had she gotten to? Once again, there was no trace. Nothing to track at all. I grew more and more disturbed by the image of what looked like blood-spattered hair she'd been hiding. Steve didn't have that.

Something was quite wrong. I just knew it. I headed straight to the dungeon tower to see that tower-dweller once more.

"Where is she?" I demanded.

Steve stretched contentedly and climbed out of his cot. "Good morning, Zieglon," he said, squinting with bed-eyes. "Happy to help if you care to explain what you're talking about."

"She told me all about what you did to her. Now she's disappeared just like my son."

"Your wife, then. Do you mean to say you saw her disappear into the monad?"

"All I know is she disappeared with riding gear at some point last night but didn't take her horse."

"If Shran's still gone, then even as his mother, she couldn't break the monad barrier. So, that narrows it down a bit more."

"I need real answers. Where is she?"

"How should I know that?"

"Because you tricked her, did sick things to her and she hasn't been the same sense."

"True. No mortal can stand in the light without being burned, but she's been given a great gift."

"Should I douse you with a bucket of hog blood and call it a gift?"

Steve looked shocked, perhaps for the first time ever, at that. "You don't mean to say she looked like that?"

"I do."

"I'm afraid that would mean she's taken a human life. If she hasn't told you about it..."

Despite the instinct to immediately call him a liar, I remembered the way she'd acted at dinner: the vacant stares, the silent tears she brushed away. Something even worse had indeed happened to her since that afternoon.

The next moment, Hothen's signal bell rang, indicating the riders had begun readying to move out soon. Steve looked at me expectantly, but I didn't signal back.

"Steve," I said, "you brought my family into this mess—don't deny it. I'm sick of failing, despite doing nothing wrong. So, you tell me. What am I supposed to do? What am I supposed to do when everyone disappears with no rhyme or reason?"

Again the bell rang, and I didn't signal back.

"What should you do? You should answer the call where you're needed."

"I want to know my family's safe."

"You can't. No one can. Yet, I find that simple obedience has the strangest tendency of leading exactly where you need to be. What will you do, Zieglon?"

I led my men up an old cart path to the northern forest. The party of fifty fully armored cavalry trotted behind me in the early morning sunlight. Thordin held the foreguard, with a hand-picked party of his own.

"So, Zieglon," Hothen said, riding beside me, "are you sure we'll be able to beat that abominable giant this time?"

"In any ordinary battle, ten to one odds is optimal. Given the stature of this enemy, ten times that will be sufficient if we keep our wits about us."

"That's counting Thordin's party. What if he goes rogue again to try and steal away the prize?"

"For his sake, pray he remembers this is a battle, not a hunt."

Hothen chuckled. "That'll be the day."

Aside from the archers and spearmen, I also stationed four men at the corners of the party with purrium core spears. Those riders left the sister platelets behind so they could strike the exposed core for an unimpeded ring. The sound seemed to prick at the giant's temper so violently that we might be able to draw him into a position of our choosing. I brought a similar throwing spear for myself, should the need arise.

As we approached the tree line, I myself started to second guess the plan. Ohha Forest made for a fine hunting ground under normal circumstances. I enjoyed the feeling of being dwarfed by the towering pines and making use of the generous cover offered by its old oaks and alders. Now, an enemy of uncertain cleverness waited somewhere therein. As the shady foliage enveloped the last of Thordin's riders, I even questioned who hunted whom.

We made our way deep into the forest, beyond the berry patches and other vestiges of civilization.

Thordin's party separated off as we sought out the clearing where we'd first met the giant. Their party had a similar setup to ours but a completely different strategy. Soon as they got a few hundred yards off on our left flank, they started striking their purrium spears, resounding for all to hear. He'd bring the beast down on top of us on its terms instead of our own. There was simply no reasoning with that man.

Soon enough, there came a distant rushing through the woods like I'd heard before. Thordin must've heard it too, because the purrium ring suddenly fell silent. Then the rushing stopped.

I heard men shout and horses scream from Thordin's party. Bows twanged, and a guttural, inhuman voice yelped, perhaps more surprised than injured. Then more chaos ensued. Thordin's horn blasted a call for aid. There was no open ground there for a proper cavalry charge. Yet we had to respond.

We headed for Thordin's party, barely able to gallop through the brush. The melee fell silent while we still had no visual on the party or the foe. There came a scream and dry snap—presumably one of the purrium spears—and another missed volley.

Our only option was to draw the monster out, then strike. Once we got a visual on Thordin's party, on my order, one of the front spearman struck his purrium core spear and cast it into a tree. It rang out in full view of both parties.

As predicted, the beast sprinted out from his hiding spot, large feline ears twitching angrily. The instant he had the spear between his teeth, we loosed a volley, several arrows sticking into his leathery back. He grunted, but disappeared again before we could do any serious damage. We had to get out of those thick woods and take him with the spear. I sounded a retreat, hoping to draw the monster to an ideal battleground.

It wasn't far to the clearing, but he pursued ferociously. Archers fired backwards, never landing a decisive hit. It towered well above the tips of the raised spears and swiped two men from their mounts in his approach.

At last we broke into the clearing and galloped into its center. As I turned my men, readying to charge, the beast did not emerge when he ought have. Instead, that crashing gait carried on around the edge of the clearing.

That greasy beast knew its strength was in cover and kept to it. The clearing was a lot longer than it was wide, and he kept moving towards the spot.

171

I cursed and directed the party to face the giant's most likely location.

At my command, one of the rear corner soldiers struck his purrium spear. The giant quieted behind the trees, too quiet now to hear over the ringing spear. He should have charged straight at us, yet held back.

A moss-covered rock large as a man came hurling down on us. The soldiers scattered out of its path. It bounced and crashed into one rider, his horse squealing. Then came a log, spinning horizontally, at our right flank. The men cleared an even larger path, further upsetting our formation.

The trees rustled frantically before us. He'd be charging out any second now. "Spears at the ready," I said.

The six-meter fiend came swinging tree to tree, launching itself right for the middle of our ranks. He shook the ground on the landing, in the hollowed-out center of the formation. We had him surrounded but with no room to charge him at full speed. I sounded my horn, calling for Thordin's aid. Where had the man gotten to?

The monster swatted spears out of his way, barely scathed, as individuals tried to poke at him. He carefully worked his way to the ringing purrium. Even the archers couldn't get a good shot without endangering fellow soldiers. He kicked and punched at disarmed men, horses screaming as riders fell to the ground. The men were breaking up further.

"Close ranks," I ordered. We couldn't let him get his prize. We had to delay. The terrified men heeded my command, the crazed monster still flinging weapons and men to the ground. Even he couldn't protect all sides at once. As the circle closed in, several spears found some purchase near the loins. He shrieked in fury, kicking and stomping as he shook free. But he favored a now-wounded leg.

The chorus of Thordin's charging horses overtook the sound of the melee, but they were still some distance away. The purrium bait-spear silenced as the monster approached. The corner spearman must have lost his nerve.

At last, I struck my bait-spear and cast it towards the approaching cavalry. "Make way!" I ordered. The spear landed amid the grass. My riders parted, forming a corridor for the oncoming charge, even as the monster ran after my spear.

Thordin's cavalry met him at a full gallop. They pierced deep into his abdomen, shafts breaking off as the cavalry passed between our ranks. He cried out in pain, grabbing up a horse with his rider and flinging them into the trees. Yet more men struck him, blood spurting.

Clutching at its wounds, the monster loped off into the woods. He would be going back to whatever hovel or bog he lived in. Soon, he would keel over on his own if we followed long enough. So, we held a close enough following distance to keep him at a jog.

He crashed and tumbled his way through the brush until he neared the steaming lake, a landmark most avoided as a bad omen. He entered a hole so tall he barely had to duck on his way in. It appeared he'd only recently excavated it.

Undeterred, I commanded, "Charge!" and the contingent of my men galloped into the hole with spears readied. It gradually sloped a long way downwards, more than long enough for all my riders to fit inside. Oddly enough, at the end of the tall passage, sharp, blue light illuminated another cavern with a perfectly circular entrance. But the giant never made it there.

He erred greatly by choosing this location. Now his silhouette stood out clearly against the blue background, while we remained cloaked in shadow.

We struck true, piercing deep into his abdomen. Yet even as he squealed, he grabbed a club the size of a log and swung blindly, knocking a few men against the tunnel wall. Then the archers released a perfect volley. Arrows sank into his neck and open mouth. The beast fell backwards with a thunderous thud. In a few heaved breaths, his heart struck its last. His prognathous head, as long as a man, smacked the dusty ground.

I dismounted to inspect our trophy. His breath stank of rotten fruit and meat. He clearly ate a similar diet to a man, with none of the delicacy. "Excellent work," I shouted to my riders. "Let's get this carted off before Thordin claims it for himself."

Barely a moment later, Thordin and his party arrived. He dismounted a mere meter away, eyes blazing with the will to fight for his claim. Solving a difficult problem is one thing. Proving you did it is a whole 'nother beast.

"Thordin, no," I said preemptively.

"Zieglon, my man, you can't possibly believe you won this prize on your own," he said, centimeters from my face.

I refused to let myself back up a hair's breadth. "First, we had to answer your call for aid—the result of your foolish tactics. Then, as you can see, we killed the giant ourselves."

"Nonsense, Zieglon. My cavalry struck the decisive blow when you were in a full retreat."

"Really? How many giants have you slain up till today?"

"I guess you weren't listening to Falen the other night. This giant was no more than a particularly nasty breed of pre-Storm human. If you don't recognize a decisive blow on a man, I suggest finding a new profession."

"You will not take this from me, Thordin."

He grinned. "Fine. I suppose we'll split it, say fifty-fifty."

"How about eighty-twenty," I said.

"My favor?"

"Of course not."

"Be reasonable Zieglon."

"You had your way last time, destroying my catch. And you would've been dead twice over at this point."

Thordin chuckled, shaking his head as he stepped back and paced the floor. "Perhaps you have a point. I'll think about it while we wait for the carts."

To make Thordin budge on a claim such as this was a feat almost unsung until now. This time, I would get my prize. That's what I'd give my family: the right to say, a Mattian killed the giant.

I found Hothen staring at the kill and clapped him on the back excitedly. "We've done it, my friend," I said. "We've saved the mayorship."

"They better carve us a statue for this," Hothen said.

"Two statues. One for my left side and one for my right."

We laughed as I hadn't laughed for days.

After a few moments, Hothen asked, "So, what is this place anyway?"

The floor of the entry hall was covered in dirt, yet as my eyes adjusted, I saw the walls and ceiling formed a smooth metallic arch. "Whatever it is, this brute didn't build it," I said.

We walked through the circular gate whose massive metal door hung wide open. The cavern within, really a much larger, squared-off room, looked reasonably defensible, with most of it raised up on either side of a long entry stairway. As I approached the stairs, the glint of a small metal object caught my eye. I picked it up and knew beyond a doubt, it was the monad-holder necklace, the necklace I'd given to Liza.

Chapter Twenty-Two

Shran

I dusted off Siever's old top hat and placed it loosely on my head. Lady Courtlya still wouldn't respond, and she probably needed her rest.

"What are you doing, Shran?" Glinta asked.

"You made me realize I really can do it. If I've got to fall down every funnel hole in this place and end up back here, I'm going to do it, going to win my light back, going to win Courtlya's title back."

"That sounds *hard*."

"Yeah," I said resolutely and still felt nervous for what I was about to ask. "So, Glinta, I ask you to possibly—"

"Of course I'll help you!"

The two of us set off across the bridge, went partway down the crimson hall, and entered a side passage. Glinta kept a few paces behind. On my own, I still couldn't see my hand in front of my face, but the light tracking her gaze warmed my back and lit some of the path in front of me. Though this wasn't the most convenient form of spelunking, it allowed two of us to see instead of only one. That left it up to me to seek out a waterbud.

As a thank you for coming along, I passed Glinta a handful of the dried fruit still left in my side pouch. She gobbled it all up immediately and asked if I had any more.

"Sorry, that's it," I said, and she groaned, disappointedly.

We'd walked a fair distance through the passage when Glinta asked, "Who were you talking to earlier?"

"What do you mean?"

"You know. After you fell out of the funnel mouth, you talked like there was some man there."

I had to rack my brain to figure out what she meant. "Oh. You mean All Father."

"Who is that?"

"Well, he's the one who fathered everything and keeps it from turning to pure chaos."

"How come you think he listens to you, if you don't mind me asking?"

At that I laughed. "If he's holding everything together, he's got to be able to hear everything too."

"But how do you know he's listening? I didn't hear anyone talk back to you."

"No," I said, and we walked on a bit further as I thought it over. "But you did."

"So?"

"Lots of songs say how he speaks in many ways at just the right time."

"How come I can see everybody else but not him? Is he listening from out in your world?"

"He's even beyond that, but he must be holding this place together the same as my world."

"What a strange person this All Father... did you see that, Shran?"

"See what?" Nothing but cave and blackness surrounded us.

"Wait. There it is again." She coned her hands and shouted, "All Father, Sir."

"What are you doing?"

"I'm trying to save us some time," she said and went back to shouting. "Please give us some water already."

"You'll only get us punished, asking for an easy-out like that."

"Your dry snacks made me thirsty," she groaned.

"But you can't just… and don't make fun of my snacks."

Something caught my eye off in a side corridor. It glowed bright as day, a fat woody thing growing out of the wall with a few large green leaves. "Waterbud," I announced.

Glinta looked too, lighting up the corridor leading to the distant plant.

"Incredible," she said, hugging me excitedly.

We ran off for the waterbud. I had a bit of a lead, and unfortunately, she didn't survey anything more than a few paces in front of me. Since most things were black, I didn't notice the dark chasm until I was right on top of it.

I skidded to a halt, turning to laugh sheepishly right as Glinta bumped into me at full speed. I completely lost my balance, saw nothing to grab onto, and in my last-ditch effort, leapt as far as I could.

Glinta screamed as I sailed out across the abyss, hoping against hope something waited there for me to land on. Glinta's gaze illuminated solid ground on the other side, but I'd already peaked out. No way could my feet reach it. I caught the ledge practically by the fingertips and slammed into the rock face below.

Gasping for the breath that had been knocked out of me, I strained to pull myself up, with no foothold. Grunting and straining as Glinta cried out from the far side, I managed to get my chin onto the ledge. That bit of rest left me enough strength to roll onto solid ground.

"I'm so sorry," Glinta said, clutching the top hat I'd apparently dropped.

"I'm alright," I said, climbing to my feet, then wincing at the pain in my side. "Well, I've had worse."

"I can't jump that far. It's too scary," Glinta said, looking into the chasm. It went way down, with no soft landing or ledge to climb across.

On my side, the waterbud still shone with its own daylight a few meters away. I walked up it, and Glinta lent some light to my feet. This one also had a nice pool of water at the top, not nearly enough, but we'd have to fill our quota somehow.

"Here, Glinta. Throw me that hat, will you?"

She tossed it over like a discus, and I got to work. After scooping the meager puddle into the upturned hat, I realized how utterly grueling this task still was.

"This'll take a *really* long time," I said. "Unless…" I painfully pressed my shoulder into the plant. It barely gave in at all and made an agitated rumbling noise like the one from earlier.

"Stop! That's hurting it," Glinta said.

"But we need a lot more water than this," I said, seeing that the pool remained quite empty.

"What do you expect, treating it like that?"

"Then what do you recommend?"

She blew a few loose strands of white hair out of her face. "Something else."

Half a dozen ridiculous ideas passed through my head: how to make a magic plant do its job faster? I shook my head and sighed aloud. And there it went. The pool rose slightly, while I'd sighed.

"Oh," I said.

"What's happening over there?"

"I think it likes sound."

180

"Well, keep doing it."

I sighed exactly the same way, but nothing happened. "It's not working anymore."

"Maybe it's bored. Try something more interesting."

I laughed at the thought of a bored plant. Then yet again, the pool appeared to rise ever so slightly. "Okay. How about this," I said, and hummed the scale from the lowest through to the highest note I could reach. The little pool filled up quickly, and I scooped more into the hat.

"It likes music notes," I said, chuckling. I'd figured it out so easily. Yet the next time I went through the scales, the pool only filled about halfway and continued to have diminishing returns after that.

Then it came to me in a flash: singing. I had to sing to it and knew just the song. Thinking back to that moment in the hedge maze, I remembered the song Nella sang, the song from lessons with a beautiful new melody. Almost like magic, the words came to me as soon as I needed them.

I sang it, mumbling it quietly at first, but the plant seemed to have a volume preference as well. So, I sang with my full voice, loud enough even Glinta could hear it across the way. Clear, crisp water cascaded down the sides of the plant. With the help of the broad-brim top hat, I easily harvested all of it.

On and on I sang, making up a similar melody of my own for the parts I hadn't heard, until the hat was full. Then I turned to my partner, clutching the two-liter hat in my arms.

Glinta sat as if mesmerized. "What was that?" She asked with shimmering eyes.

"Oh, it's only a song from our lessons. I heard someone sing it like that once."

"It was beautiful. Your voice sounds so vibrant, so full of love."

My face flushed with embarrassment, but I just said, "Thank you." She nodded, and I considered my next move. "I barely made it over here before, and I can't jump back across here with all this water."

"Then how are we gonna get it back and pay your fine?"

"I'll have to slide down another one of those funnel holes and get back up top from there."

"Do you see any?"

"I still can't see anything you can't. But it sounds like this passage keeps going a ways off to the right here. I might be able to feel my way to one."

"What if there's another chasm?"

"That's what I thought too. I wish I could do it on my own, but... I still need your help."

"My help, how?"

"You've got to jump across, Glinta."

"All the way across that? *You* barely made it, though."

"I know. That's why I'm gonna catch you, if you trust me."

She started hyperventilating. "Oh, I don't know, Shran."

"Then I'll just have to feel my way on my own."

She finally caught her breath. "Okay, but you better not drop me."

"Alright," I said, grabbing a solid rock and leaning over the drop-off. "Ready."

She froze as she gazed straight down the chasm.

"Don't look down there. Look at my hand," I couldn't even see the thing in front of my face until she looked up again. "Try getting a running start. It's more than I had."

"That's just because you're good at that stuff."

All the same, she backed up, took a deep breath, and dashed forward. I guess she really wasn't much of a runner. She jumped a bit too early, peaking out before I could snatch her flailing hand. Still clinging to that rock, I reached as far as I could stretch. Our fingers brushed, then somehow, we both closed fists as strong as steel. She slammed into the wall below, nearly yanking my shoulder out of joint. I gasped and squealed in pain.

"Grab something," I said, my shoulder roaring with pain. After not a little more kicking and pulling, Glinta crawled back onto solid ground.

We walked off down the new passage, water sloshing around in the hat as we went. It felt so peaceful to have a real-life friend, knowing she didn't have to help but chose to. Soon, we found a funnel hole. Some of the water would undoubtedly be lost on the way down, so we both took a nice swig off the top.

I shouted "Tallyho," and jumped.

Glinta slid down after me, her screams echoing across the polished surface. As we swerved this way and that, I caught glimpses of yet more shoots feeding into ours. The cave system seemed absolutely massive.

At last, we landed on the bone pile, up top once more. Siever and Funnella were already there waiting for us.

"Fantastic," Funnela cheered as some of the water splashed straight onto her bright face.

"You did it, lad," Siever said, nabbing the hat and guzzling water from it triumphantly.

"Oh, let me at that darling," Funnela moaned, licking the droplets from her lips.

"Wait your turn," he growled between gulps. Once he'd emptied about three-quarters, he passed her the leftovers.

She yanked it to herself, daintily puckering her lips and sipping down to the last drop. Then she slammed the soggy hat back onto Siever's head.

He merely straightened the brim before turning to me. "I see you've succeeded in the first stage of your fine. Now onto fruits. You'll need to procure the fruit of the honeyoak, a temperamental old breed to harvest from, as I hear it."

"And how do I find them?"

Funnela went wide-eyed. "You've got to go... deeper."

I gulped.

"Not to worry," Siever said. "We've brought a fellow here who has an appetite for danger."

"Who?" I asked.

"Oh, I think you've met before." Siever put two fingers in his mouth, grimaced slightly as his lips curled over those very sharp teeth, and made a shrill whistle. "Diver, come follow the young man."

Even as Siever and Funnela walked away, the young man— who looked more like a boy—ran into the topside cavern. As he neared us, I recognized him as the same wave-crazed boy I met on the beach. He sneered when he was a few paces away. "Oh, hi Shran."

Chapter Twenty-Three

Liza

Zieglon went to sleep quickly, while I couldn't catch a wink of it. My heart thumped and thumped as I tossed and turned. Both moons waxed full, the blue moon, Sartir, right behind the red moon, Albier. They created that strange violet moonlight through the shredded curtains, and part of each shadow still had that faint orange and blue around it. The longer I tossed and turned, the thinner those outlines became.

After quite a while, the last vestige of blue and orange linings shrank to nothing, marking Albier's bi-annual eclipse and my time to leave. I looked over to Zieglon and silently lamented yet another night of sleep we wouldn't share.

Quietly as possible, I pushed off the covers and slid out of bed, then donned warm riding clothes for wherever we were headed. Last of all, I ever so carefully fastened the strange necklace around my neck and went out to meet Haldra. Fiddling with that empty iron pendant offered my only semblance of comfort as I crept alone through the dim halls.

I found the lady near a secluded hallway on the east side of the palace.

"So glad you could make it, Lady Mattian," Haldra said.

I nodded, attempting not to look scared out of my mind. "So, where are we going?"

"Right this way," she said, and led me to the dead end of a secluded corridor.

"Didn't you say we'd be riding somewhere?"

"Mmhmm," she said, then unpinned a broach and lightly flicked the metal backing. The broach emitted the familiar sound of a purrium link, and she twisted it with some effort against thin air. Something clicked inside the rear wall, and the two of us pushed until it swung inwards. Behind it was a long stretch of blackness. With that, Haldra lit a lantern and ushered onward.

The musty, hidden corridor must have had a spider web every two paces, and I could hardly bear it. Scores of broken cobwebs dangled next to freshly repaired ones, mocking anyone fool enough to try cleaning the place up.

Suddenly, I sensed a living thing land in my hair. Without even looking, I perceived its exact form and essence: an eight-legged spider. I frantically smacked it dead before it could bite me. The clear-as-day spider essence disappeared faster than a puff of air.

I had had the misfortune of killing a fair number of spiders in my life before coming to the palace. All that time, the only worry that remained was getting rid of the infernal goo they left behind. Yet this time, well after I'd snuffed the creature out, that vivid essence of the spider crawled around in my mind. I had seen it— known it—in an instant.

The tunnel twisted gradually downward until we emerged at the base of the cliffs below the far side of the palace. The two of us approached a nearby group of about ten cloaked figures, who had enough horses for everyone. Both the full moons were already visible again, casting those funny orange and blue-tinged shadows behind the people in cloaks.

One of them stepped forward, a man in his early twenties whom I recognized as one of the apprentice palace bards. "So, she's the one, Lady Haldra?" he asked.

"That's right, Fixten," Haldra said. "Lady Mattian will be helping us tonight."

Fixten pursed his lips, eyeing me suspiciously. "What does she know?" he asked. It surprised me to see a mere apprentice bard questioning a lady of Newmund like that, yet Haldra seemed to take no offense.

"It's not what she knows," Haldra said. "It's what she can do. She's smart enough to do the right thing once it's all been explained to her. Right, Lady Mattian?"

"Mmhmm," I said hesitantly.

One of them, whom I recognized as a palace maid, approached me excitedly. She had red hair, bright red lips, and an almost boastfully upriver accent. "The name's Talna," she said. "I knew we'd see another lady in our ranks soon enough."

I didn't dare bring up the circumstances that had led to me joining them, especially with one of the maids. "Just happy to be here," I said, forcing a smile.

With that, we mounted horses and set off. Between the chill in the early morning air and the never-ending worry of what might be coming, I stayed quite alert throughout the whole ride.

Deep into the northern forest, only a few sharp moon-rays penetrated the vapor cloud over the steaming lake, the air ever so slightly tinged with the odor of sulfur. The whole place took on a surreal temper, making me question whether I'd stepped into a dream after all. Not far from the shoreline, we dismounted at a massive hole. One woman stayed back to water the horses, while the rest of us headed underground.

Smooth sheets of metal arched overhead instead of a dirt ceiling, making the hole look like some enormous metal tube. It gradually descended deeper, growing darker until we could only see by the light of Fixten's lantern.

We emerged from the tube into a much larger cavern with a disk-like metal gate hanging wide open. Fixten flipped a small lever on the wall, and a bone-chilling buzz echoed across the large chamber. Many circles of piercingly bright lights flickered to life, flooding a large space with their bright indigo hue. With that, Fixten blew out his lantern and set it aside.

"What are all those lights?" I quietly asked Haldra.

"It's a pre-Storm technology," she said. "This is just one of the sites that survived the Storm."

Fixten led us up a stairway to a broad area that wrapped around and overlooked the entrance. A few levels of catwalks jutted out from the plain walls, each spanned with metal doors every several paces or so. I wondered how the whole thing didn't collapse, since there wasn't a pillar in sight.

An array of square tables with one-legged stools covered most of that level, something like a mayor's court, I supposed, though not nearly as festive and without a high table in sight. Hundreds of people must have dwelt there all those centuries ago, though I couldn't fathom why.

"Isn't it amazing what the pre-Storm folk created?" Haldra remarked as our procession crossed the room. "Such expandability. Such efficiency!"

"But what is this place?" I asked.

"Only a faint remnant of the high civilization the Storm destroyed."

"How could pre-Storm people build it? I thought their brains were all mush in those days."

"Bah. That's those old schoolyard songs talking again: 'All man's knowledge was drained, Till he learned once again, And made song his strong cane'. It's pure balderdash. Pre-Storm folk didn't need children's songs and walking sticks to remember things. Just look at this place. It must have saved hundreds, perhaps thousands of people, all living here in comfort with all their needs met... complete freedom."

"Freedom?"

"Absolutely. In those days, everyone got to eat, drink, or experience whatever they wished, whenever they wished."

"Experience anything?"

"It's like I said: pre-Storm technology. Practically any experience they could imagine was at their beck and call. It was a truly marvelous age," Haldra said.

"Oh, it'll be fantastic," Talna said. "Aren't you excited, Liza?"

"Sort of," I said, seeing everyone now listening.

"More than Sort of," Talna persisted. "It *will be* fantastic. You'll see."

The more I thought about it, the harder I found it to believe. How could any mayorship grow enough of every crop, both in and out of season? And how on Tew could pre-Storm folk bring everyone's imaginations to life all at once? And if they really could, why did the aesthetics of this pre-Storm structure leave so much to be desired?

I settled on another question. "What would become of nobility in a world like that?"

Haldra shrugged. "I don't suppose pre-Storm folk had much need for a noble caste. How could they, once they conquered so many of nature's silly limitations? You see, they didn't need thousands of farmers to get a good harvest, didn't need an army of servers to make a good meal, nor did they need legions of spinstrisses and tailors to make them clothes. They had machines perform that kind of menial task so all humanity could pursue more happy endeavors. No one had to pretend she deserved more or less than someone else. She simply got what she wished when she wanted it."

"So, you would give up your nobility?"

"Anything for humanity to reach where the pre-Storm folks reached," she said, and the others cheered in agreement.

I started to relax a bit after that as we walked deeper into the mysterious complex. After all, it was only a dim remnant of the ancients' world, not the whole of it. This group wanted good things for everyone, not merely for themselves. I still wondered who these people were. "Lady Haldra, what is this group?"

"We're the tip of the iceberg," she said. "A word of advice, never worry about the name. Names must be adapted to the circumstances. I think of us as Keepers of the Secret—the Keesec if you prefer."

"So, all of this has to stay secret?"

She giggled. "There you go, paying more attention to the name than the content. We want everyone with us eventually. But not everyone on Tew—especially the rest of my family—is ready to accept the ancient ways. Until then, we need to limit the Keesec to those we can trust. You, Liza, you're special. You understand where others can't. That's why we want you with us."

As we went, the dread with which I entered that complex transformed into curiosity. How deep did the secret go?

Chapter Twenty-Four

Shran

"So you've got a name after all," I said. "How's your back doing, Diver?"

"Better, no thanks to you," the scraggly-haired boy said. "They said you're looking for honeyoak fruit and hogging fresh water too, so I've got to come with."

He had also brought a pair of what looked like hollowed-out gourds strapped by some rough twine around one shoulder and hanging across his chest.

"Are those for holding the water?"

Diver sniffed. "Yeah. I invented them."

So, Siever and Funnela headed off to business with some other young folks wandering across the bridge, and the effort gained a new member.

Next, I found Courtlya. She had finally stopped stammering and now lay asleep. I nudged her shoulder. "Come on, Lady Courtlya."

She woke up as if from a bad dream. "I'm not a lady. The almighty Siever declared it himself."

"If he's that almighty, he wouldn't need people like me to go get him a sip of water."

"He took your light away, though. You are only a dark spot when no one is looking."

"That doesn't stop me from treating you like a lady."

She thought for a few long moments, and then the last of the haze left her eyes. "Thank you Shran Mattian."

I held out my hand in a courtly manner to lift her back to her feet. "Will you accompany me on the quest to pay our fines?"

"I will," she said, taking hold and rising to her feet. "Aren't you forgetting something?"

I kissed the back of her hand. She didn't yank it away this time but smiled and nodded proudly. "Oh, and you can just call me Shran."

She sighed. "Skipping surnames is not the most courtly thing to do, but if you insist."

Then Courtlya, Diver, Glinta, and I set off across the bridge and into the crimson corridor. We spiraled farther down the red corridor than before, walking off into a side passage where Glinta said she'd seen fruiting honeyoaks. Oddly, she didn't know exactly where she saw them.

It was significantly easier to see and navigate through those caves with three more pairs of eyes lending me their light. I stayed behind Diver and ahead of Glinta and Courtlya, who lit a path for my feet.

The cave grew larger and larger as we went. Stalagmites towered to the ceiling, and colorful moss dotted all over the place. To me they resembled a splotchy night sky wherever no one else was already looking.

We wandered deeper and deeper into that mesh of tunnels and caverns. It was no surprise Glinta didn't know where she'd seen the fruit. Yet, my excitement grew, seeing how much there was to explore. Despite the many twists and turns, the presence of funnel holes made it impossible to get truly lost.

Some of our group were quite parched, but found relief at another waterbud. Glinta joined in with me, singing Nella's song as Courtlya and Diver looked on disapprovingly. They changed their tune when Glinta and I had our fill of fresh water. Those two guzzled it down as if they'd never seen the stuff before. Diver also filled his gourds to overflowing and poured some over his head.

"So, how did you guys get water down here before?" I asked.

"Wave water doesn't taste very good," Diver said. "That's why I invented these water catchers."

"I fear the rest of us have had mere drips to sate us until now," Courtlya said.

"What about food? And where do you actually live and all that?"

"Food, Shran?" Courtlya said. "Not just everyone has had that pleasure. As for where we live, even you cannot be that blind. Here we are."

We continued wandering the caves in search of the honeyoak fruit. The more I pondered along the way, the more it seemed all the monad-folk had simply popped into existence within the past day, with nothing but the clothes on their backs. They had no buildings, no sculptures, no agriculture, no deep history, no ancestry, even. They had no sense of day or night, due to the peculiar sky lights that never went off, except in cases like mine. They only knew about the honeyoak fruits at all based on Glinta's, increasingly suspicious, report.

Eventually, we reached a ledge overhanging a cavern too deep to see even the bottom. Just below our ledge, something like an enormous root system had grown sideways out of the cavern wall. It branched off in all directions, each arm anchoring itself to countless other paths on our level of the cavern. The thing was also clearly dead, because no light shone upon it except where others were looking. The top of that enormous dead root system was flat enough to make for a broad walkway, if a precarious one.

The others scanned all around, allowing me to make out many knotted-up sections of the branching path, like little islands in the blackness. More reasonably sized trees basked in daylight, even to my eyes, along with a sprinkling of other small plants growing on many of the islands. A few of the fluffy critters from outside had even wandered onto the branching path.

"Those are them," Glinta said, excitedly pointing. "Honeyoaks."

Each of these trees had several large boughs that rose high, bent sharply and drooped until nearly touching ground. Now and then, their boughs swayed gently, though there wasn't much wind in the cavern. With sparse few leaves, they almost resembled gigantic hands, a thought that sent a chill down my spine.

On the center-most island, something stood out to my unlit gaze: a single pear-shaped object probably the size of Diver's torso, hanging on the spindly end of one drooping bough.

"There," I said. "A fruit."

We carefully held formation, so I could still see my feet as we marched for the center island.

"This place is incredible," I said, imagining how many other such caverns it had to explore.

Courtlya shook her head slowly. "Incredibly unsafe. An incredible way to plummet to our doom. Incredibly unladylike for that matter."

"Thanks for coming anyway."

"Well, noblesse oblige and so on."

The pathway branched off with such complexity that we kept needing to stop at each branch-point to reassess our route. Taking one wrong turn would lead us somewhere completely different.

First straight, then off to the left, then a left and a right, then straight. On and on it went.

We came across a pile of wet bones and bits of fur discarded in the middle of the path. The crunched-up skull looked like it belonged to one of the long-snouted critters. Glinta shuddered and looked ready to cry, while Courtlya's eyes went wide and her face got even whiter than usual. I ushered us along double-time without another word. We passed by another pile a bit farther on.

As we approached one little island, a horrible hairless beast, about the size of a large bull, emerged from behind a cleft in the distance. It appeared to have eyes poking up from the top of its head like a slug, while a pair of meter-long mandibles felt around on the ground in front of it. It walked its back end on two muscular hind legs and had no legs in the front. Instead of front legs, it treated its chin like a third foot. When it caught sight of us, the beast popped its jaw wide open, which propped up its head the same height as its back end. Its mandibles opened wide, twitching, eager to clamp down on prey.

"Scotor," Glinta cried, pointing at the snarling beast.

"What's a—"

"Shran, run," Courtlya said.

The scotor charged, chin skipping across the ground in the distance like a stone over a lake. With each chin-step, it kept its jaw hanging wide open, ready to swallow anything whole.

The girls fled screaming into a hollow log. Diver chuckled, "Cool," and ran straight for the beast.

"Diver don't," I called, but he wouldn't listen. The beast's gaze locked onto him, whereas I suddenly stood in darkness once again. Only a few stray patches of moss gave the slightest hint of what was a walkway and what was a bottomless pit. I could either run off with my friends, the girls, or help the boy who said I wasn't any fun.

I chased Diver, trying with all my might not to waiver from where he'd stepped. A single false move and I would probably be dead.

Diver called back angrily, "I saw it first. I've got first rights."

"On what? Getting eaten?"

"On getting to ride it."

"That thing's a super predator. It lives to eat people."

He scoffed, "You didn't say that before," and kept running for it. I'd almost caught up, so I could try tackling him, but that'd only worsen our chances at escaping. Already, I heard the scotor's ravenous panting as it skipped its open mouth towards us.

"Then why are you trying to beat me to it?" Diver asked.

"To stop you from getting yourself killed."

"Prove it."

Hadn't Diver seen the piles of coughed-up bones? I supposed I couldn't immediately prove what had put them there. The barreling beast would be right on top of us within seconds.

If only I could show the boy how to feel about that. I skidded to a halt and imagined the charging beast was a statue. In that half heartbeat, I eyed it from bottom to top as they did in the schoolyard. The scotor's song composed itself in an instant, and I sang it out loud: an infernal voice-cracking scream at the top of my lungs. I had never made such a sound in my life, much less in front of other people. Then I sprinted back the way I'd come, yelling, "Retreat!"

At last, Diver too shrieked in terror, and some of his gaze sporadically lit bits of the path ahead of me. He was following me again, the rhythmic clacking of his water-catchers at a fever pitch.

Even so, I saw nowhere to escape to, unless, "Diver, we need to jump to another branch."

"Oh, that sounds like fun," he said and started looking all over for a narrow-enough gap. One portion of another path happened to snake its way very close to our own in one spot.

"Okay, get ready," I said, bearing down on the gap. When I was a few paces from it, Diver's gaze swerved away, leaving me again in darkness. No wonder he did, since the scotor sounded like he was right behind him.

With no time to spare and no way to see where the ground ended, I screamed and leapt as far as I could imagine. Why hadn't I told Diver to look at me? Hurdling through darkness, I feared I'd gone a pace too early. When I peaked out, Diver's gaze returned, giving a glimpse of where I'd land.

I crashed into the hanging walkway, clawing at the dead bark as I scampered up to safety.

Diver followed shortly after me. He was a master jumper if nothing else.

The scotor popped its chin high and leapt right over the gap with its hind legs. I had hoped it would be too clumsy to make the jump. It was aiming straight for Diver, to chomp down on him even as it landed.

We wouldn't have another chance to find the scotor weak. So, I smashed both fists onto one of its disgusting outstretched mandibles. The scotor tipped off course, bumping its chin on part of our path. It nearly stopped him mid- air. Nearly.

The scotor heaved its hind legs into something like a headstand. It was trying to flip itself into a somersault and finish us off, but it could only stretch so far. I braced my feet against a large rock and pushed against his upper jaw. The scotor must have weighed a bit less than a charging bull, and it took all my might to stop him from rolling forward.

The beast changed tactics. It slammed that enormous mouth shut, catching onto a knot in the walkway, then swung its hind legs sideways. They scratched and kicked to get a hold on the dead bark, enraged eyes glaring at me from the top of its head.

Then Diver rammed into the beast's side, sending its hind legs thrashing in open air. In a moment, its jaws lost their grasp, and the whole thing fell into the black pit.

Diver and I both sat back, catching our breath in relief.

Glinta's yelp echoed out the mouth of the nearby hollow log. I watched as first their gazes and then the two girls themselves crawled from their hiding place and came our way.

"Are you okay?" I asked them.

"I *was* okay," Glinta said, then buried her face in her hands.

"What happened in there?"

She stifled a sob. "That scotor just died horribly."

"We do not necessarily know that," Courtlya said. "He may have landed on something soft."

"No," Glinta said, wiping her nose on a sleeve. "He got dashed on the rocks. Actual rocks. Actual dashing. I saw it all."

"He fell way down into the blackness," I said. "How could anybody see that, Glinta?"

"The same as always," she said.

"That is absurd," Courtlya said. "I saw nothing from inside that musty old log."

"It was through those ceiling holes. How do you think I saw that poor waterbud when it disappeared forever?"

"Glinta, you can't be saying you see everything everywhere all the time," I said.

"Of course not," she said.

198

"Well, what do you see then?"

"Only all the people and plants and animals and whatever they look at, from all those lights in the sky."

For once, Courtlya and Diver stared in confusion along with me. How much more bizarre could this place get?

"Then why didn't you tell us you could see all that stuff earlier?" I asked.

"You'd think I'm weird," Glinta said.

"Okay," said Diver, turning his back on everyone. "What face am I making right now?"

Glinta broke into a giggle. "A silly one."

"I could have guessed that," Courtlya sighed.

The four of us zigged and zagged the rest of the way through the branching path to the island with the fruiting honeyoak tree.

When we set foot on that giant knot in the dead roots, Diver rushed ahead. The single fruit hung within his grasping distance, but as soon as he grabbed for it, the branch lifted out of reach. Diver stumbled and stammered curses in his fashion.

I jumped for the fruit, but again the branch lifted itself out of reach. "Why won't it let us have it?" I wondered aloud.

Courtlya walked up behind me. "Why would it? The honeyoak, lord of all trees, has something valuable, so it tries to keep it for itself."

"Not if I have anything to say about it, and I do," Diver said, rushing the tree trunk and beginning to climb it. "I'm coming for you, you wormy little..." Several whip-like branches laid lash upon lash on his back, and he immediately yelped and retreated. "This tree's broken," he said.

"No. It's a good honeyoak," Glinta insisted. "Maybe it's not ready to give its fruit away yet."

199

Courtlya humphed. "You wailed for a plant and for a vicious predator, but not for Diver? Hypocrite."

"Those died horrible deaths and disappeared forever," Glinta said. "Diver isn't in serious pain, are you, Diver?

Diver brushed a hot tear off one eye. "Guess I'll live."

Glinta continued, "I'm sorry. I can't very easily focus on everything at once. In fact, it's really, really hard."

"Let's get back to business," I said. "Courtlya, why would a honeyoak attack someone like that?"

"Clearly, it took offense at something."

That gave me an idea. I stepped up to the tree, just out of whipping distance. Then I spoke to the tree, "Excuse me, Honeyoak tree..." which, coming from my own mouth, sounded even more ridiculous than in my head. "Honeyoak... tree, I'm sorry we tried to steal your fruit."

"What are you doing, Shran?" Courtlya asked.

"I'm trying to reconcile."

"That does not seem very gentlemanly, engaging in such foolishness."

"Have you got any better ideas?"

She rolled her eyes. "I suppose it will not hurt."

I continued talking to the tree. "I'm not trying to steal your fruit for myself, even though I'm really hungry. You see, we've got to pay off a fine in fruit, just because I spoke the truth. I don't know how this world works, much less why it works the way it does. Does any of that make sense?"

The honeyoak seemed to twist slightly one way then slightly twisted the other way.

"It says no," Diver said. "Come on. Let's all rush it at once."

Maybe I was losing my mind, but the tree *had* almost resembled someone shaking his head no, the way it moved.

"Wait, Diver," I said. "Sorry again, tree. What I wanted to say is, you didn't just pop up here for no reason. You've got a rare gift. If you're anything like the trees back where I come from, you don't need to eat anything, and yet you make food that you can't eat yourself. Is that true?"

The more I spoke, the more I doubted my own sanity, yet it seemed like the tree slightly jerked its boughs upward, then let them fall again in a way analogous to someone nodding for yes. So, I kept at it.

"I don't know if you can see it, but there's a very long drop all around you. That fruit you're holding is eventually going to break off, whether you protect it or not. If we're not here, it will either roll off the edge and splatter into goo, or it will have no room to grow in. If you let us have it, we can plant its seeds somewhere better. You'll help someone else have something to eat, and you'll help the rest of us to pay off a severe fine."

The tree lifted the fruit yet more out of reach.

I looked to Glinta, who smiled hopefully. I looked to Courtlya, who wore a "why are you stopping now?" sort of expression. I looked to Diver, who said, "You tell that tree, Shran. I'm hungry."

So, I did tell that tree. "You're more than just yourself. You think you just popped up here in the middle of the abyss for no reason? Well, I mean, maybe you did. I don't think I know anything here."

The fruit continued to rise, a little more slowly.

"But maybe you're here for a purpose. You can make food when we can't. We can eat food when you can't. So, you tell me: are you merely a pile of soon-to-be-dead wood, clinging for dear life to a bit of fruit that's turning to rot soon? Or is there a reason, a real purpose for all of this?"

At that, the fruit stopped rising. After a long pause, the stem snapped, and the torso-sized fruit dropped. It smacked into my arms, heavier than I'd expected, so I nearly toppled headlong.

The fruit shone like silver and seemed just slightly above room temperature rather than cold. The others gathered around to touch the fruit delightedly.

"Gimme a bite," Diver said.

I pulled it away. "I've got to pay off the fine with this."

"That's no fair," he said. "I came all the way down here, nearly getting eaten alive, so I deserve my share. And I want a big piece."

All that effort getting it away from the tree, only to have to fight over it with my own companion.

"You almost got both of us killed by that scotor," I said.

"After you brought us here."

"I didn't ask you to. Siever sent you along."

"Shran," Courtlya said, "I can hardly believe this. Diver is your soldier, conscripted by the almighty Siever himself to serve under you on this mission. A gentleman can hardly go about capturing territory without dividing the spoils among his men. Diver helped survey the tree and took a lashing in the process. You wouldn't let that service go unnoticed, would you?"

I definitely hadn't thought of it that way before, but she had a point. I tried to think as a commander ought to do, as a noble would. "Diver, is it true what Courtlya said, that you came here as my soldier? Or are you only here for yourself?"

"What she said," he grunted. "So, give me some fruit."

"If you're my soldier, then you've got to follow my orders or you won't earn a reward. Deal?"

"Okay. Give it here then."

"I didn't order you to run to that tree trunk, though. And you disobeyed when I said to stop racing for that scotor, didn't you?"

202

He groaned, "Fine."

"But, you can get your plunder from the next fruit, I promise you that."

"Then what are we waiting for?" Diver said. "Let's get more already."

"Glinta," I said, "do you see any more honeyoak fruit? You know, from all those ceiling holes?"

"I see all of it, but I can never tell quite where it is. Everything's so jumbled up, it's hard to piece together."

"Are there any in an area like this?"

"Yes, but they could be anywhere on this level."

"Is there more on other levels?"

"Lower down, a lot more, more of everything."

"Great. Let's head there next."

"More fruit," she said with a shudder, "and a lot more danger."

Chapter Twenty-Five

Liza

We assembled in a room lined with tall metal boxes that constantly hummed, I figured, through more pre-Storm technology. In the far side of the room lay a hideous, hairy giant in a heap of leaves and straw. I yelped as it sprang to life and scampered right for us.

"No need to fear, my lady," Fixten said. "Nestor is our defender. He follows all our commands."

Talna, the jubilant palace maid, ran halfway across the room to meet the big, harry thing. "Here, Nestor," she said.

The giant panted excitedly, picked the woman up, and licked her. She just laughed and patted his snout.

I didn't even have to think about it. I knew it was Nestor who had left those tooth marks in the silver stag. How reliable was a "defender" that killed what they only meant him to catch?

The giant carried Talna to where we'd gathered. Then he sniffed the air and growled at me.

"No, Nestor," Haldra said. "This is Liza, our new friend."

The growl turned to a toothy smile, and before I knew it, he scooped me up too. His visage looked more hideous up close: bump-ridden, oily skin, pointy ears sticking out the sides of his head, and that horrible grin. I froze as he licked me from waist to face, fearing he would snap me in half if I as much as twitched.

205

As foul as he smelled, the writhing vibrance throughout Nestor's body fared even worse. I felt it, tasted it, almost heard it: an endless clash between the essences of man and animal. I could only guess someone had haphazardly forced equal bits of both those essences to merge into a single body, and every tiny unit within hated its neighbors because of it. Not nearly soon enough, he set us back down.

Fixten called the group to order once Whira returned from tending the horses. We formed a semicircle in front of him and the giant.

"Dear sisters of the Keesec," Fixten said, "we gather here tonight for the betterment of all humanity." The rest of the group cheered in agreement. "Yet many of those in power continue to deny humanity this betterment. Despite our wholly benevolent goal, we remain weak. Weak and powerless."

The sisters booed indignantly, as did Nestor, who seemed to half follow about half of what Fixten said.

"Shall we be forever relegated to these clandestine meetings, kilometers from home, to make our plans and decisions?"

"No," the circle replied in unison.

"That's why, grotesque as he may appear to the ill-informed, we need, and indeed we value, the likes of Nestor. We'll actually need more like him if we're going to succeed. Through him and his future brethren, we will reveal the folly of those in power."

Talna raised a hand, promptly hiding it back in her riding cloak before speaking. "What about our plan with the silver stag and that?" she asked.

"We've got a better plan now," Fixten said. "Isn't that right, Lady Haldra?"

Haldra nodded. "In our position, we must be adaptable. Now we have a new ally far better than that old stag: my friend Liza," She nudged me towards the middle of the circle.

"For what?" I hissed.

"Go on out there," she whispered. "Now is your moment. It all comes down to you."

My pulse pounded as I stepped in the middle of everyone, my eyes darting from one person to another, wondering if they would pounce. They only stared back in quiet awe.

"Haldra," Fixten called, leaving her personal name to hang denuded of its title, "would you do the honors?"

Haldra smiled in feigned modesty and went to one of the humming chests. The metal door hissed, pouring out frost as she procured a small glass vial with leather-gloved fingers. The circle began a strange chant as she sauntered towards us, waving the little vial overhead. They grew louder and louder until she ceremoniously handed it to me.

The vial stuck to my fingers from sheer coldness as I wondered what they expected me to do with it. Though significantly muted by its frozen state, I sensed vibrance inside, clashing within itself just like Nestor. Then I realized exactly what they intended me to do.

Fixten waved for silence. "Liza, you have the potential to change the world, to better all of Tew."

"How do I know this will change things for the better?"

"It's about what's best for all," Haldra said. "Thanks to the incredible technology of the bygone age, these precious creatures have managed to survive until today. So, it's our duty to ensure they have a place in our mayorship."

"Why now? Why here?" I asked.

Haldra shook her head. "They face extinction. If these vials thaw without the proper care, they will die."

"This could be really dangerous."

"You don't know that," Haldra said. "All we've got to do is treat them like anyone else. Then they'll undoubtedly do the same."

Had I judged too early based on too little? Had Nestor ever chosen to be what he was? The constant battle between his dual natures put me off horribly, so how much harder would that be on him? Maybe instead of hatred, what a creature like Nestor deserved was pity.

This was finally a chance to be part of something. If I didn't help, the Keesec could find another way to raise these creatures. Perhaps if I stayed with them, I could steer things in the right direction. Still, I sighed, fatigued. "I don't even know if I can do it."

Talna barely hid a giggle with a cupped hand. "Lady Mattian, pre-Storm folk never asked what they could and couldn't do. They just did it. Look at this complex, they made it last so people like us could do as they did. They give us a job, and it's up to us to do, best as we can."

No one could deny the skill required to build the massive complex we stood in—one that lasted centuries at that. If they made better technology, wouldn't they also know how to make better societies? Perhaps then, countless other young men like Shran wouldn't be mistreated and excluded from those around them.

What had I received my gift for anyway? Merely to steal life from people I feared, or to give life to those who needed it? The people were chanting my name now, cheering. Choosing to be confident in it, I pulled off my hood, throwing out my crimson-spattered white hair for all to see. "Okay," I said.

The chanting fell silent, and everyone froze on the spot.

My heart raced as I took a deep breath. Then I poured a lot of vibrance into the little vial. The frozen thing inside grew rapidly, breaking the glass in my hands. It gained size and weight so that I nearly dropped the now dog-sized creature before laying it on solid ground. The circle cheered me on, as I knelt down and sent more life into it. It soon grew into a full-sized giant, sleeping on the floor.

Sisters shook my hand excitedly as others touched the giant in disbelief. I'd never felt so powerful in my life. They needed me. And for once, I really had helped them.

Haldra brought another vial. This time I perceived a female giant there, hibernating. I grew her to full size, all but exhausting my reserves. Haldra handed me a third vial, all the same. I mentally squeezed the last tiny remnant of vibrance into the frozen vial, then fatigue set in. The giantess in the vial swelled slightly, but didn't even break the glass open.

"What's the matter?" Haldra asked.

"My reserves, they're empty." As I said this, I absentmindedly twirled a few locks of hair and realized it lacked that almost glowing quality, and the apparent spattering of red had finally disappeared.

"That's no good," Fixten said. "If there's only one female, what happens when she's in heat?"

"Fratricide," Whira agreed. "The males will dash each other into oblivion for the chance to mate."

"You see, Liza," said Haldra, "we need at least one more female to balance this out."

"But I'm all out. There's nothing left to give," I said, and felt it. The present, stark reality wiped away the thrill of a few moments earlier. I'd invested all of Penna's stolen life into these monstrosities.

"This question goes above our heads," Fixten said. "I call a motion to speak with our Guide immediately."

"Seconded," Whira said. She was a tall, sharp-featured woman whom I recognized as a guildmaster's wife. In keeping with the nobility, Whira had barely as much as greeted me up until that night.

Everyone raised a hand, saying "Aye."

Haldra nudged me. "Liza, state your vote."

I whispered, "I don't know what's happening," though everyone seemed to be listening in.

"We already called for a motion," Whira said, sternly. "No further discussion. Give us your vote, please."

Everyone else nodded in agreement.

"I don't know what I'm voting for."

"Are you voting against the motion?" Whira said, not for a second deviating from the procedure.

"No. I need more information."

"Remember her as an abstention," Haldra said.

"The ayes have it," Fixten announced. "Everyone around Nestor."

The ladies and Fixten formed a large circle around the eldest giant, the only one already awake, and I followed suit. Haldra removed a glove, letting it drop beside her. Before I could ask her what she was doing, each of them pulled out fine-tipped little knives and pricked a finger.

"Come now," Haldra said, reaching for my hand.

"What is going on here?" I said, hiding hands in my cloak.

"Lady Mattian," Whira said, "just because you abstain from voting doesn't mean you can abstain from the verdict."

"What's even happening right now?"

"It's just a bit of blood, a matter of procedure and nothing you can't heal in a moment," Haldra said.

"What procedure?"

"You're one of us now. You'll learn all of it soon enough, but we want to get you home sooner, rather than later. Here, it's easier if someone else does it for you."

"Ouch," I blurted, when the blade poked deeper than expected.

Everyone raised a finger in the air and started to chant some name a dozen times as they walked a circuit around the bewildered giant, "Bar-thoon, Bar-thoon, Bar-thoon..."

Then they started dragging their pricked fingers across the cold floor, whispering, "Go to sleep." We each simultaneously drew a segment of the circle around Nestor, until each person's finger met the beginning of the next member's segment.

This faint circle drawn, we remained stooped around the giant with our fingers to the ground, and a drowsy haze fell over Nestor's expression. My finger throbbed painfully as I kept pressing it onto the damp path. Meanwhile, Nestor appeared to notice himself nodding off. He shook himself awake a few times, but soon laid himself down within the large circle and let sleep take him.

At that point, I tried to heal my fingertip before it got infected. Of course, my reserves had run out, so I instinctively tried to suck my finger. It was sticking to the ground. I yanked, and the trail of blood held on with the strength of ten men, pinning me to that spot through the open wound.

The rest of the Keesec simply knelt where they were, pinned like me. I looked to Haldra, hoping for comfort and saw her self-assured confidence had faded away.

A thin column of mist rose from the edge of the circle. It seemed to emit a certain intangible essence, something powerful and hungry. The mist gradually worked its way inward until it completely engulfed Nestor and rushed into his nostrils. He convulsed so violently I tried to retreat but got painfully yanked to the ground again.

Suddenly, Nestor spoke in a deep, refined voice. "There is someone new." The giant face turned to look at me while the rest of the giant's body lay limp as a rag. "Who is this?"

Haldra answered, "Lord Barthoon, sir, this is Liza Mattian. She's joined us in Penna's stead."

"Where has Penna gone?" he demanded.

"She died for our cause, sir," Haldra said, "but not in vain."

Nestor's face glared at her suspiciously. "And what of the silver stag I all but handed to you for the task?"

"I'm sorry, my lord," Fixten said, and Nestor's head jerked to look at him. "Villagers sighted it, and the mayor's armies got to it first."

"Half-truths, I hear in you," the voice said. "Don't think you can hide it from me."

"It's the truth," Fixten said. "Nestor returned to us full of small harpoons. The mayor's men must have killed the stag before we had a chance."

It amazed me how little the Keesec seemed to know about the silver stag. From all the time I spent fixing it up, I knew that Nestor bit and mangled the poor creature to death. I never saw signs of man-made weapons. Clearly, this giant could find a target, but what happened after that depended on the swings of his mood.

Haldra spoke to the being inhabiting Nestor's head. "With Lady Mattian, we won't need the silver stag."

"You can't be serious. Explain yourself, Liza Mattian."

I wished the floor could hide me from whatever this being was, this Lord Barthoon, as they called him. It terrified me to think he knew my name. "I grew those two defenders tonight," I stammered, pointing at the sleeping giants with my free hand.

Barthoon perked up. "You truly have this ability? And you've joined our cause?"

I nodded, though I couldn't bring myself to say the word yes.

He chuckled, dubious. "You will."

I didn't know what that meant, and dared not ask. As their conversation carried on, it only grew more confusing.

"They'll need their own drivers, of course, given the time frame," Barthoon said. "Is that the only reason my children summoned me?"

"Only a trifling matter," Fixten said. "We need another giantess, to prevent mating tensions, but Lady Mattian ran out of vital force. We hoped you could lend her some more."

Barthoon shook Nestor's head. "That's not how it works, my son. Blood for blood, life for life: perfect balance. That is the sum of all. It comes down to the simple question of who *decides?* So, *that* I will." The being took a deep, satisfied breath.

Nestor's head fell limp, and his arm sprang to life, as if this Barthoon entity had relocated there. The arm reached out to the edge of the circle. Starting with Whira, Nestor's hand prodded her, as if inspecting cattle in the market. Whira's expression went stiff and her face quite pale. She didn't as much as breathe until the giant hand moved on to the next member of the circle.

By some good fortune, it passed right by me. The hand continued, inspecting Lady Haldra, Fixten, and then, it came to Talna. The arm fell limp, and Nestor's face lit up.

"Please, my lord. Not me," Talna screamed.

"No, no, no," Barthoon said. "I offer you deliverance."

"I've been loyal, by thunder. Ask any of them."

213

"Be silent, Talna," he said. "You will keep your life, minus the burden you carry."

"Oh my," Talna said. "Thank you."

Barthoon grunted approvingly. "The decision is made. I'll have the drivers ready." The mist poured out of Nestor's nostrils, spreading out in all directions, and evaporating as soon as it left the circle. Nestor returned to a deep sleep, and the trail released me from its grasp.

Talna skipped over to me as I found my feet. "It's perfect," she said. "That man had his way with me, then wanted nothing to do with me the very next morning."

"Who are you talking about?" I asked.

"Guilen Stohvan," Talna said. "Here. See for yourself."

She held my hands to her stomach. Few might have noticed the swelling therein. Yet with my new sense, I felt it clear and crisp as crystal: the full-bodied vibrance playing its song within. It was a son there, unmistakably.

"Thank Barthoon for you, Lady Mattian. There should be just enough here for you."

I pulled away, stunned. "He's your son."

"Guilen tricked me, used me. And he'll be dead soon anyway, and the president—"

"Talna!" Haldra cut in, angrily.

The more I backed away, the closer she followed. "Please, oh please, Liza. You must do it. You must take it." She was grabbing my collar when I slapped her hard across the cheek. She sank to the ground, weeping.

"Liza," Haldra said, "that's no way to treat a sister of the Keesec. Sacrifices must be made."

"Go to the grave, Haldra," I said coldly. "You're nothing but murderers, all of you!"

"Lady Mattian, don't do this to yourself again. We're friends here. I'm your friend."

I didn't care anymore, didn't fear Lady Haldra anymore. I looked her right in the eye, said, "But you don't act like one," and strode straight for the exit.

Whira spoke first. "Well? Someone stop her."

"No," Haldra said. "I've already seen one sister die that way."

"Send Nestor," Talna said in a rage.

Seeing no one yet following once I reached the exit, I ran for my life. Who knew how long it would take them to wake a sleeping giant? Soon, I'd reached the large man-made cavern overlooking the circular entrance and heard an inhuman howl, indicating *that long.*

Even sprinting, how could I outrun him to the horses? And could horses outrun such a creature? Fleeing the same way I'd entered was not an option.

Enormous footsteps thudded up the hallway. Earlier, Nestor had recognized me—or rather, not recognized me—by smell. I noticed myself clenching the pendant of the monad-holder necklace, palms dripping with sweat and a slight smear of blood coming from my dripping finger.

A few paces to my right was the entrance to a side passage. How had clinging to that empty necklace helped anyone so far? Unfastening the chain, I twirled it overhead and threw it as far as I could. It flew over the edge, landing somewhere out of sight. Hopefully, that would lure him off my scent long enough.

Careful not to touch anything with my sweaty hands, I slipped into the side passage and let it quietly seal behind me. The narrow corridor I ran through had the unfinished appearance of a server's hall. I soon came to a room dominated by several objects, that resembled huge metal casks lying on their sides. Something inside

215

them churned loud enough to drown out the sound of me catching my breath. Then, to my relief, I found a ladder leading to a trapdoor in the ceiling.

Chapter Twenty-Six

Shran

Back up top, Siever and Funnela were elated to get their hands on the fresh honeyoak fruit.

"Superb job, young man," Siever said. "You've nearly paid off your fine." Then he and Funnela walked off with the fruit. As he went, he called over one shoulder, "Glinta, give him his light back for good behavior."

Why was he telling her? Wasn't Siever the one controlling all the lights? Glinta just nodded. Then, once again light warmed my whole body, and everywhere I looked shone with daylight from holes in the ceiling.

"So, Glinta," I said, "was it *you* keeping me in the dark all that time?"

She nodded, ashamed. "They've been telling me what to do ever since I met them."

"So, you see everything living and control the lights too?"

"I guess so. Yeah."

"How?"

She shrugged. "It just happens. It's like I have my own eyes in my own head, and then I have a thousand thousand other ones in the sky that don't work the same. I basically just closed all the ones that were looking at you, until now."

"Can you put out anyone's light whenever you want, then?"

217

"If I know who it is. But I can't just go and disobey Siever and Funnela."

"How would that be disobeying?" I asked.

"They laid down the good law that every living thing gets to see and be seen, except as a punishment."

I ran up to Siever, who was gorging himself on the large fruit. "Mister Siever, sir, would you want to wait around a long time for Courtlya's fine to get paid off, or do you want it sooner?"

Siever choked down a juicy mouthful of fruit. "The fewer delays, the better."

"And make him get us more water, darling," Funnella said, "I'm a smidge thirsty."

I ushered Diver over, who brought the parched woman one of his mostly full water-catchers.

"Now out with it," Siever said. "What are you hoping to request?"

"Only to help get more of what you want faster."

"Meaning what?"

"I request to be deputized for this mission, so I could expand your range of authority to punish creatures that get in our way."

Funnela spat out her mouthful of water in disgust. "Only the almighty Siever and I had the right to dole out punishments."

"How right you are, dearest," Siever said, shaking his head in solemnity. "However, seeing as we've got to eat again soon, meet Deputy Shran Mattian. He's going to help us dole them out on unruly creatures."

"Splendid," Funnella said.

I went back to our group and announced my new position. Courtlya looked more impressed than I'd ever seen her.

If the lower levels held more dangers, we needed to be on guard. Yet none of the monad folk had even heard of a weapon before.

I dug through the bone pile and found some kind of leg bone long enough to craft into a spear. I hoped the spear combat I'd already learned in the schoolyard would be enough to defend ourselves. The girls were hesitant to use, "what did you call these again, 'weapons'?" but consented to carry a spear each. Diver picked up swinging and thrusting perhaps too jubilantly.

Fully armed, the four of us set off down the crimson corridor. We spiraled a fair amount deeper than before, taking a side passage about halfway to the bottom of the red hallway. There, Glinta said we could find a lot more fruit.

The new cave system bustled with more of the fluffy, long-snouted critters. Glinta called them "meshors," because of the way they chewed their food, and the name stuck. She had a knack for naming things, helped in no small part by the fact she saw all that lived in the monad world at every moment.

At one point, Glinta stopped to pet some of the meshors while Diver found a nice waterbud to refill his water-catchers at. Meanwhile, Courtlya held perfect posture as she perched on a rock, deep in thought.

I set aside my spear and found a spot next to her. "What are you thinking about, Lady Courtlya?"

"Oh, nothing really," she said. "It's just, you are an official deputy of the almighty now. Could that mean you can make me a lady again, officially?"

"I wish. Siever only gave me authority to dole out punishments."

"It was a silly thought. As long as you treat me like one…" She laughed a gleefully courtly laugh. "Anyway, I suppose you should know, I was right all along, Shran."

"What about?"

"You know very well what."

"I don't have a clue."

She sighed. "You do look better now."

I smiled, wanting to say she'd looked pretty since we met. Those eyes of hers were pure silver. And she was looking at me too, sharing one moment, just the two of us. Then out of the corner of my eye, I spied Glinta pause from what she was doing. The acute awareness of someone else always watching yanked me right out of the moment.

"What are you sitting around for?" Diver said, strapping his topped-off water catchers over his shoulder again.

"Right," I said, hurriedly picking up my spear. "Let's get moving."

The deeper we went, the more the cave gave the impression of a garden. Green or pale plants grew anywhere with dirt.

The caves also had a healthy population of the bat-like critters that Glinta called "Fletors," for obvious reasons. She said they liked the fruit, which was more plentiful down there.

Diver soon asked, "So, where's all the fruit? Where are the honeyoak groves?"

"I promise," Glinta said, "I see plenty even as we speak. It's just too hard to figure out exactly where."

We eventually reached a lush cavern, filled with tall leafy trees on a small hill. Towards the highest point, I spied the drooping tops of many honeyoaks. Diver started jogging up ahead of us, and Courtlya gave me a nudge and a look that said to start leading already.

"Diver, back in ranks," I called after him.

"They're right there, though," Diver moaned.

"That's an order, soldier." I felt like an idiot saying that, but Diver actually listened. We all hiked the hill together. Towards the top, the fruit trees started to thrash furiously. The cause of the disturbance remained obscured behind all the other trees.

"Do the honeyoaks know we're coming?" I asked Glinta, hoping they wouldn't be in a bad mood.

"I don't think so," she said, then went pale the same time as a chorus of agitated chirps erupted from up around the thrashing trees. The chirps grew closer until a large swarm of fletors passed overhead. "We shouldn't be here," Glinta said.

"How come? There's fruit up there," Diver said.

"Danger, guys. Danger!" she screamed. It echoed across the cavern, and the trees stopped thrashing. Several basketfuls of honeyoak fruit rolled downhill a little ways to our left, a bit smaller than before and therefore easier to carry. We couldn't leave when the prize was so close.

"I think you mean fruit," Diver said, visibly fighting the urge to run off after the cascade of honeyoak fruit.

"Just grab it quick," I said, and the two of us began scooping up as much as we could carry.

"But there are writhors in here," Glinta cried.

When my arms were full, I saw it: one huge nightmarish animal. It walked like a four-legged spider, knees splayed up and out, while its body hung just visible above some of the treetops. Crocodilian jaws protruded from the relatively small body, readied to rip prey to shreds. I froze up, trying and failing to believe it was only a nightmare.

Courtlya shrieked in sheer terror, fleeing in the open and drawing the writhor's gaze. He sprang to full height—higher than most of the trees—and charged after the fleeing lady. He went right past us. To my shame, I was still frozen, too scared to do anything. Only after he'd passed did I begin the desperate chase. "Glinta," I called, as she and Diver followed, "put out Courtlya's light."

"Now's no time to punish her," Glinta said.

"We're punishing the writhor, so he can't see her."

"Okay, there," she said. Courtlya's gaze disappeared, her body still bright as ever. The writhor gained ground all the faster as she stumbled in the dark.

"She's still lit up," I said between breaths.

"He's still looking at her, and so are we."

"Put out his light too, as a punishment for—"

"There are so many creatures that look the same. I can't tell them apart," Glinta said.

He was almost on top of Courtlya. Meanwhile, Glinta tossed me her spear and stopped in her tracks, grunting as if to make herself think faster. I could only imagine the vast volumes of sights she was sorting through, trying to match exactly one onto the scene before us. "And I've never done this before," she said.

"Just keep trying," I called back as Diver and I chased with spears raised.

Courtlya scampered into a clump of trees.

"Nobody look at her," I said, a challenge for me as much as them. She needed as much darkness as we could give her.

The writhor snarled angrily when Courtlya disappeared into the trees. It crouched down and fished around with a spindly-fingered claw that made my skin crawl. I resisted every urge to look where Courtlya hid, praying the darkness would buy her time.

Courtlya screamed, "Shran help me!" She was already in its grip, thrashing, kicking, and completely disarmed.

I howled in desperate rage, hurling my extra spear, and it scraped the writhor's leg. The monster squawked and advanced on Diver and me, still grasping Courtlya in one claw-footed leg.

Then Glinta declared, "There you are," and the writhor's gaze went dark. The shock made it collapse in a heap. I hoped he'd broken something in that fall. And Diver and I stabbed like madmen at its muscular appendages. At that, the writhor threw Courtlya aside and hobbled out of sight.

I rushed to Courtlya. She lay silent, limbs contorted. "Lady Courtlya, are you okay?"

"My leg hurts," she said.

"Can you move it?"

She yelped in pain. "It hurts."

"Don't worry. We've got you," I said, grabbing an arm to hoist over my shoulder.

"No, Shran. Don't move me."

"We have to get out of here before something worse comes."

"No, I…" Her eyes glazed, and she started shivering.

At that point, Glinta caught up to us.

"She must be too cold," I said. "Glinta, can you light her up again?"

We found that her leg was broken, and even as the light returned, her shivers turned to convulsions.

"What's wrong with her?" Diver asked.

"It must be shock," I said. "It's all my fault. I should never have dragged her along."

More things roared from somewhere in one of the side passages.

"We've got to get out of here," Glinta urged.

"Not without this," Diver said, holding half a dozen fruits in his arms.

223

"Not without *her*," I said, making to lift Courtlya no matter how much she shook.

Glinta took the fruit while Diver and I put Courtlya's arms over our shoulders. Courtlya cried out in pain, then fell silent again. I tried to comfort her, but she couldn't stop, and neither could we.

We made a clumsy retreat down the hill, Glinta barely able to keep the fruit pile stable while Diver and I struggled to keep our pace in sync, carrying an extra forty kilos between us. The spear walking sticks only made the retreat harder, but I was far too scared to get caught without them.

Once we'd gone a little ways into the new passage, a familiar panting noise came into earshot. It grew louder and louder from back in the forested cavern. Along with the panting came a plodding three-legged gait: a scotor. Despite the zigzagging of the new passage that kept him out of view, we had nowhere to hide. Eventually, it would catch us.

"Where's a stinking funnel hole when you need one?" Diver said.

"There's bound to be one soon," I said. "Glinta, can you make us go dark without dousing our gazes?"

"Okay, but it won't help much if he's looking right at us." Not a few heartbeats after, we all went dark. I could see my hands when I looked directly at them but not out of the corner of my eye.

The scotor rounded the corner. His gaze fell upon us, with little else to look at in the narrow passage but us.

"Now turn that thing's light off," I said.

"Way easier said than done," she said.

"Hurry up, the super predator's coming," Diver said.

"I'm trying."

"Why not turn all the scotors off at once?" I said.

"Just change a thousand things at a time instead of only one," Glinta scoffed.

"Oh, come on Shran. Let's spear that chin-scuttler," Diver said.

"But he might get past us and get Courtlya."

"You're gonna get all of us killed for this girl."

Light as Courtlya was, I couldn't keep running much longer carrying her. The scotor closed in on us moment by moment.

"Aha," Glinta said. Dropping most of the fruit, she twirled around with one of them in her arms and tossed it like a human sling. It went right at the scotor. He swerved to catch the fruit, leaving us darkened once more.

Just as the fruit went down his gullet, Glinta said, "I see you," and the scotor's gaze died. He grunted confusedly, then hobbled in the darkness towards the only light left in the passage: our gazes.

I spotted a funnel hole ahead, but it was too far away. Even at his hobbled pace, the scotor would reach us before we got there. Then I remembered when Glinta and I first entered the cave, how her shadow blocking the lights nearly boiled my feet. "Hey Glinta," I said, "try only looking at the scotor's eyes."

"What?"

"Focus all his body light onto his eyes."

"Shran, I don't want to hurt any creature."

"He's trying to eat us," I said as we rushed for the escape. It was simply too far away, and she wouldn't listen. "Okay Diver, I was wrong. Ready spears."

"Yes sir," Diver said. We set Courtlya down and turned to the scotor. We planted the spear butts in the ground and gazed high.

"Aim for the back of his throat," I said. The scotor wouldn't even know what he'd hit before the tips pierced into his wide-open mouth.

Suddenly, Glinta ran between us and the scotor. "Don't kill him," she pleaded.

"Glinta, save yourself," I said, but she refused, through tears, to move.

"Out of the way," Diver yelled, swinging the blunt end of his spear and hitting her temple. She fell headlong, and everything disappeared. Not a glimmer of light remained, yet the little world ambled on.

The scotor glanced past the tip of my spear. He must have shifted course, aiming for Courtlya where she lay, thrashing in the darkness.

"I've got him," Diver said, and I heard a spear plunge into flesh. The scotor growled, and seemed to be whipping one way and the other.

The passage was too big and too strange in the darkness. I swung my spear here, then there for the elusive target, and finally tapped something soft. Without a second thought, I ran and thrust with all my might. It seemed to pierce right the way through, then stuck. The scotor gave a few more belabored pants and breathed its last. Diver wheezed somewhere by the scotor.

"Did he get you?" I asked.

"We got him," Diver said, a faintness in his voice. "What about Glinta?"

I stumbled around in the darkness, searching for the girls. I found Courtlya by the faint rhythm of her shaking. She was safe for now, thank All Father.

Soon, I found Glinta. She breathed irregularly, and her forehead was wet with something. I wanted to believe it was only sweat and tears but couldn't see a thing. "Diver, I found her."

"How is she?"

"I don't know. Glinta, please wake up."

She twitched. Everything flickered for a few heartbeats, then daylight returned. A trickle of red smeared down her forehead, from where Diver's spear had struck. And I felt the tears roll down my cheeks as she feebly spoke. "Shran?"

"Are you okay, Glinta?"

"I see everything the light touches, remember? I sure don't look okay." She laughed to herself, regret in her voice. "All this and I couldn't even save that scotor."

"It's at peace." Then, looking back, there was Diver wheezing as he lay on top of the dead beast. My spear had skewered through both of them! "We've got to get help," I said and tried to pull Glinta upright. She screeched, and everything flickered until I set her down again.

Diver coughed. "What's to help?"

"Isn't there someone who can fix you up?" I asked.

"I don't think so," Glinta said.

"In my world, we have physicians, people who heal wounds like this. You don't have any of those?"

She shook her head, wincing. "If only you could bring one here,"

"How? They don't even know where *here is*. Is there even a way back at all?"

She closed her eyes, and the light flickered again, but she got an idea. "Yes. Yes, you can."

"Where do I go?"

"Well, take my hands, Shran. I think it'll help."

I obliged, holding her feeble hands in confusion.

"Ever since you came here from outside…" she trailed off, looking like she was about to sneeze. "Come back soon, Shran," she said.

Then, some unseen force yanked me upward and outward. In a fraction of a heartbeat, it stretched me like spaghetti through the ceiling, everything whizzing by me in a blur.

I found myself standing in what looked like one of the palace workshops. Above my palm floated the demi-monad.

Section Three

Out of Darkness

Chapter Twenty-Seven

Zieglon

The little hollow globe dangled at the end of the necklace.

"What is that?" Hothen asked.

"I gave it to Liza just last night. Must have taken this with her early this morning."

"But if this is the giant's hovel... that's not a good sign."

I clicked the little globe flat and concealed the necklace under my collar. "Wherever she is, we'll find her." That's why I had to come here. It had to be.

Hothen motioned towards a spot on the cavern floor covered in fresh laid tracks. "What do you say, Zieglon? Looks like maybe a dozen people came and left. We might've just missed her."

I crouched down and scanned the many different pairs of tracks, recognizing the shape of Liza's boot print among them. There she had walked in and then... "No," I said, slowly rising. "She came in with the ones who left all those prints but didn't leave with them."

"She's still inside somewhere."

Then the mission changed. "Tewin," I called.

The young medical officer hurried over. "Yes sir?"

"Go see to the wounded in the clearing."

Tewin rode off without delay. The rest of us formed battle-ready ranks and climbed the stairway. Archers held bows at the ready until we reached the main floor. The last vestiges of dirty boot prints faded away on this broad, sterile surface.

"Looks like no one's home," Hothen said.

I had presumed the place was some kind of pre-Storm prison, yet as we checked the many cells lining the walls, none of them appeared to lock from outside. Who would willingly live in such conditions?

Deeper still, we found a basement, full of humming metal contraptions and what must've been the giant's sleeping pallet. As I pawed through that massive pile of rotting leaves, Hothen cried out, "Dashing blazes. What's this about?"

He'd noticed a circle streaked in blood around a large section of floor. It was dry to the touch but not yet fully browned, certainly no more than a couple hours old. Was that a fingerprint? They performed some sinister ritual. "What did Liza have to do with it? And where did she go?" I asked.

Hothen looked on gravely, not venturing an answer.

There was the incessant humming of those metal chests, large enough to hold a full-grown woman. I flung open the nearest one, revealing hundreds of frozen vials on little shelves. Then I threw open the next, and the one after that. Soon we'd cracked every one of them wide open, mercifully finding no human remains.

I pushed back every nagging thought, how that same giant had nearly swallowed me whole two days prior.

"She was here with them, Hothen," I said. "That's all we know. Keep searching here for anything unusual." With that, I headed for the door.

"Then where are you going?" Hothen asked.

"For a walk."

As I left, I imagined seeing it through her eyes. If not the main exit, where would I go from there?

I stopped just before the complex's main open area. To my right, I noticed an unassuming door that hadn't stood out on the way in. Pushing it open, I jogged down the little server's corridor inside. A mechanical churning reverberated from the far side of the corridor.

"Liza?" I called.

No answer.

I rushed through to the room at the end of the corridor. Inside stood a few metal drums taller than a man, the source of all the noise. They reminded me of an overworked watermill, only sealed all around, with no clear place to grind grain. The contraptions certainly had no crevice to hide in.

Then, I spied a ladder against one wall, leading to a trapdoor in the ceiling. Fresh dirt lay sprinkled around its base. Had she escaped? I flew up the ladder and pushed and pounded at the hatch. More dust rained down from the edges. Beyond that, the door wouldn't budge. This simply had to be the way Liza tried to escape, and she hadn't made it.

I gripped each rusty rung of the ladder on the way down as if to crush the treacherous iron. Stepping off the ladder, I rested the back of my head on the plain wall. Denial had run itself dry. How had things gone so wrong so fast?

All too soon, Tewin came up the corridor with more bad news. "Lord Mattian, sir, I just returned from checking the wounded."

"How are they?" I asked.

"Twenty wounded, some of them severely. Two, I had to put to the mercy knife." He gave their names. Two fine men—my men—stripped from this world under my command.

I only nodded.

"And sir, we've got to hurry. Thordin's stolen off with the giant's head."

A giant's bloody head? What did that mean to us now? "Let him have his twenty percent. Let's hope he forgot our arrows in the thing's mouth."

I spat, disgusted. What was the meaning of it all? Shran lost, Liza gone, some ritual in a monster's hovel, the same one that killed the silver stag? Indeed, it had to mean something, something stifled by that oppressive subterranean atmosphere. "Good work, Tewin," I finally said. "It's time to get out of here."

Chapter Twenty-Eight

Shran

It must have already been late Sunday morning as I pushed at the workshop door. Someone had bolted it shut from outside. With no lamps lit, only a few high windows illuminated the place. Presumably, no one else expected me to be there either. It beggared belief, but somehow, someone had moved our little world all the way to the palace workshop without any of us even noticing.

I grabbed an empty crate and slid it below a window. That gave just enough of a boost to see the courtyard outside. It was still full of booths set up for the New Moons festivities.

The window bolt took a good tugging, but pulled loose soon enough. The grimy hinges gave some resistance too. Nothing a well-placed punch couldn't solve. I slipped the monad in my side pouch and climbed out the window.

The delicious scent of roasting meat wafted through the courtyard air from the temple, making my empty stomach growl. I reasoned it must be Sunday morning, so I headed for the palace's temple wing, where everyone had gathered.

The common folk filled the temple's first tier, while the nobility, mayoral officers, and their families congregated on the second. Those waiting to give an offering proudly displayed their freshly groomed animal on the broad stairway to the third tier.

Up there, I saw the priests inspecting each offering and leading it to the altar beneath the Throne of No Man. Every week, they blessed each offering to All Father as if he sat right there, then divided it into its key portions. They had already burned up some of the fat from several animals and begun cooking the extra meat for the common folk's feast, creating the savory aroma. If only time would allow me to eat something too.

The crowd sang a festive hymn in one voice as I hurriedly pressed my way through. Many on the first tier danced and clapped along with the song, allowing me to rush by without drawing too much attention. I needed to find a physician and a good one at that.

Soon, I broke through to the central stairway, only getting a few annoyed nods from those lined up with their offerings as I climbed by them to the second tier. The palace physician had to be up there. While far fewer people danced on that tier, they stood much farther apart, providing better visibility.

I sighted the head physician: Ston Mevrin, the only one I knew of who'd cured wounds like Diver and Glinta had. I carefully made my way to him and tapped his shoulder. "Excuse me, sir. My friends need your help."

Mevrin gave what sounded like a well-practiced reply. "Come by my office during working hours."

"They're badly wounded, Mister Mevrin."

"Then they'd better learn not to go hunting and warring on Sunday morning."

"Please, sir. You don't understand."

Mevrin sighed. "If I had half a gram of copper for every time..."

His wife, finished for him, "Then you'd be the richest man in the presidency. You promised me no work today, dearest."

"That I did. Unfortunately, my lordling, there's just nothing I can do."

I hung my head as I walked away, with no idea where to go. To my surprise, I heard the mayor's voice and saw him delivering a speech from the third tier. I thought only priests and those giving offerings were allowed at that level. Even he wasn't supposed to be up *there* without one.

"I present to all of you, the most rare and beautiful creature known to the forests of Othark: the silver stag!" The mayor motioned towards the entrance, where a throng of young men marched in. Most of them played flutes or drums while several in the back wheeled in a very beautiful but very stiff silver stag. Its hide shimmered in the afternoon sunlight, and its antlers really were as clear as polished glass. The crowds ooh'd and aah'd as the young men brought the stag to the third tier, displaying it beside the mayor for all to see.

Mayor Guilen motioned for quiet and continued his speech. "The legends tell us the pristine pelt of the silver stag grants prosperity and peace to its owner. I, Mayor Guilen Stohvan, freely offer that same peace and prosperity to all my loyal subjects." He paused as the crowds applauded once more. "However, to those few who foolishly oppose their rightful mayor, forever commit these words to memory: calamity awaits you. Yesterday, the ruler of that impregnable tower, which casts its grim shadow over Newmund each day, was captured. Even now, he sits imprisoned in my dungeon tower."

First murmurs then cheers chorused throughout the crowd.

An idea suddenly came to me: if I could only get to Steve, perhaps he could revive my friends like he revived my mother. But how to get there? I rushed back out of the temple, down the central aisle, drawing the ire of not a few onlookers. Leaving right in the middle of a mayoral speech would have been terribly embarrassing, except for my firm conviction I could not delay.

Out in the courtyard, I paused to consider my next move. The dungeon tower stood dozens of meters tall, with the first iron-barred windows on about the fourth story. I concocted a plan to get up and inside, starting with retrieving the missing half of my purrium platelet.

Since my half lacked a strap, I kept it securely inside my side pouch as I reached in and flicked it, summoning its other half. The ringing platelet slightly tugged the pouch in the direction of our chambers, which overlooked the far side of the palace courtyard. A second later, it jolted slightly, suggesting the other half had struck a wall or something. That must have meant the other half now sat by the nearside wall of the family chambers, unable to reach me from where I stood.

From my spot in the courtyard, I could see all our windows hung wide open. So, I just needed to maneuver the other half onto the windowsill and summon it from there. For that, I silenced my platelet and linked it instead. Blindly feeling around through thin air in the middle of the courtyard, I must have looked pretty ridiculous. Then my platelet seemed to bump into the bottom of something, which had to be the protruding edge of the windowsill.

A hand clapped onto my shoulder and spun me round to face its owner: Jaldane. "What do you think you're doing, little Mattian?" he said.

"Nothing much." I could hardly let him in on my scheme to infiltrate the mayoral dungeon.

"Then why were you causing a major disturbance during my uncle's speech?"

"I was just looking for something."

"Yeah? Let's see what you've got there then," Jaldane said, grabbing for my hand in the pouch.

"It's mine," I said.

He grabbed the pouch, my arm still in it. It sat stiffly in mid-air, stuck on the floor and wall where the linked platelet sat. Just how much force did it take to destroy a military-grade purrium link? Jaldane hesitated, confused. I seized the opportunity, maneuvering the other platelet over the windowsill and running around behind him.

He caught hold of my pouch. "You're not getting away this time, you little skid."

With my arm still caught in the bag, I desperately flicked as hard as I could. The platelet sang out an earsplitting purrium ring. Even as Jaldane tried to cover his ears, I felt my fist yanked into his unsuspecting gut. He gasped like I'd knocked the wind out of him.

As he keeled over, my platelet pressed out of reach so I couldn't silence it. If I waited a second longer, the other half would smack straight into his back, perhaps piercing straight through him for all I knew. Unable to risk that, I grabbed him with my free hand and popped the demi-monad between two fingers.

Instantly, it sucked both of us inside. We landed exactly where I'd left the monad-folk, lying in their helpless state.

"Thank goodness," Glinta said. She'd only grown more pale as the blood oozed from her temple, her fingers seeming to twitch at random. "I knew you'd find help, Shran."

"What are you playing at? Where is this?" Jaldane demanded.

"I'm sorry, Glinta," I said. "I'm still looking for help."

"Then who's he?" she asked in a feeble voice.

"I'm Jaldane Stohvan, and I will not tolerate this nonsense for one second longer. Shran, get me out of this dump immediately."

Now Courtlya chimed in for me, her leg still badly broken but her wit back at full force. "How dare you talk like that to a deputy of the almighty Siever!"

As the two of them quarreled, I saw Diver, still breathing but pallid from blood loss. We didn't have a second to spare, and I couldn't get help if Jaldane went blabbing about everything upon release.

Ignoring it all, I checked for my side pouch. It hadn't traveled through with me this time, which is what I'd meant to do. Somehow, the demi-monad took my intentions into account when I entered, and hopefully would continue to do so.

"Glinta," I said, "I need to get back outside for help."

"Ready when you are," she said.

"Do it," I said. Even before I could take her hand, she nodded, and I felt the world yank me out onto the palace courtyard again. I grabbed the second platelet, threw on my side pouch, and ran off to the dungeon tower.

At its base, I craned my neck to spot my destination. The lowest cell window sat a good four stories overhead, and Steve could be in any of them.

No guards patrolled the area at ground level, presumably because the only entrance was from deep inside the palace. The stone walls were far too smooth to climb if one were so bold, and the bars in the window were too narrow for even a child to fit through.

Nevertheless, I prepared to sneak in right there. I secured a purrium platelet in a little pocket near the mouth of my side pouch and hung the other one around my neck by its leather strap. Then, I placed the pouch directly below the barred window and committed its height to memory. It seemed to me that, if Father had carried the monad all the way to the palace workshop without

240

shaking everything inside, my side pouch could do the very same thing: motion outside the monad didn't affect motion inside of it. Moving something as light as my pouch was easy enough at any distance by purrium link, so why not from inside the monad?

Satisfied with the placement of the pouch, I tightened its mouth until it was just wide enough for me to reach in and grab the monad without letting it easily escape. With a deep breath, I popped back into the monad, leaving the pouch and its contents behind.

"Still no help?" Glinta asked as I found myself down in the cave again.

"Not yet," I said. As she struggled to stay awake, all the light flickered along with the flutter of her eyelids. "Oh graves. What am I even thinking?"

"Huh?" Glinta said.

"I needed to climb up something tall in here and then get sent back out again. But there's no way I can bring you with me like this, with who knows what else lurking around these caves."

"Well," she said between breaths, "I calibrated for you already… it should be fine… just signal when."

"That's not going to rip my arm off or something?"

She laughed slightly, but it looked painful. "Hopefully."

We agreed I'd give a thumbs-up signal whenever I needed to be yanked out again. Glinta would see everything, as always.

With that, I ran through the corridor to the forested area full of fruit trees. I picked a very tall tree with a good number of climbing branches, looked up and imagined the tree was the dungeon tower back outside. From my spot next to the tree, I carefully visualized which branch grew at the same height as the cell window I wished to reach.

241

Committing that branch to memory, I lightly flicked the platelet hanging around my neck. It hummed steadily, reorienting itself as it linked to the platelet outside. I lifted and moved my half around a bit, feeling the weight of my pouch where I'd left it in the world outside. Satisfied with that, I climbed, the weight of my pouch hanging from my neck by the purrium link. To anyone watching, out by the dungeon tower, the bag would appear to be levitating.

Higher and higher I ascended, refreshing the link with a light flick whenever the hum started to wane.

About halfway up, I heard something moving through the strange trees. I recognized the sinister quadrupedal gait from before: It had to be a writhor. Sure enough, I glimpsed its horrible, toothy visage as it emerged above the foliage like a periscope.

I tried to hide on the far side of my tree, but that leather strap around my neck dug into my jugular as I pulled against it. The platelet held firm in midair, exactly as if it were stuck against the dungeon tower where I'd imagined it to be. In that delay, the writhor sighted me and ducked out of view once again. His footsteps hastened ever closer.

I nearly signaled for Glinta to send me outside again but realized what a horrible idea that would be. I'd emerge several stories in the air and fall to my death.

I could only escape by reaching my target branch and getting that pouch safely inside the window in the world outside. So, I scrambled up the tree, fast as my limbs could carry me. The tree trunk got smaller and started to curve inward, making the petulant platelet pull against me once more. I had to awkwardly lean away from the tree trunk to breathe.

The writhor rose to full height as I reached the right branch. Hanging on with one hand, I grabbed the end of the strap on my

242

neck and pushed it where the window should have been. Instead, the platelet seemed stuck against more brick wall.

The writhor carefully positioned himself as if taking aim. Meanwhile, I flailed about with the platelet, feeling for the window to my left and right, but it wasn't where it was supposed to be. I'd remembered the height so clearly, positioned the bag so carefully, and never let the link die out once. It had to be the right spot.

The writhor opened his jaws wide. He'd lunge at me any moment. Then I remembered I hadn't accounted for my own height when I linked the platelet. I ripped the leather strap off, holding it high in one hand and jumped an extra half meter, narrowly dodging a ferocious chomp from the writhor.

He wound up again, and I felt around desperately for the barred window. Then there it was. I shoved the platelet till it dragged the pouch between iron bars and signaled thumbs up for an exit. The monster lunged again. I screamed, then felt myself yanked back to the outer world.

Now I found myself standing in an empty holding cell, the barred window right behind me, side pouch in my hand. For a moment, I just shuddered, seeing, almost feeling those horrible teeth coming straight at me all over again.

I could only find Steve by searching the rest of the holding cells. Before that, I'd need to escape this one. Of course, they left the cell door locked. So, I kept the side pouch around my hand, held it right next to the cell door, squeezed my fist around the monad and popped its outer shell once more.

In I went, finding myself hanging up in the tree exactly where I left off. The writhor hadn't gone anywhere but kept sniffing around for its lost prey. I linked the necklace, at which point the monster spotted me. I moved the platelet until it felt like I'd dragged the side pouch through the cell bars and signaled thumbs up for an exit, before the writhor could snap down on me. The world yanked me outside again.

Now I stood freely in the middle of the dungeon hall. Travel by monad wasn't the most comfortable way of getting around, but it worked wonders nonetheless. I marveled to think I'd snuck into one of the most secure spots in Newmund with little more than desperation and a few minutes of planning.

I searched the dim hallway of empty cells as it twisted and turned up through the tower. Soon, a lonely prisoner called out to me. "Shran my boy, is that you?"

Chapter Twenty-Nine

Liza

On Sunday, I emerged onto an unkempt patch of forest, bathed in the sharp-angled rays of early morning sunlight.

I shut the hatch behind me, then looked around for a large rock to roll over it. Seeing none, I selected a large enough aspen that looked beyond its prime, growing a few short meters from the hatch. With one hand on the aspen, its complete form sang itself out in vibrant detail. The sheer size made it a lot harder to absorb the living power spread so far across its branching body. After absorbing with all my might for a bit, the leaves browned and cascaded to the ground in a flurry, leaving hundreds of dark, stiffened branches behind. The snag creaked in the wind but remained standing.

With who knew how little time left to spare, I felt around on the dead roots for different kinds of life. There, I discovered fungus and innumerable tiny creatures living off the aspen. I poured the new reserve of plant vibrance into them, leading their growth with my fingers into the near side of the trunk. They released a dense cloud of rotten fumes as they seeped in and ate away the inside of the tree. I kicked at the bark, revealing the newly formed cavity and focused more of the power into the weakest points. I pushed and heaved against the far side of the trunk until the whole thing cracked, and groaned as it fell to the ground. It landed right on the escape hatch, forcing any pursuers to take the long way around.

Then I ran. I recognized nothing in the forest but the rising steam cloud from the nearby lake, telling me at least one way not to run. Soon enough, I lost sight of that too, getting completely and utterly disoriented. The thicker forest canopy blocked my view so fully that I could scarcely even point out the sun. I decided to try climbing a tall tree to get a bearing. If I could only glimpse the Great Tower, that would point roughly homeward.

I absorbed more vibrance from many small plants as I went, until judging that I had a good amount in my reserves. Then I found a nice tall pine with no branches at my level. Undeterred, I laid my hand on the pine and carefully focused some power into a spot where a branch had meant to grow. It sprouted out, just in reach, and it soon became my strong foothold when I made another branch grow above it. I climbed and climbed like that until I reached some existing handholds.

Eventually, I penetrated the canopy. The sharp silhouette of the Great Tower stood out clearly against the morning sky, and I concluded I'd been going the wrong direction for quite some time. Hopefully that would at least throw off anyone trying to track me down.

Something huge came plodding through the forest, followed by several riders. Nestor and the Keesec. How had they found me so quickly? Then I scoffed at myself. Of course, Nestor must have sniffed me out. I realized even now, a little droplet of blood oozed from my fingertip. I tried in vain to heal it with my reserves, but clearly, plant vibrance lacked some crucial flavor needed for human life. And in fact, the stuff made me recoil like I'd just inhaled a pine needle whole. Even if I stopped the bleeding, I'd already left a trail of it all the way up the pine tree. So much for covering my tracks.

First, I grew a bunch of new branches all up the trunk, camouflaging my ladder of handholds. Next, I smeared a good throwing stick with blood and hurled it off for another diversion. Scanning the nearby treetops, I wondered if I could grow myself a bridge, but what then?

Before I came to an answer, the whole tree quivered slightly. Way down on the forest floor, bits of Nestor appeared through gaps in the foliage. No time left. Here I would make my stand. I took a deep breath and made the pine grow enough needles to hide me from prying eyes. The Keesec would have to work to catch this target.

I peered through a small gap in the foliage, to see what happened. Nestor loped right up to my pine tree—which again quivered slightly at each step—grunting excitedly as he sniffed around the area. Anger rose within me. Had that abomination even bothered to notice the diversion stick I'd thrown him? I figured probably not when he started sniffing at my tree's roots, then a bit higher, then a bit higher.

"Old Nestor's found something," came Whira's voice from among the approaching riders.

Suddenly, he jerked his head in a completely different direction. His ears twitched, and then I heard it too: several shrill and sustained clanks, like metal on purrium, resounded from some party off in the distance. Nestor growled and charged off to whatever poor souls made the offending noise.

The Keesec riders called after him, to no avail.

Whira huffed, "Where's he going now?"

"Off in search of trouble," Haldra said. "Face it. Nestor was a dud. We'll just have to hope two is enough."

"What about Liza?" said another. "She'll go blabbing to everyone, no doubt."

"She'd only discredit herself," Haldra said. "Hurry now. We've got to get those drivers in before we miss our chance."

They galloped back the way they'd come. What did it all mean? What was two enough for? And what were these "drivers" they needed? What exactly was I going to blab about?

As soon as I believed they'd actually left, I started climbing back down the tree with reckless abandon. I dropped from branch to branch, relying on my gift to precisely image each footrest. As long as I touched it, I sensed the whole tree clearer than sight, whether I looked directly at it or not. Then my foot snagged on something unexpected: a dead branch, invisible to my special vision. It sent me plummeting and grasping for anything, but I only scratched my palms on fistfuls of pine needles.

As the ground approached, I poured living power out into any twig that would have me. At last, something grew into my waiting hands. The glorified twig checked my descent just long enough to let me dangle right-side up before it broke. I fell the last few meters, twisting my ankle.

I cursed at the pain shooting up my leg as I rose to walk. Naturally, I tried healing myself from my reserves, and again it did nothing but make me recoil in disgust. There was no choice but to get moving.

Wincing at each step as tears rolled like beads of sweat down my face, I tried in desperation to absorb vibrance from my own body to heal the ankle. But my own body seemed to be the sole anchor by which I absorbed anything. A man would've stood a better chance of lifting himself off the ground by tugging at his own ears. In the end, only a sturdy walking stick brought a bit of relief on that homeward hobble.

It still nagged at me. What were the Keesec planning to do? They wanted their new system implemented at any and every cost. And it had something to do with the giants. They definitely wanted me. Wanted me to grow more of them, perhaps many more.

And what had Talna said just before I slapped her? She expected Guilen to be dead soon, and the president too.

Was that their next move? Kill the men at the top?

It all started to make sense. To put in their new system, they'd get rid of those in power, and then take their place. But there was the succession to worry about. Everyone in Newmund knew only the eldest of the line had the right to rule. Haldra being the youngest, the people would never accept her and her son as rulers unless... Unless they were the only ones left.

She said no one would believe me. And as I hobbled onward, I wondered if even I would believe myself, so outlandish was her scheme. Who could plan such reckless evil against her own family, for no wrong any of them had done to her?

But what could I do about it anyway? They had horses and giants. They had secret connections in the palace, and secret tunnels *into* said palace. I was lost and alone and barely able to walk.

After some time like that, the first meager sign of civilization appeared: a bridge over a quiet stream, lashed together from a few narrow logs. Bunches of market-variety mushrooms grew up all over, definitely someone's special patch.

Never one to steal unnecessarily, I sat down, taking the weight off my throbbing ankle and touched one of the broad caps. Through it, I sensed the whole underground network and poured in some vibrance of plants. Several new mushrooms sprouted up nearby, and I started eating them, raw. Not the heartiest meal, but anything beat an empty stomach.

"Good morning, stranger," came an elderly man's booming voice.

I spun around to see a tall, cloaked fellow leaning on a scraggly walking stick. Many tiny wrinkles surrounded his deep green eyes, belying his old age. Behind him was a fine white horse, stopping to nibble at a tuft of grass.

"I wasn't stealing," I said.

The man's voice was deep and full of years. "On the contrary, it looks like you've got a knack for making your own food."

I held my tongue, hoping not to give any more away about my strange ability.

"Whoever you are, good woman, you don't have to hide your gift from me. I'm here to help."

"Thank you for your kindness, good sir. But I don't think anyone in Newmund can help me. You're better off not getting involved."

He let out a chuckle. "I'll be the judge of that. Come now. Get on this horse before you cripple yourself."

Chapter Thirty

Shran

Steve and I hung from the same tree I'd previously climbed, and the same old writhor immediately spotted us.

Steve leapt into action, swinging out of the way, and I followed suit. The writhor made to chomp down on us, but amazingly, the tree grew a new bough where we'd dangled a moment earlier. The monster snapped down onto the bough, which wriggled up his gullet. Dozens of small branches grew from the bough, binding themselves around his crocodilian jaws, so it couldn't draw away. He writhed and clicked angrily, but the branches grew thicker until he could hardly move.

I had expected Steve to have some very special talents, and still this went well beyond my wildest hopes.

The writhor grasped for us with that vile three-fingered claw. More branches fastened around its crooked wrist, freezing the limb in place. With that, the monster panted and ceased attacking us.

Steve and I raced down the corridor until we found the others.

Steve knelt beside Diver. "By All Father, this boy's nearly gone." When he laid a hand on the pallid pale boy, the life came back to his young face, but he still had a spear stuck through him.

"I'm sorry. This is going to hurt," Steve said, motioning for me to come help. The two of us heaved and hoed until we

251

removed the bone spear. Diver shrieked like a wild animal, but Steve immediately touched the wound and healed it before our eyes.

Diver jumped up and laughed. "That's incredible, old man. I feel like I could dive right off a tree."

Then Steve had Courtlya and Glinta back on their feet in short order.

"Splendid job, Shran, finding this miracle worker," Courtlya said.

"I'm just glad you're okay."

"How do you do such incredible things?" Glinta asked. "Are you this All Father Shran told me about?"

"No no no. Merely a man following his call," Steve said. "Which reminds me, might you be the girl who sent Shran back out to our world?"

"Yes I am," Glinta said.

"Do you know what that means?"

Glinta shook her head.

"It means you, Glinta, are the prime perspective of this demi-monad. You and this little world are essentially one and the same. It's a mighty responsibility for you and in a way for Shran as well."

"Me?" I gasped. "All I can do is come and go in this place. I don't have any special gifts at all."

"On the contrary, only you or your offspring can link our world to Glinta's. You used to be an only child, but now I present, your sister."

Steve let that sink in as I stared in confusion. I guess we did both have the same mother. Then I looked to Glinta and noticed, for the first time, those familial features in that toothy one-sided smile.

"And the truth is, I'm not just any relative," Steve said.

"You aren't?"

"No. Your father's father's father's father—a great many generations removed—is me."

"Hooray," Glinta cheered, jumping excitedly and grabbing my and Steve's arms. "Grandpa Steve, we're all family. That means you get to stay here forever."

"I hope to visit often," Steve said, "but Shran and I have got to be going for now."

"What do you mean?" I said. "Aren't we finally safe, now you're here?"

Steve laughed. "Safety is a gift for the led. You're meant for something else altogether. A deykti they once called it."

"A what?"

"Deykti, one who points the way, points not for his own benefit but to the benefit of those who follow."

"But no one listens to me out there. No one even wants me there."

"Whether anyone listens or not, whether anyone wants you there or not, your purpose doesn't change. Your place is with them."

Out of nowhere, Glinta gasped. "Shran, that lordling you brought here is in danger."

Only then did I realize we'd lost him. "Jaldane? Where did he go?"

"Down the funnel hole," Diver said, "as soon as he heard those were the way back. It sounded like he got a really fun ride out of it too."

"What kind of danger?" I asked, now worried myself.

"It does not take an all-seeing army of eyes to answer that," Courtlya said. "That old wretch seeks power and domination. It was only a matter of time before he started battling the almighty Siever."

Glinta nodded in agreement.

What would the nobility do if Jaldane got hurt—or worse—on my watch? "Glinta, you've got to send him back out of here," I said.

"I've never even touched him," she said. "It's like you were saying about losing an arm or who knows what. Siever and he keep tussling around, and I can't calibrate. You've got to help him."

By some strange impulse, I immediately ran for the funnel hole. "Shran wait," Diver said.

But without another word, I dove in. I slid through it really fast this time, the funnel zigzagging and spinning me upside down as it plunged deeper and deeper. One tunnel converged into another and another until I shot into the main chute. I tucked into a ball as I fell, crashed onto the bone pile, and rolled down to the cave floor.

In a dizzy spell, I spotted Jaldane and Siever in a full-blown tussle near the bridge. Funnela cheered her dearest on from the sidelines. I ran for them, yelling to stop it, in vain.

Then Siever got the upper hand, grabbing Jaldane's neck. "Gather me my fruit, you insurrectionist cur."

"I'm the...president's grandson," Jaldane said between gasps. "I'm not giving you... anything."

"Then you shall die," Siever said, opening his mouth as wide as he could muster. Those sharpened teeth glistened in the ceiling light as he—presumably—readied to bite Jaldane's head clean off.

Jaldane kicked and shoved, only delaying the approaching teeth.

"No!" I yelled, nearly to them.

Funnela quit her cackling. "Dearest, Shran's gone insurrectionist too."

Siever growled and shoved Jaldane to the drop-off. Jaldane shrieked, narrowly grasping a handhold as the rest of him toppled over the side. Siever leered at me. "Defy me twice, Deputy, and you'll lose your light for life."

"You don't control the light, Siever. You never did."

Siever pounced in a rage, pinning my arms with his knees and grabbing my head. I cried out for help, unable to do more than flail about.

"I am the almighty Siever, master of the light. May you never see it again." Then he started pressing rough thumbs on my eyeballs as if to blind me.

I screamed for help again. Suddenly, Siever released me, clapping palms to his face. Through my teary vision, I saw a white-hot light beam piercing between his fingers into his eyes. The beam tracked his movements so precisely that he couldn't escape it, no matter how wildly he shook.

"Make it stop, Glinta. Please make it stop," Siever cried.

Thin plumes of smoke rose from the gaps between fingers, the sickening odor of burning flesh growing stronger and stronger. He leapt off of me, desperately pressing his face into the ground. The beam redoubled its intensity on the tiny gaps that remained.

A whole group of people crashed onto the bone pile at once. One of them spoke even as they ran for us. "Glinta, that's enough," Steve shouted.

"He tried to blind Shran," Glinta said, running up with Steve and the others. "He's a wicked, mean ruler."

"That doesn't make you his judge and executioner," Steve said.

The white-hot beam went out, leaving nothing but smoke behind. I didn't dare look at Siever's face as he whimpered in pain. Steve went straight to him, placing a palm on the wounds and healing them just like my friends'.

Glinta followed behind him. "I'm sorry," she said, and hugged him where he sat. Siever barely seemed to notice the girl as he marveled at his renewed eyes.

About then, I was pulled away by someone who seemed to believe a dry handkerchief could dab away eye pain. "Shran, you poor thing," Courtlya said, "don't worry. It will be alright."

"Ouch."

"Sorry!"

Then Funnela was yapping at Glinta, "Treasonous girl. How dare you?"

Steve interrupted, "Lord Siever, may your name be loved forever."

Siever slowly rose to his feet. Finally noticing Glinta, he yelped and pushed her away like a poisonous animal. "And who the blazes are, you, old man?"

"Your servant is but a humble traveler on a mission for peace and prosperity," Steve said, holding out a water-catcher, full to the brim.

Then came Diver, carrying all the fruit we'd gathered and laying it in front of Siever, saying, "I can't believe you guys forgot this stuff."

"Alright, but who are you?" Siever asked.

"Steve is my name. I had the pleasure of joining these young folks in their quest to harvest your fruit and water."

Amidst their discussion, I approached Jaldane. He still lay by the edge where he'd nearly fallen into the lake.

"Are you alright?" I asked, offering a hand. He took it, eyes vacant until he got back to his feet.

"That madman nearly killed me before you got here," he said.

"I guess I'm glad he didn't."

Jaldane laughed. "That's right. You'd have your head chopped off if anything happened to me, eh?"

"Well, assuming they'd even believe me."

"Say, Shranny, how do we get out of this stinking place?"

"Don't worry. I'll show you."

Steve and Siever were still negotiating, fruit and water still at Siever's feet.

"I accept this payment for your original fines," Siever said, "but that doesn't begin to pay for how this girl just burned my—"

"Burned the almighty Siever?" Steve finished for him. "Impossible." Siever stared, confused, as Steve continued, "Look and see. You are in perfect health. I've rarely gazed on a pair of eyeballs as smooth and fair as yours." In fact, Siever looked a lot more kind, now the dark rings were gone. "Never let it be said that *you*, of all people, could have been injured by a young white-haired girl like this."

"I'm so sorry, Siever," Glinta said. "I promise I'll never do it again."

Siever glared down at her, but just as he opened his mouth, he appeared to have an epiphany. His expression turned into a father-like smile. "I'm sure I have no idea what you're talking about, Glinta." With a satisfied look at the pile of goods before him, he said, "Thank you all for your offerings. Now disperse while I figure out what to do with them."

"Almighty Siever, sir," Courtlya said sheepishly, "if I may be so bold, the title that I lost?"

"Yes, yes, Lady Courtlya, it's been reinstated. However, I can't just give such titles away willy-nilly. Someone's got to keep that screeching grass in order. I'm putting you in charge of all the grassland outside."

"In other words," Courtlya said, "I have lands?"

257

"Call it what you will," Siever said as Courtlya grinned from ear to ear.

"Oh, thank you almighty Siever."

"And what about some fruit?" Diver said. "I'm really hungry." And my stomach growled ravenously in agreement.

Siever sighed. "All of you, clear some of these bruised ones off the top of my pile. Then get outside already."

We each grabbed a fruit large enough for a good meal and started up the corridor towards the grassy plane outside. I devoured the fruit until I had no room left. Nothing ever tasted so delicious, so full of crisp, rejuvenating flavor. It tasted so good, all the hardship endured up to then seemed like a trivial price to pay. I tossed the core aside, sure to be finished by some fortunate cave critter.

Outside, the pale grass swayed gently in the sea breeze, bustling with meshors. They scampered around smoothly as ducks on a pond. Off in the distance came the chorus of breakers on the shore, just above a whisper. And once again, overhead was that enormous, hazy red tapestry full of stars that weren't stars, lending us their light.

It seemed quite a long time since I first went underground, or to "the top," as Courtlya put it. Somewhere in there, I'd lost myself. Somewhere, I found who I was meant to be.

All the countless lights in the hazy red sky smiled down on me. Indeed, I knew exactly who watched from each one. I smiled back up at them and just said, "Thank you."

"Me?" Glinta asked, looking up from the juvenile meshor in her arms.

"Yes, you, little sister." The last word felt strange and foreign to my mouth.

"Well, thank you, big brother. You did save us, after all."

"With a lot of help from you, not to mention Steve. All I did was—"

"Bring us together," she said.

Having taken the sights in, Steve walked over. "It's a fine little world," he said. "Just like people, no two demi-monads are quite alike."

"Grandpa Steve," Glinta said, the title ringing quite oddly to my ears, "if I'm this 'prime perspective,' what am I supposed to do?"

"Use every gift you have to seek the good, the true, and the beautiful," Steve said.

"Like seeking this cute meshor or something?" she asked.

"Soon this little critter—"

"Meshor," Glinta corrected.

"Soon this meshor will die. Everything you see now will eventually die and rot away."

She looked legitimately shocked, covering the meshor's ears as if to protect it from the injurious words. "That's not beautiful at all. Don't say that, grandpa Steve."

"It's not beautiful but is true."

"But then, nothing's really all three of those things," Glinta said.

"Nothing you can see now," Steve said.

Jaldane walked up behind us. "Come on, little Lord Mattian. Get us out of this nutty place already, will you?" Though his verbiage hadn't improved much, he didn't seem as disgusted towards me as before. He almost seemed to be asking nicely, in his way. "And… thanks again for helping me with that madman. You're not so bad."

Nearly dumbstruck, I managed to say, "Thanks."

Steve gave us the exit plan. Glinta would send Steve out first, allowing him enough time to toss the monad safely out his window. Then, she'd send Jaldane and me out to re-emerge in the courtyard, leaving no one the wiser about my little break-in.

Glinta grabbed Steve's hand and started looking like she'd sneeze again. The moment she relaxed, Steve stretched up and above the stars like a reversed bolt of lightning and disappeared into the red haze. Only a tiny puff of air gently swayed Glinta's hair as the man left our locality.

I looked once more at my new friends, wondering how long before I'd see them again. Diver chased a couple of meshors while the newly reinstated Lady Courtlya surveyed the lands, eyes filled with the joy of a dutiful worker. I walked up to her. "Goodbye, Lady Courtlya."

She curtsied politely. "I bid you safe passage to that strange world of yours. May you gain many lands like me," she said, stifling a sniff, "and you better come back soon."

"I sure will."

Then I returned to Glinta. "I guess we're ready."

Glinta sniffed and wiped wet eyes on her sleeve. "I'll be watching for you, brother." She grabbed mine and Jaldane's hands, squeezing hard. The little world yanked Jaldane and me up and out in a moment. We hadn't emerged in the courtyard as planned. We stood beneath the old barred window of Steve's cell.

"What are we doing in here?" Jaldane said in disgust.

"My question exactly," Mayor Guilen said.

Chapter Thirty-One

Zieglon

We stopped a short way south of Ohha Forest for a very late breakfast, finally free from our oaths of secrecy. The small open village had a fair-sized brewery with a tall thatched roof. Outside, each man tied up his horse wherever there was room.

As we stepped inside the cozy brewery, the sweet sound of lively locals at table nearly masked the odor of burning tallow.

"What'll it be, my lord?" came the raspy voice of the brewmaster behind the counter.

"Food and drink for all my men and lodging for our wounded," I said.

"I can sure help with the food, my lord. There ain't no inn here, but I guarantee we'll find a few families happy to lend a bed."

Hothen and I grabbed a small table while the rest of my men mingled with the locals, who were perhaps already on their third course of ale.

"Can I ask you something, Zieglon?" Hothen said.

I put away the hollow necklace I'd been fidgeting with. "Alright."

"How are you doing? With a dozen of the men injured, two dead, and your wife…"

"I'm doing," I said. "Just doing. I thought I knew the right path, but it brought us to this. How am I to understand any of it?"

Hothen nodded and pressed me to eat. At least the food wasn't bad.

Soon enough, Tewin led my soldiers in an impromptu song:

We killed the giant

While horses screamed and brayed

We killed the giant

Let all foes be dismayed

We killed the giant

Yes, Zieglon saved us all

We killed the giant

It took a mighty fall.

The locals applauded and clambered over to our small table. Some of the youngsters begged and begged, "Please show us." Hothen tried to shoo them away, but I stopped him short. How could I foist my somber mood on the folk? I felt myself oblige as they ushered me to the front of the dining hall. I conferred with a few of my men, and Hothen volunteered to play the part of an unnamed, particularly haughty nobleman.

As I acted out hunting the silver stag, Hothen pontificated on "his" plot to steal the beautiful prize for himself. Before he had the chance, another soldier roared like a giant and stole off stage with both of them. We brought over one of the spears with an exposed purrium core, and I made it ring loud and clear as I re-enacted rescuing the nobleman. Many in the crowd covered their ears at the shrill sound of the purrium summons.

Once I, too, escaped the giant's grasp, we started the re-enactment of the morning's hunt. The spark in the eyes of these common folk of all ages nearly made me forget my worries. A few soldiers acted as the haughty nobleman's party, obnoxiously clanking on the butts of our three spears with exposed cores, making as much noise as possible. And then of course, the giant hopped out from behind a wood sculpture, sending them all into a flurry.

The crowd roared with laughter. If nothing else, I'd lifted the spirits of the small village. Yet something was wrong. I motioned for silence. As the confused crowd quieted down, there it came again: the dull sound of enormous feet in the distance. It reverberated ever so slightly through the dirt floor.

"Take cover!" I shouted, grabbing my helmet. "We've got company."

Each able-bodied soldier leapt into action as the village folk huddled on one side of the dining hall. They lacked any fortifications, and didn't even seem to have a deputy present. The only protection was us.

Outside the door, I saw not one but two giants approaching and not a single horse left where we'd tied them. "Where are our mounts?" I called out to the brew-master.

"By thunder," the brew-master cursed, rushing out the front door. "I had them brought to the stables." He shakily pointed to the building a few hundred meters across a wide-open field—too far to run before our unexpected guests would arrive.

The disappointed sigh I let slip must have flayed the man beyond words as he stared at the approaching giants in disbelief. He'd only meant to help, dash it. "Hurry now, brew-master, signal a warning to the palace, before those things get here," I said.

He shook his head. "The sheriff's got the only purrium bell for kilometers." And the said sheriff's castle was several minutes' gallop away.

Here the man had only done right, yet found himself to blame all the same. How could we possibly beat the things without proper cavalry? Yet I would not let him suffer in vain. "Get inside," I said. "Protect them in there. We'll deal with these."

"Aye," the brew-master said and bustled inside again.

Each man held his spear at the ready. I donned my helmet and turned to Hothen and all my soldiers. "Men," I said, "you will keep your heads about you. Until we've sent the palace fair warning, permission to die is completely and utterly denied."

"Yes sir," they said as one.

The two new giants ran for us. Both bore hideous visages, now clear and distinct. One looked just masculine enough to make a mockery of the sex, while the other mocked all that was feminine. On top of that, their stiff, inhuman ears stuck out the sides of their heads, twitching as they listened. The many folds of their loose furry skin flapped at each step, grease glistening in the afternoon sunlight.

In mere seconds, they'd reach our position. Without our horses or the bows left hanging thereon, I doubted the dozen of us stood a chance against two giants. I gulped and pondering how they got here. And why? At last, a moment of clarity dawned. The purrium! That's what they were after, or so I hoped.

"Who has those bait-spears?" I called.

A few of the re-enactors piped up, saying they did.

"Throw them now," I commanded, assuming too much.

They did so without making them ring first. I stared in disbelief as the platelet-less spears sailed through the air and planted themselves in the ground without a sound. The giants were nearly there already. They passed over them without a second glance, apparently not registering the silent spears as the source of the offending sound as they ran for the crowded brewery.

I threw my hunting knife with all my might. It narrowly missed the lost spears as the giants came ever closer.

"Dashing graves. What do we do now?" Hothen said.

"We draw them away," I said.

With that, I linked to the knife which lay uselessly beside the lost spears and waved my fist like crazy. The knife clanked against one of the exposed cores, ringing it loud and clear. The giants spun on their heels, going straight for the spears. Yet in a moment, they'd still come for us.

Then I chucked my spear as far as possible and summoned back the hunting knife. "To the stable," I ordered.

We ran furiously as the giants backtracked. In those precious moments, I fished another platelet from a pocket. When we'd got within ten meters of the stables, the snarling giant and giantess were right on top of us. I held the platelet high overhead and clinked it loud and clear with my hunting knife. The abominable pursuers roared, whipping their heads around as the shrill ringing object whizzed through the air, back to my cast spear.

That bought us enough time to reach our horses—blessedly still saddled. We freed them from their pens and mounted up, haphazardly filing out for a cavalry charge.

By the time the horses were ready, the giants had destroyed the spear and ambled off in the direction of the palace. We'd saved the village, after a fashion, but the giants must have had another target. I considered trying to chase them down. With twice the giants and half the men, I decided against it. We had to warn the palace before anything else.

* * *

We reached the sheriff's castle, a fare trot from the village. There we met a throng of village folks enjoying their Sunday on the castle lawn. Several men just started to pick up pole-arms as we drew near. Hothen and the other riders watered the horses as I hurried to the chief deputy, the only fully-armored man present, with the lesser deputies in rank behind him.

"Good afternoon to you, Lord Mattian. State your business."

"There's foul danger on the loose. We need to signal the palace immediately."

"I can send a rider," the chief deputy said.

"We have horses already. I need to use your purrium bell."

"My apologies. It's out for repairs to the core."

"Why didn't you just request a new one?"

"Request? No, General. Lady Haldra came by this morning, insisting it needed repairs."

"If she knew that, why didn't she start by bringing the replacement?"

"Well, rare stuff, that purrium metal, as I hear it."

"The signal bells have always been low grade—it's all you need for linking those little things. It couldn't possibly be worth the extra trip."

"Unless the lady didn't want us to be able to signal the palace," he said.

"True. All too true."

I went back to the watering trough, hopping on my horse. "Mount up. We're going home," I said.

Hothen followed suit. "I was going to ask, how do you signal 'two more giants on the move' by waving a bell around a diorama?"

"It's more than that, my friend. If I'm right, there's a traitor on the loose."

Chapter Thirty-Two

Shran

"Uncle Guilen," Jaldane cried, "the tower-dweller tried to trap us in some underworld. We barely made it out alive."

"Exactly as I thought," the mayor said, motioning for the jailer to unlock the door. "Out of there, you two, before the man poisons your minds."

"But Mister Mayor," I said, "Steve helped save people. I don't think he meant to hurt anybody."

"So, you're his accomplice now, are you? I'm afraid I rescued you too late."

The mayor had the door locked as he led Jaldane away. Not only that, but he took my side pouch with all of my things in it. It came down to me and Steve, trapped in one small cell.

"I can't believe it," I said. "So, this is how Jaldane repays us? Some people are just evil, no matter what you do."

"I'm sorry," Steve said.

"I'm sorry now too. Now I've lost everything, and you didn't do anything to stop the mayor."

"I'm sorry, my boy—"

"But you have to do something and get us out of here."

"I wasn't finished. I'm sorry you feel this way, but you've got to learn. Learn to trust our true father."

"Haven't I learned enough? Besides, what's that got to do with being betrayed and trapped in here after all I did?"

"Everything. The father of all meticulously sculpts every event for the very best interests of his true children. And I mean everything."

"How? How is there anything good about being even worse off than before?"

"If I knew that, I'd be him. How could I use the very gift he gave me to oppose the ones he's chosen to place in authority—for a time—over me?"

"Mayor Guilen doesn't deserve to be in authority."

"But he is."

"So, he can just do whatever he wants and you'll never do anything to stop him?"

"The second he ceases to be mayor, I have no obligation. The second he commands me to disobey an even higher authority, I have no obligation to oblige."

"How is that good enough? What about... what about..."

"Because I don't subsist on fair treatment. The stuff is more fleeting. In the end, I have only one sustainer."

What a dumb thing to say, especially from a man who seemed so wise, especially at a time like that. With an angry sigh, I found a seat on an old clump of straw in the corner and remained quiet for a while. Steve gazed out the window, as if mesmerized by the narrow patch of sky. After some time, he still didn't appear phased by long bouts of silence but seemed to peacefully relish each moment. When I couldn't stand it anymore, I finally blurted, "So, what are we going to do?"

"I myself was planning to keep silent, until the time was right. Now they've got you here, as a suspected accomplice..."

"But I didn't do anything wrong, besides breaking *into* jail, I mean."

Just then, the door at the end of the hall opened again. The dark figure of Falen strutted our way.

Steve quietly whispered, "If you would, try not to tell him everything."

Falen led me off to a small room where the interview would take place. Never in my life had I managed to tell two convincing lies in a row. Beyond that, the bard knew me well enough from schoolyard to pick from my brain like dates from a dish.

It started before I even knew what was happening. "Shran, my lordling, have some roast," led to, "Oh, aren't you starving?", and "Why not?" That led to, "How did you get in Steve's cell?", "What's a scotor?" and "What do you think about the lordling, Jaldane?" And ultimately that led to questions like, "Why run away?" and "What happened to your mother up in the Great Tower?" And what would happen if my story and hers didn't match? In short, after landing firmly back in the real world, I almost immediately caved.

To my surprise, the mayor held Steve's trial from the third tier of the temple, encouraging the large crowd of onlookers to watch as they ate their Sunday meat. The whole thing had more of an air of festivity than any trial I'd ever seen. Odder still, he had Jaldane and me join him up on the third tier even before bringing Steve out. It was all so wrong. We weren't supposed to be up there.

He motioned for silence. "People of Newmund, at long last, I present to you the criminal inhabitant of the very tower that casts its dark shadow across our homes each day." Stark silence fell over the whole temple. The people seemed to hang on every word, surely amazed to hear any news about the mysterious tower.

"I want to be straight with all of you gathered here today. This is no trial. Today, we declare a victory a thousand years in the making. I merely bring this man forward to display for all of Newmund why he deserved his final defeat. Bring him forward."

Guards led Steve through the temple archway and up the center aisle. Every neck craned to glimpse this strange tower dweller: some curious, some glaring even as they strained to see him. Steve stood out from the crowd like a sore thumb, head held high, shoulders back, and each step a thing of grace. Once he reached the third tier, he seemed to tower over the mayor. Though, as I looked carefully, they had to be the same height.

The display-that-wasn't-a-trial started like this: The bard Falen gave a long list of crimes attributed to Steve over the past day and a half, including kidnappings and torture of innocents, with me, Mother, and Jaldane being the chief victims. Falen used us—the two available witnesses—like silent props in a drama, garnering sympathy from onlookers. Glancing all across the second tier, I wondered where my parents had gone. It seemed I was alone again.

When Falen finally asked for a response, Steve simply looked to Mayor Guilen and said, "Not guilty, Mister Mayor."

The mayor shook his head and sighed. "This isn't a trial. You aren't permitted to deny any of this. Yet, for the benefit of Newmund, we will hear from the first witness."

Falen brought Jaldane to the foot of the throne that no man could sit upon. The seat of the throne dwarfed them, well above both their heads. Jaldane placed his hands at its base and looked skyward.

"Do you, Jaldane Stohvan, swear by this throne and the unseen one who sits upon it, that your testimony today is true?" Falen asked.

"I do," Jaldane said. Though I noticed he began removing his hands from the foot of the throne just before speaking those words.

Falen proceeded to question Jaldane about the events of that morning at the front of the third tier. My fists clenched and jaw tightened with every new outlandish claim and every fresh word of willful ignorance. With each question, Falen sculpted Jaldane's testimony, forming some maniacal villain in place of the kind—if misguided—man I knew. Jaldane didn't appear to care. Worse yet, I knew in a few short minutes, Falen would use my own words to do it all over again.

Next, Falen brought me to the foot of the throne as well. I placed my hands on the smooth, polished stone. Behind it, I could see the spire of the Great Tower where it disappeared into the bluing of the sky as Falen recited the truth oath for me, as if speaking an incantation.

All I was permitted to say was, "I do."

Mayor Guilen looked down at me as I took my place at the front of the third tier. "Shran, as a sworn witness in the Newmund Mayor's Court, all you must do is provide the facts of that which you witnessed. You shall not supply superfluous details, conjectures, or personal opinions. Understood?"

"Yes sir, Mister Mayor," I said, and he nodded contentedly.

Then, he sicced Falen on me with a perfectly sequenced battery of questions. "Shran, pray-tell, where did this man Steve first find you?"

"Outside the..." I didn't dare talk about the forbidden Great Tower here, of all places.

"It was near that sinister spire where we captured him. Wasn't it?"

"Yes sir," I said, resignedly accepting his framing. On and on it went. The more he mangled my every memory to force it into his special interpretation, the more my fear of the nobility turned to hatred.

Falen carried on. "Remember: just the facts, Shran," he said, later followed by, "Shall I have to define the word kidnapping for you?", and, "Once he lured her into the glass room, describe what happened next."

How I wished I could re-enter the demi-monad, which was still locked up with my effects somewhere.

Soon enough, Falen nodded in satisfaction. "No further questions, Mister Mayor."

Mayor Guilen addressed the deadly silent audience. "There appear to be no more witnesses. It breaks my heart to announce that the lady, Liza Mattian, the mother in question, has disappeared without a trace. I can only venture to guess why. Therefore, all that's left is for me to declare Steve's punishment."

"Wait a moment," came an elderly man's voice from the temple entrance. There, a cloaked man was walking in, with a cloaked woman on horseback behind him. The sound of the man's heavy boots and the clopping of shod hooves echoed across the whole temple area. As they neared us on the center aisle, I realized the cloaked woman was none other than Mother.

"Shran!" she called excitedly. The cloaked man helped her off the horse, just shy of the third tier. She limped the few steps it took to come and hug me. I hugged back, happier and more relieved to see her than ever before. Somehow, this time, things would be better.

As the mysterious man removed his hood, the mayor uttered one astonishing word: "Father?"

Chapter Thirty-Three

Liza

T he elderly stranger led the way out of the forest and made course through the hilly fields towards the palace. He had such a way about him, I couldn't put my finger on it. But he seemed to know what he was doing to the point I didn't have to.

"So, why are you helping me?" I asked from atop his horse.

"It's my privilege," he said, not slowing his brisk walk.

"And seeing me grow a patch of mushrooms had nothing to do with it?"

"It had everything to do with it. It's not every day some wight gets a chance to assist one of the Eldenvolk."

"The what?"

"You joke," he said.

"I do not. I never heard of the things." Though perhaps the word rang a bell.

"One of the ancient benefactors, wise elders ageless from generation to generation, able to harness life itself for the good of all. Thus... the mushrooms."

"Well, that's not me, sir. I tried to do the right thing. Tried to help my family, but that only made everything worse. Now all I hope is to warn Newmund before it's too late."

"Family, you say? And how old are you, then?" he asked.

"That's not a very polite question, is it?"

He shrugged. "That young? In that case, you'll learn to do better soon enough."

"How can I? Officially, I am a lady of Newmund but *only* officially. We don't have any blood ties to our rank. So, all the Newmund nobility think I devalue the whole institution."

"That's not so," he said.

"It's no matter of opinion. I was fleeing from one of them just now, I tell you."

"As it happens, I'm something of a nobleman myself."

"But sir, you're too old. You can't be of the Peltern line."

"What did we just say about the age question? Anyway, my wife was of their line."

"Oh. So, you escaped the siege of Newmund palace?"

"I helped lead it, actually."

My jaw slackened as I blinked. He did bear a striking resemblance to certain statues in the palace. "You can't be. The president?"

Shran helped keep me off my bad ankle as we watched President Dessidon the Second shake hands with the mayor atop the palace temple. Who would have guessed two strange reunions of parent and child would happen at once for all to behold?

"Well, this is quite the surprise, Father," I heard Mayor Guilen say. "We kept watching for your entourage, but none came."

"Those spectacular entrances always seem to muddy things up. Make it incredibly difficult to see what's really going on," Dessidon said.

"Yet here you are."

"Yes," the president sighed, glancing at the crowds watching below. "The spectacular has a way of smoking me out eventually. Regardless, a few urgent matters have come up."

"By all means, Father, but we were just in the middle of an important display."

"Lady Liza," Dessidon called.

"Yes, Mister President," I said, and Shran helped me walk over to them, my ankle still quite tender.

"Would you kindly stand witness for this man you told me about?"

"Yes sir," I said. "Though standing isn't my strong suit at the moment."

Steve stepped forward. "Not to interrupt, but may I?"

He offered a hand, and when I took it, a jolt of energy shot through my twisted ankle. I gasped as the wound rapidly healed itself. Mayor Guilen gripped the hilt of his sword. "Hands off the lady, Steve. I warn you."

"It's fine, sir. It looks like I can stand just fine now."

Guilen stayed his hand but didn't advertise the healing incident at all.

Falen took the stage as Steve's prosecutor, and had me sworn in under the Throne in short order.

"How old are you, Lady Mattian?" Falen asked.

Why did everyone on Tew suddenly care so much about my age? "Twenty-seven."

"Yet you don't wholly look it," Falen said, the nerve of such a comment. "Has your hair always been this color?"

The very last thing I wanted to do in front of all Newmund city was relive the terrifying experience that had given me the whiter than white hair. Yet, what choice did I have? If my story didn't match up with whatever Shran had said, one or both of us would be sorely punished. That left no other option but the truth.

I still couldn't put a finger on exactly what I thought about Steve. As Falen asked me the questions and I gave truthful responses, the bard kept molding my every word to suit his desired conclusion. He'd chosen me to play the role of victim but for all the wrong reasons.

In the midst of it, I increasingly realized Steve's fate and mine were sewn together. Whatever happened to him, as a true Eldenvolk, would happen to me eventually. We couldn't let him lose the trial. Yet the longer the hearing went on, the more I discovered Steve was not allowed to be innocent.

All too soon, Falen announced, "No further questions, Mister Mayor," and the case was closed.

I went and stood by Shran in the moments of stark silence as the mayor pondered. Shran looked at me, equally disheartened.

Finally, Guilen addressed the crowd. "Now that our final witness has spoken, after some consideration, I have decided Steve's punishment. He will be beheaded."

"No!" I yelled, and Mayor Guilen shot a quizzical look.

"No delaying indeed," he said with a smile. "We will hold it at sunset."

Guilen was always swift with justice, but how was this even possibly just? Who would dare treat such a person like that, without even giving him a chance?

Suddenly, Dessidon approached Guilen. "Thank you, Mister Mayor, but I have something else in mind for Steve."

"My apologies, Father. If beheading isn't enough—"

"No no no," Dessidon said. "I mean to pardon Steve on all counts."

"Pardon?"

"Absolutely. I found the evidence less than compelling and the prosecution less than thorough. Why wasn't this man even afforded time to question the final witness himself?"

Guilen looked to Falen, who kept stone silent, both hands clasping his standing stick. "Forgive me, but you arrived very late, Mister President. This is not a trial but a victory display. There's no need in this special case—"

"Rather in all cases, Mister Mayor. Justice is not optional for you: justice is your very life. I came to your mayorship in secret, hoping to find things in good order before greeting you as a father ought. Now you've left me no option but to administrate."

"You don't understand," the mayor said in a hushed tone. "We've finally got a victory amidst this endless civil war with your uncle. We got a victory over that impregnable tower. You can't take that away from me, from Newmund."

"You breached the Great Tower?" Dessidon asked.

"Not exactly 'breached.' I did see this man leave the Tower and personally captured him before he could slink back inside."

"Guilen, my son, don't you see? Steve is one of the Eldenvolk. He came to us of his own volition. Now more than ever, the Presidency needs allies. Steve and Lady Mattian will be our allies, if we can keep them," Dessidon turned to Steve. "What say you, Steve? Will you ally with the true Presidency of Othark?"

"I hope to be your presidency's best guest and proudest neighbor," Steve said. "Of course, I must follow the will of the Father and my conscience. Still, as for you, Mister President, I would gladly be your friend." And the two shook hands in resolution.

Dessidon turned to the crowd and announced, "Let it be sung in Newmund, we have a friend in the Great Tower."

As he spoke these finishing words, I looked to Shran beside me. I knew now things would be very different.

Chapter Thirty-Four

Shran

Before we dispersed, President Dessidon asked Mayor Guilen, Steve, and my mother to join him for a private meeting.

"Happily," Steve said.

"Could I wait a bit?" Mother asked. "I've got to catch up with my son."

Dessidon sighed. "You've got the hour, Lady Mattian. Guilen, Steve, shall we?" and the three men went off to wherever they hold secret meetings in the palace.

The preceding trial—or whatever it was—cemented one thing in my mind: even if the president sought justice, none of the Newmund nobility did. Whether Jaldane or Nella, or Mayor Guilen, they'd all betray you as soon as convenient. Now, rather than fleeing, I only wished to get rid of them.

As my mother and I left the temple, a guard returned my pouch. It hit me as I felt the sparse contents: the tiny demi-monad granted me real-world power—if not the power to do anything, certainly the power to do something. But I needed all the help I could get, needed allies.

"Where's Father?" I asked.

"I don't know," she said. "I was away for a bit this morning, but Shran, you did so well."

"Thanks." I wasn't sure about that. She hadn't seen how the mayor had made a puppet of me until the president arrived. He alone won the day. He won because he had the power. What happened when he left again?

We walked off toward the festivities in the palace courtyard, and Mother took my arm as if I were escorting her in Father's place. "And son," she continued, "I think things are going to be a lot different now."

"What do you mean?"

"Do you think what just happened is the end? No. Maybe before, you and I could hide in the background—could go unnoticed from time to time. I think those days are all but done. We've been to the highest point of the highest tower in the world for a reason. They'll be watching us, everyone."

"We're important then," I said. "We've got to do whatever has to be done, right?"

"Yes. So, come on, let's enjoy these festivities while we still can."

We strolled through to the main courtyard, still packed with many booths and little performances. They seemed small, distant almost. I told Mother all about the adventures I'd had, this time in my own words, including how I'd escaped and been betrayed by the same lordling I'd rescued.

Some people I didn't know seemed to crane their necks, listening in on the stories. When they did, I found an excuse to move along. The story wasn't meant for them, wasn't ready for them yet.

We found our way to one packed area, watching some traveling acrobats throwing each other in the air and completing back-flips just before striking the cobbles. That seemed distracting enough to keep off the prying eyes. There, I told Mother more about

Glinta, how she was like a real sister to me, and I held up the demi-monad for her to see.

"That's so sweet," she said, then winced at the words. "There I go again. What it really shows is your strength. You can find friends in the worst of places, and you fought for them."

"Yeah, I guess so."

"So, you can just pop in there as easy as that, then leave at will?" She tried doing it herself, but the orb only shot out from between her fingers.

I snatched it out of the air before it escaped into the crowd, who were still distracted by the acrobats. "Steve said only I can break the barrier. But I did manage to drag Jaldane and Steve along with me. So, you can come visit too." I lowered my voice. "I could even trap Jaldane in here again if I wanted to, or the mayor. Wouldn't that be great?"

Shock flushed over my mother's face. She opened her mouth as if to speak but said nothing. Maybe I didn't much like the sound of it either as I said it, but still. "Mother, they're unjust. Someone's got to do something about it. Now I can."

"Shran, do you have any idea what that would do to you?"

I just kicked at a stray pebble, and she went on. "Well, do you have any idea what I've been through today, why I twisted my ankle, who I was running from?"

I shook my head.

"I'm like your friend Steve now," she said. "I used that power, ignored my better judgment, and now I see... see evil is on the move."

Before I could ask what she meant, the high tower started ringing its most disconcerting rhythm: "danger," and it was no drill. Newmund hadn't had invaders in my lifetime, so I rushed towards the gate to glimpse whomever it might be. Mother called after me, but I slipped through the crowds anyway, certain I could take cover after a quick look at the attackers.

On the way, I heard mighty hinges creaking as a dozen guards pushed and heaved the palace gates closed. The doors shut with a dull thud, locking hundreds of us inside. Guards above the gatehouse cocked crossbows, readying themselves by the murder-hole. Others lit bonfires under the tar cauldrons. In no time, the palace seemed ready to take on any siege.

Worries rushed through my mind in a moment. Would we be trapped under siege like I'd learned about in the schoolyard? How long would we have to hold out? And how long could the palace feed so many stomachs before turning to more desperate measures? I prayed this siege would be a short one as I neared the wall with a bunch of other youths.

At the very base of the stairs leading up onto the catwalk, the guards blocked our way, demanding everyone take cover indoors immediately. Why did they have to make such a fuss?

Then came the sound of a very large and very heavy form beyond the wall, coming closer and faster. The footsteps ended abruptly. One woman screamed and pointed at something atop the wall: a hand, so enormous its grimy fingers curled over several battlements at once. Then a second hand grasped the battlements next to it. The monstrosity was already climbing straight up the wall.

Panic erupted through the courtyard while I stared in disbelief. Even with what I'd seen in the bizarre world of the demi-monad, I never imagined anything like this could happen out in the real world, much less the safety of the mayoral palace.

In that moment of disbelief, I hadn't kept up the pace with my countrymen. Many families ran in long lines, gripping hands like daisy-chains, but I'd rushed off alone. When I turned to move with

286

the crowd, someone's boot caught my ankle, someone else bumped into me, and I fell headlong. More and more feet scurried all around. Kick after frantic kick struck me as I curled up in the fetal position, until the traffic thinned out.

I looked up, now clearly seeing a hideous giant poking his long, protruding face over the battlements. The several guards up on the gatehouse loosed crossbows. The giant ducked, then quickly heaved himself onto the catwalk.

The guards nocked new bolts furiously as the giant sprinted for them. His massive feet barely fit atop the walkway, and his calves alone rose higher than any of the guards' heads. Before they could loose another bolt, he'd already reached the gatehouse and swatted a few of them clean over the edge with one arm.

There came a second giant popping over the wall, this one with a grotesque mockery of a woman's face. She clasped a hand onto one guard as she climbed up, and I heard his armor crunching against the battlement. We didn't stand a chance against the things. I scrambled to my feet and fled.

To my shame, only then did I realize I'd put my own mother in harm's way too by running off as I'd done. "Mother?" I called out. Useless within the hundreds of screaming passersby. The current of crowds flowed off towards the inner palace. I pushed and shoved my way further in, gradually nearing the last spot where Mother and I had spoken.

A dull thud reverberated through the ground. I spied over my shoulder. Both giants loped freely across the courtyard. They honed in on several more guards. Perhaps that bought the rest of us some time, though we would be all the more defenseless soon.

I kept pushing through, barely managing to cut across the flow of people to reach my destination. Mother soon turned up, having taken cover under an abandoned fruit vendor's booth. Her eyes projected pure horror as she sat there, rocking with knees under her chin. When she saw me, she buried her face in her palms.

"We've got to go," I said, barely able to stand in place as others pushed past.

She barely seemed to register my words as she spoke. "It wasn't supposed to be like this," she said. "She deceived me again. She always, always does."

"Mother, we'll both die out here," I said, tugging at her limp arm.

Finally, she appeared to notice me again. "Oh," she said. Then she crawled out from the booth and rose to her feet.

We should have been dead already, hundreds of Newmund folk should have. Why were the giants still attacking guards, risking injury? Why had they attacked the single strongest place in the mayorship instead of the many unfortified villages? They had a deeper motive, but what?

We'd fallen far behind the rest of the fleeing crowds. Almost everyone had passed by us. They pressed on towards the inner palace's main doors. That left little chance for us to reach safety inside. We needed another way.

"Come on, Mother," I said, and she allowed me to steer us towards the servants' entrance. All the pillars made this way less crowded and prohibitively tight for pursuing giants. They would easily fit in the main entrance, where the general public were flooding in.

Mother breathed heavily, still barely responsive.

"What are those things?" I asked.

"My fault. All my fault," she murmured.

"What is?"

"Those abominable monsters."

"They came out of nowhere, Mother."

288

"Lady Haldra tricked me into growing them. She figured out I'm just like Steve now. They'll be searching for me this very minute. They want more of them, and…"

"But we're safe in here," I said. "Those monsters couldn't fit in this door."

"Not the giants. This is a servants' hallway. At least two of them were on her side. We've got to go. Now."

We jogged into the public corridors, weaving our way between the folk taking refuge in the palace. The closer we got to the main entrance, the more crowded it got. In all the commotion, Mother explained the worrying turn of events that had happened since we'd been separated.

"So," I said when she'd finished, "all along, Lady Haldra was with these Keesec folks, revolting against her own family?"

"That's what I gathered. Only after she tricked me into helping her did I get the courage to escape."

"But why?" I wondered aloud. "Why attack now?"

"The President, I think."

"Yeah!" I said, "he could declare her incompetent."

"If he's alive, that is."

"So, he's in even more danger than you," I said. If only Father were there. He'd surely know what to do.

Chapter Thirty-Five

Zieglon

I paced in front of the palace wall, the rhythm of the emergency bell ringing out from the high tower. "We're getting in there," I said.

"It's barred shut and no one home in the gatehouse," Hothen said.

"Then we'll just have to open it ourselves." I turned to the contingent of soldiers. "Every man with an intact purrium set, spread out along this wall, and give yourselves a wide birth. We don't have any time to go spearing each other."

They did so as I launched my spear as high as I could manage. It peaked out as it overshot the battlements. Before the weapon could plummet any further, I snapped my gauntlet into an ear-splitting purrium summons, clinching my fist to keep the glove from escaping. The spear planted itself in a cleft, like a makeshift grappling hook and yanked me upwards.

As soon as my feet left the ground, I felt myself swing towards the broad face of the palace wall. I threw my feet forward and ran up sideways.

A volley of spears thrown by the soldiers below flew past me on either side. They began to ascend right behind me.

The closer I got, the stronger the purrium pulled. I sprinted faster and faster until I couldn't keep up. My foot slipped, and I clattered into solid stone. My armor screeched as my whole body twirled and scraped its way upwards. Grunting angrily at such a rookie mistake, I shoved off the wall hard. The wind whizzed through my helmet as I got right way around again and skipped onward.

At peak momentum, I silenced my platelet. That arced me the last meter over the battlement, landing feet-first onto the catwalk. With one more snap of my finger, the spear tugged itself free and flew into my waiting palm. The rest of the men followed a moment later, retrieving their weapons in like manner.

Before we could climb down to heave the gates open, two unwanted visitors approached from the palace courtyard. The same monstrous couple that met us at the brewery had already infiltrated the palace. I silently cursed. They kicked aside the vacant booths in their path like so many dead leaves, enraged again by the sound of purrium.

I shouted, "Into the palace!" We rushed across the walkway and into a narrow soldier's entrance, leaving our only chance at a cavalry charge locked outside.

In the main entrance hall, we found a disorderly mass of the folk puttering around as the remnant of palace guards faced the main doors with spears raised.

"Where is Berrin?" I asked the remaining guards.

They shook their heads.

"And are you mad?" I asked the ranking officer.

"No, General," he stammered.

292

"Then get that door barricaded already."

"With what?"

"Get every man you can find, bring everything we can lift."

Anything was better than seeing the common folk milling about with nothing to contribute. If we were thus favored, it would even buy enough time to prepare a proper defense.

In the meantime, I took my men to the barracks and had squires fasten sharp spurs at all my joints. I'd have a little surprise ready if one of the abominations tried snatching ahold of me again. I strapped on an extra sword, slid fresh platelets into both gauntlets and summoned their spears into my waiting hands.

"Are you sure about this, Zieglon?" Hothen asked, armored in like fashion.

"Sure as I can afford."

"Lady Haldra can hardly have stolen every signal bell in the mayorship. We'll have our reinforcements soon enough."

"For the city, yes. As for the palace, we're on our own."

"I just don't get it," Hothen said. "How could Lady Haldra join league with these things—against her own people, her own *kin* even?"

Shaking my head, I sighed heavily. "Pray that I'm mistaken, Hothen. I don't want to be right."

Suddenly I caught sight of two familiar faces in the crowd, two wonderful faces I feared I would never see again: Liza and Shran. I went straight to them, scooping the two up in my arms. "Thank All Father. How did you escape?"

Shran produced that strange orb from his side pouch. "You wouldn't believe it, Father, but there's a whole 'nother world in here. All I had to do was ask the right person to let me out."

I laughed aloud. Steve had been right all along. To think how much we'd worried. "Shran, I've learned one thing today. Our own

293

world is stranger than we like to imagine. And, Liza, what about you?"

"Hmm?" she said with pretend innocence.

" 'Hmm,' is what I said when I found this." I produced Steve's necklace from a pocket.

She stared in shock, and ushered us into a secluded corner. "Zieglon, the president's finally here, in the palace. They mean to kill him, and probably the entire noble family."

"You mean Lady Haldra?" I asked.

Liza shook her head and whispered, "her and at least a dozen others had control of these monsters the whole time, down in that ancient complex."

So, indeed, the worst was true. How deep did the conspiracy go? I checked my corners and, satisfied for the moment no one was eavesdropping, turned back to Liza. "And what happened? How did you manage to discover this and escape that place?"

She sighed, and tears filled her eyes. "I helped her do it. It's my fault."

I held her tight, silently cursing that we had any part in this.

"I was afraid," she said into my ear. "I didn't mean to, but I let her deceive me. They spoke with something—someone—evil. Some entity from another world, it seemed like. And then I knew I had to get out of there if it killed me."

"And you *did* escape," I said, smiling as I released her. "You're alive! How did you do it?"

She sighed, "I had to kill a tree, make it fall right on top of the hatch I came from. I had to grow a ladder for myself up a tree at one point, and just before they found me up there, some poor soul drew him away."

"Liza, you never cease to impress me. What you did took bravery, and what you lacked in strength, you made up for with sheer ingenuity."

She smiled as she wiped a few tears away.

"That must have been the giant we killed already. There aren't any *more* we need to worry about, are there?"

Liza shook her head.

Then, I held out the necklace to Shran. "Here, son. Steve said you could use this."

"What is it?" he asked.

"It lets us see inside the monad." I showed him how it opened and closed.

Shran grabbed the necklace, secured the orb inside the rings and snapped the little cage shut around it. Once again, an untrained eye could confuse it for an amber stone.

Shran peered through the stacked eyepieces and sure enough, saw something. "There's Glinta, clear as day. Here, look and see," he said, then held it a bit farther from his face and waved. "I think she sees me too."

He held the little amulet out where all three of us could see into the eyepiece at once, with all our heads close enough together. A reddish haze clouded the image as before, certainly not clear as day to my eyes. Yet there I saw the same young woman as the night before, now sitting in a field with a strange critter in her arms.

She waved at us excitedly, clearly saying something, but none of us heard her. As we were straining to hear, an unholy roar and a mighty pounding on the main doors gave us all a start.

I unstrapped the family sword, hastily fastening it around Shran's waist. "Take care of your mother and use this when you need it."

"Can I keep it?" he asked, excitedly.

"Keep it sharp. Now get to our chambers, the both of you."

"Yes sir," he said.

The three of us hustled to the main hall, where we separated by the main entrance. There I found Hothen, surveying the barricade with the others. They had propped tables and chairs against the main doors, along with a large pile of toppled sculptures. Only by our bard songs could we restore or rebuild them one day. Until then, they bought us precious, precious time.

A couple dozen meters from the door, a few ranks of overworked spearmen and archers held their place, ready for combat. Some more soldiers had joined our last line of defense, but not nearly as many as I'd hoped.

By the looks of it, most of the women and children had found cover elsewhere, while rough-handed men, young and old, stayed put. These commoner folk continued to stand behind us, even as the doors creaked and bulged farther and farther inward. Some brandished decorative spears, poleaxes, and other weapons borrowed from the palace displays, while many a man gripped only his walking stick.

I addressed everyone present as the first signs of a crack appeared on the main doors. "Soldiers of Newmund."

"Sir, yes sir," came the reply of only my soldiers.

"This day, some of us faced a giant in its own habitat. We destroyed him. True, our number waned a bit since this morning, but as I gaze at your brave faces, I tell you the strongest portion remains!"

Some of my men cheered, and a few others. Not nearly the spirit we needed.

"True, we lack the benefit of armored horses at present. That only multiplies the weight of glory we shall soon bear. In a short time, we will meet two more of those hideous monstrosities who are clearly starved for punishment. So, let us sate their appetite. That's an order!"

More men joined in, "Sir, yes sir!"

Would it be enough? A few more mighty thuds shook the oaken doors, the barricade still holding firm. But the crack grew larger, splinters spraying outward blow by blow.

"Protect our mayor!" I barked. "Protect our home! Protect our folk!"

One of the main doors split in half, swinging on its hinges until slamming into the side wall. A grizzly visage peaked through the gap. This prognathous, vaguely feminine form bellowed a triumphant howl. Then she reached inside and began shoving aside the barricade. She withdrew, and right behind her came the fever-pitched gait of the other giant.

I took my place in the front line, shouting, "Hold!"

We planted spears on the stone floor, points extended outward as far as they'd reach. The male giant burst through the door, raining the biggest storm of dust and splinters yet. We held firm, even as some desperately wiped their eyes clear.

Archers loosed a volley, but the giant leapt over our ranks in one bound. The arrows fell low of his vitals. Still, to my relief, he fumbled the landing, collapsing with a thud that shook the whole entrance area. Down but only for the moment.

Even while he crash-landed, the giantess followed. She was covered in hair over all except her hideous face: a female, yes, but womanly she was certainly not. She ripped off and hurled a broken half of the door like a discus. It tore through half of my soldiers and into the commoners. When the archers loosed a second volley, she shielded herself with the other half of the door and cast the arrow-riddled remnant back at us.

Many managed to sidestep this time, but still some folk weren't so blessed. The two missiles had bought her time to close the distance between us and thrust a mighty kick. Several spearmen flew across the room before they could land a hit.

By then, the first giant recovered from his fall and charged at our rear. When our backs were to the wall, I thought we stood a chance. Now they outflanked us, I clenched my spear, hoping, praying at least my family could escape.

"Hey, up here!" a woman yelled from atop the stairway. The first giant perked up to see who'd spoken. There, stood Liza and Shran. "Come and get me," she continued, and the two sprinted off towards our chambers.

The giant skidded his bare feet on the smooth tile and scrambled right for them.

"No," I gasped. How could Liza do this? I struck all the exposed purrium I could find. The platelets for my spear, my spare sword, but they only clinked together and silenced. The giant kept his course.

Chapter Thirty-Six

Liza

I looked down at the main entrance, horrified as my creations tore through the Palace Guard. I couldn't let Zieglon and so many of our countrymen pay with their lives for my mistake. Now the monster was coming for me.

"Hurry Shran. Get out of here," I said.

"Not without you."

The giant had already begun bounding up the broad stairway, so Shran and I both ran through the hall towards our chambers. "I've got to stop him long enough for you to escape," I said on the way. "I might be able to drain his life before he does me in."

"'Might?'" Shran said. "How long does that take?"

My son had a point. At that thing's size, perhaps too long. And perhaps he could turn me to jelly before I could do real damage.

We'd made it halfway to our chambers, the giant too close, crawling on all fours to fit in the hallway.

"Shran, we've got to hide."

"I'll pop us into the monad."

"Then what?" He would surely then carry us away even more easily.

Shran shrugged, uncertain as well.

"Okay, this way, then," I said, pointing up a nearby stairway. We climbed madly to reach the next level. The giant was hindered by the narrowness of the stairway.

"Where now?" Shran said when we were in the upper hallway.

One of the doors creaked open. A dark-haired young woman poked her head out of Thordin's family chambers—Nella. She beckoned to us. "In here."

"We can't trust them," Shran said.

"You have a better idea?"

He shook his head, so we hurried inside.

A wide array of trophies and sculptures littered Thordin's entrance hall, with still more sitting on shelves and hanging from the rafters. The artifacts barely left space to walk through to the adjoining chambers.

Nella bolted the way behind us. "Are you alright, Shran? Lady Mattian?"

Shran said nothing, and I shrugged in exasperation. "We're pretty far from alright, all of us."

Shran whispered, "We shouldn't have come here. It's never safe with them around," eyeing the ladyling by the door.

"Not safe?" Nella said. "Not safe? Actually, my father had this door doubly reinforced for situations like this." She pounded it with a firm fist. Satisfied with the dull thud, she rested her back on the door, peaceful as a kitten.

In the moment of silence, I heard sniffing from out in the hallway. I briskly motioned Nella to come away, but she'd frozen with fear. Shran, too, held still beside me, and then the sniffing stopped.

I held a finger to my mouth, backing up as quickly and quietly as possible. Nella looked to us, her eyes asking what to do, and a fearful squeak escaped her lips. The sniffing stopped abruptly.

"Run, dash it," I said, too late.

The whole room quivered as something huge struck the door. Dozens of trophies and sculptures toppled, right over me. My foot was jammed under a sculpture. I pulled and pulled but couldn't get loose.

Shran managed to stay free, while Nella lay stunned by the tall splintering door.

"See!" Shran yelled. "They always betray us."

"It was an accident," Nella said. "I didn't mean—"

Everything shook again and again, until a gargantuan fist broke through. The giant peered inside with one beady eyeball and grunted excitedly at the sight of the ladyling.

Nella screamed and hurried to get back on her feet. "Help me," she cried, struggling to flee while stepping around the fallen trophies.

"Please," Nella mouthed in desperation. Just as quickly, the giant scooped her up and slowly pressed his oversized head through the doorway.

Shran drew the family sword and charged at the monstrosity.

I fought all the harder to free myself, to stop him from such a reckless attack. That knocked a few taxidermy critters down in front of me, blocking my view completely. The giant squealed as if he'd pricked a finger and then I heard its enormous jaws snap shut.

All fell silent.

I desperately cast aside every object in my way and finally pulled free.

There at the entrance, stood Lady Haldra while the giant leered in behind her. "Lady Mattian, are you alright?"

"Where's Shran? What did you do to him?"

"Sorry. I haven't seen him."

I looked for any signs of his little amulet, the family sword, a scrap of his cloak. Seeing nothing, I sank to my knees and wept.

"Don't worry," Haldra said. "We can sniff him out easily enough, but this is about you. The others asked too much of you, too soon. No one wants to hurt you, but we've got to hurry."

"Haldra, you fool. You've killed him. Killed my son."

"What are you talking about?"

"And not just that. You've killed nobility, your very own niece."

"Did I? Well, what's that to you?"

"You monster! My son! Even your own flesh and blood—"

"Is the only thing standing in our way." Haldra paced the entryway, turning over the fallen bust of an elderly man with the sole of her shoe. She gave it a little shove, making the oblong thing roll in a lopsided path. "You must listen to reason, Liza. If they grew up in conditions like this, they'd only bring forth more children like Thordin or Guilen. They're the bane of your family's existence."

I rushed her.

Haldra whipped out and threw her hidden knives in rapid succession. Sharp pain erupted in my belly and chest. I grasped at the handles, already wet with blood, instinctively pulling them loose and letting them fall as if in slow motion. Despite every effort to heal, my reserves were still quite depleted. The blades struck the floor, and the bleeding quickened.

Haldra shook her head. "I'm sorry about that. And I'm sorry for your son, truly."

I gasped for breath, unable to stand, each labored breath seeming weaker than the last.

"Oh, you can heal up from that soon enough, from all of it. The cliche bears repeating," she said. "I have but one truly valuable thing that you lack. Do you know what it is?"

I winced with each movement, crawling closer.

"Perspective, Lady Mattian. Perspective. I give my condolences, but what was so very special about your son anyway?"

"Be silent," I growled.

"We're having a discussion. With your power, you can have as many sons as your heart desires, for ages to come."

"You know nothing of love," I said, almost within reach.

"You love the idea of him," she said, "but the most freeing idea you will ever learn about the vital force we call human life: it's cheap."

I lunged, and she lost her balance backing into the broken bust. Before she could do anything, I latched onto Haldra's boots, siphoning in vibrance to my reserves. She screamed, an infernal cry of fear, hatred, and anguish. Once again, the rush of new living power took ahold of me. More. I needed more!

Something heavy slammed into my skull, knocking my teeth to the hardwood. I tried shaking the dizzying shock away, to no avail. Haldra kicked free from my weakened grasp and frantically made for the open hallway, coughing and wheezing as she went. In all the excitement, I hadn't even healed myself.

I imbibed the new vibrance, focusing it into any body part that hurt. My failing heart, searing bowels, and aching temples knit themselves back together in a burst of shock that turned to pregnant strength. I snatched up the abandoned knives and chased the noblewoman.

This time, I had a better plan. Holding one of the blades, I scraped and scraped away at the purple leather-coated handle, until it tore free. The hilt's small purrium core exposed, I struck it with the other blade.

The knife rang out loud and true, pulling at the sheath strapped to Haldra's side. The summons caught her off balance. As I leaned back, keeping an iron grip around the cross-guard, she crashed hard onto her back, and the sheath strap cinched up around her armpits. Haldra fumbled at the sheath as it dragged her across the floor.

Then the enraged giant roared and turned on me, and I was running away again.

Chapter Thirty-Seven

Zieglon

The giantess returned to her missile attacks to break our ranks. She hurled them one after another, the remnants of our blockade now her stockpile. The men who remained held ranks, common folk quickly filling gaps in the line.

For a moment, she slinked back outside. She grunted, and then came the sound of something large and heavy being dislodged from its place. She reemerged with the monument of the late Third Lady lifted overhead. The archers loosed a useless volley, as shouts of rage erupted throughout the hall.

The giantess roared back angrily and threw the monument. Tiles cracked as Clenhilda's open arms snapped off. Her likeness continued to bounce and roll at us like a fallen log. Those who could, dove over. Others were forced to meet the monument head-on.

The sneering giantess charged, an arm preparing for a back-handed swipe.

Hothen looked to me expectantly, along with the rest who'd managed to remain standing, waiting for the command.

"Charge!" I ordered. If we lacked the strong line, at least we'd meet the slatty with speed. Every soldier with a working pair of legs obeyed. The giantess nearly upon us, I aimed for her open mouth and launched a spear. She jerked to the side, letting it glance off her cheek, and I launched the second spear with all the force I could muster. She swatted this and the flurry of other projectiles away like mayflies.

We'd missed our window. She swung so quickly, I couldn't escape.

Next moment, I felt myself bounce off the side wall and slam back to the floor tile. My head spun, leaving me disoriented, and surely those without armor fared worse. Where was Hothen? What of Tewin? All had turned to chaos.

The giantess kept up her mad rampage, tearing through the feeble lines of mostly commoners who remained upright. At least she wasn't a jumper. Yet in seconds, she'd break through and regroup with her partner. That wasn't an option.

She bobbed and weaved, swinging and flailing so that no one could come close enough to land a hit. Then Hothen headed the foremost assault, dodging her every blow and holding her back by the tip of his spear. He needed help.

Unsure which in the scattering of fallen weapons were mine, I linked with a light clap of both gauntlets. Raising my arms, I saw which ones mimicked the motion. They'd landed on the opposite side of the hallway.

Now the giantess had the shaft of Hothen's spear, violently shaking it loose.

Sustaining the link in my gauntlets, I positioned myself so the angry giantess stood directly between me and my linked spears.

The giantess raised Hothen's weapon overhead, ready to skewer him with it. The man clanked his gauntlet and flew right up to meet her face-to-face, leading with his extended sword arm.

I threw my arms up, silencing the platelets so the spears continued flying higher.

She bit down on Hothen's outstretched arm and shook him like a wild dog.

With one loud clap, I summoned my spears. They shot straight at her midsection as Hothen smacked into a side wall. She screamed as the tips sank deep into her side and yanked me directly at her.

I leapt high and steadied in mid-air with the aid of two gauntlets. The shrill ring drew unwanted attention once again. As I soared faster and faster, she managed to catch my lower legs.

My front half still stretched sideways towards the implanted spears, so I couldn't even lower one hand to draw my sword. She spread her jaws wide, about to bite down on me in my vain struggle. As my last-ditch effort, I silenced both gauntlets, tucked in both legs, and stabbed with my elbow spurs. She loosened that crushing grip for the one fraction of a second I needed.

In one last clap, the ringing gauntlets yanked me for the implanted spears. I drew my sword and sliced deep across her belly. Both gauntlets reunited with their spears, which I grabbed hold of as they silenced.

She wailed while attempting to hold her innards. Then the archers loosed the decisive volley. Arrows and all sorts of implements flew into the huge open target.

She groaned and collapsed with a thud. Some kind of foul smoke poured out of her nostrils, and the giantess was no more.

I found Hothen gripping what remained of his forearm, pale and dazed. How much more would have to go just to keep off the gangrene? Nevertheless, he perked up at the sight of me. "Zieglon, my friend," he said, "forgive me. I can't seem to stand at just the moment."

"Your courage puts us all to shame. I would have you sit as long as your heart desires."

"Then with respect," Hothen said, "I would have you leave me, and put the last one to rest."

"I won't rest until *he* does."

Chapter Thirty-Eight

Shran

So there I was, surrounded by a pile of General Thordin's old trophies, about to sit by as one of the noble caste got devoured by a creature of nightmares. Isn't that what I wanted, the end of the people who made palace life miserable and unjust? Nella led the thing to us herself anyway. I had nothing to do with that. What we had to do was flee for our lives before meeting the same fate.

"Not so, Deykti," said a sudden stubborn presence in my head.

What this voice was, no one could say. I only knew I could not ignore it, nor would it ignore me. The presence shoved Steve's words into full focus, overpowering all else, the words I despised above all else: "I don't subsist on fair treatment."

I saw my mother trapped under a fallen sculpture and the ladyling in the giant's grasp. The command could not have been more clear to my mind, or more infuriating.

I drew the family sword and went straight after the giant's prey. He held her in one greasy fist, readying to snap down on her helplessly wriggling form. I jumped onto the fist with her, anchoring myself to the meaty finger with the short sword. The giant recoiled for a second, and it was all I could do to hold on. Then I threw my free arm around Nella's waist and pulled.

But the monster's grasp was back at full force. I couldn't possibly free her that way. I looked back where my mother had been, and couldn't even see her in the mess of fallen items. Now I had committed, and she was left on her own.

That same voice implored me, "*Now*, Deykti."

Nella stared in silent shock, but didn't seem aware of any voice. So now was the time to escape. But no matter how I strained, I couldn't reach the amulet around my neck. The mouthful of enormous human teeth closed in around us. I popped up my chest, bouncing the pendant the extra few centimeters I needed, and pinched the monad therein.

Not a moment too soon, Nella and I were sucked into the tiny world, leaving the ravenous monster behind.

Nella checked her arms and legs, happy to find them still where they belonged. She looked around at the quiet field in an air of mild confusion, always so very mild. "That was close. What was that horrible monster?" she asked.

"Your fault," I muttered.

"Hm?"

I roughly sheathed the sword. "I said it's your fault we're stuck in here."

"That's not very nice."

My fists clenched as I thought back on how she and her cousins treated me. "Is it 'nice' the way you treat us? My family?"

"Usually someone has to be the odd one out, and you're always running away anyway, so..."

"You helped them torment me all this time." I noticed my eyes started to water, but I persisted. "Why?"

She looked down and started kicking at the dirt absently. "Well, I'm sorry. I didn't make them do it."

"You think that's good enough? One word, and suddenly it all just goes away? I put myself in harm's way to save you, Nella."

"Like I did for you? When I let you into our home?"

"You don't understand."

"No, *you* don't understand, Shran. You're self-absorbed. You're too scared of what the rest of us think about you to even try getting to know us."

"Me, self-absorbed? Why did I ever like you? My mother's still out there, because of you, and you don't even care."

"But…" She hung her head.

Had I really just said I liked her? I was beyond all that. Right?

"Then, you chose me over your own mother."

"It's not like that. No. Something… something told me to."

"You may be a strange man, Shran, but you sure are a brave one."

There was no sarcasm or aloofness lacing her expression, only a smile that said she believed every word.

"You're not quite normal yourself," I said, "but at least you can sing."

Then we were laughing. Inexplicably, joyfully laughing. How had so much anger and worry turned to levity?

The answer emerged with the very asking: because I heeded the call. The true path had revealed itself to me, in that strong, knowing presence. It led directly towards the most dangerous place at that moment, only to bring me and a would-be victim into perfect safety moments later. Perhaps someway, somehow, we'd landed exactly where we needed to be. And perhaps, my mother would be saved another way.

Glinta ran up to us, greeting me with a hug. "You okay, Shran?" she said. "You nearly let yourself get eaten again."

"We're safe. Glinta, this is Nella, one of the Stohvans from my world."

Nella curtsied, and Glinta followed suit.

"Glinta," I said, "Can you see anything out in our world? Did you see what happened to Mother?" I asked.

"The white-haired woman you were with?"

I nodded.

"Not that I can tell. That thing swallowed us whole, and it looks like we're down in his belly right now."

And just like that, I saw the path. "Glinta, you've got to send me out again."

"But aren't we safe in here?" she said.

I clasped the pommel of my sword. "I've got to head out and save my mother too. While we have time."

"Didn't you hear me? I said we're inside its belly. It's way too dangerous."

Nella shook her head, not in disapproval but amazement.

"Look. With two giants ravaging the palace, the only place I can't get gobbled up is in its belly. And Glinta, she's your mother too."

With one solemn nod, Glinta agreed. "Okay Shran, but be careful."

I nodded back, gave a thumbs-up, and immediately emerged inside the belly of the beast, the amulet hanging around my neck. That stomach squeezed and churned me like a chunk of under-chewed roast. Little did I know it would be bathed in vinegary juices that burned whatever they touched. Only a faint reddish hue seeped through the skin, giving a vague sense of my surroundings. The slimy stomach lining pushed and squeezed so hard I could barely move half the time.

312

By the feel of it, the giant was crawl-running again, chasing after more prey. I gasped for air, catching only sour fumes in my throat. Getting right side up took a great deal of effort, and it was still hard to tell which way was which.

As if alerted to my presence, the stomach's churning turned to heaving, trying to push me out the way I'd come. If I made the giant want to be sick, the feeling was mutual, but I didn't want to get chewed up properly either. Heaves came one after the other, with a short pause between. When it pushed, I spread out as wide as possible, holding myself in place.

The heart would be about the same direction as the heaving. That was my real ticket out.

The rapid thumping seemed to come from right about... there. I guided the tip of the sword onto the spot. Here came one heave, then another, then during the brief pause, I gripped the hilt two-handed and plunged. A tough barrier resisted the blade, but the next heave of the stomach sent it all the way home.

Everything jerked erratically, and the giant's horrible screech rumbled all around. I clung on tight, the hilt serving as an anchor once again. I could only imagine the damage my blade was doing as he continued to thrash around, making it slice this way and that.

Soon enough, the jerking ended. The giant dropped and breathed his last.

I pinched the monad at the end of the necklace, popping back inside and leaving the amulet behind. Glinta appeared to be narrating all she could see from the amulet's eyepieces to Nella. The death of the hideous giant in my world clearly didn't affect her nearly as much as that of the waterbud and scotor in hers. Rather, she and Nella applauded my return as if I were a war hero. Then they clapped hands over their noses and sounded disgusted.

All I could do was gasp for breath, rolling around in the dirt to wipe off the burning stomach juices. Once I'd cleaned off a bit, I asked to be sent right back out again.

Glinta and Nella gave each other a look that said, "Yep, definitely out of his mind."

Nevertheless, when I gave her the thumbs up, that unseen force yanked me back out, into the dead giant's stomach.

Dislodging the sword from where it stuck, I got to work carving an escape. The muscly flesh gave a lot of resistance, but I poked a hole big enough to stick a fist through. After some hacking and slashing, I managed to crawl out and breathe free air again.

We appeared to be on the third level of the palace, overlooking part of the entrance hall. Down below, Newmundians of all walks of life gazed up, pointing in shock.

"Mother, are you here? Are you alright?" I called.

"Shran," she answered, from nearby. "Thank All Father!"

I let out a sigh of relief, quickly wiping off what I could on the giant's fur.

As she ran up, streaks of blood covered her face and clothes, yet she moved as if in perfect health. I grabbed her tightly and asked, "Where's Father?"

About then came the shouts and clacking boots of a few dozen men up the hallway. As they gathered around, I smiled to see my father at the lead.

He wrapped arms around both of us. "Liza dearest, Shran, well done," he said.

"What about the president?" I asked. "What about Lady Haldra?"

"I had to save you two first," Father said, "but it looks like you took care of the giant for me."

"I just saw Haldra," Mother said. "She was heading downstairs, and we've got to catch her."

"We've got to protect the president no matter what the lady's doing," Father said. "Besides, how would that look when no one yet knows the truth?"

"Wouldn't he approve?" I said. "I mean, Mother told him all about what she's up to."

"I did, but the folk don't know yet. I suppose it would still look like treason to them."

"Well," I said, "what if I just brought her into the monad long enough for you to get the president? For protection."

Father nodded with an amused smile. "Now there's an idea, Shran. You do that, and we'll go straight for him."

It so happened as Father, his men, and Mother started heading for the president, that I spied a gaunt, hobbling form rushing down the main stairs to the entrance hall. It was Lady Haldra, about to escape. No way could I get back to the nearest stairway and catch up to her before she escaped. But I had the monad with me!

Pulling the pin at the bottom of the amulet allowed me to open the little cage and release the monad into open air. It expanded as if stretching its arms after a nap. I held it over the railing, a long drop below, and popped inside.

"What happened, Shran?" Glinta asked in the field next to Nella. "I can't see anything in your world anymore."

"I know," I said, showing the empty pendant around my neck. "We're dropping a few floors down right now, and I didn't want to damage this necklace if I could help it."

"Dropping off the balcony?" Nella asked.

"No time to explain. Glinta, could you..." Before I could finish the sentence, there I was, standing near the entrance hall with Haldra right in front of me. Though she rarely wore what I would call a kind face, she now gave the impression of raw, animalistic rage. She shook her head in disbelief. Her voice had taken on a hoarse quality that made me shiver. "Shran? Weren't you dead?"

Everyone in the entrance way seemed to watch with bated breath. Unless they had very keen eyesight, it probably looked to them like I'd just disappeared and reappeared elsewhere without passing through any of the space between. Hopefully, they would give the benefit of the doubt to the one who'd just slain a giant. So, I blurted, "Lady Haldra, there's a plot to kill your family. You'll be safe with me."

"Nonsense," she started to say, but I grabbed her wrist in one hand and popped the monad with the other. In that instant, the orb pulled us both inside.

Whether the watching crowds screamed at me "Traitor" or sighed with relief, I had no idea at all. Yet more of Steve's words came to my mind:

"Whether anyone listens or not, whether anyone wants you there or not, your purpose doesn't change. Your place is with them."

Having a purpose like that finally revealed one thing: danger and fear were a pair of liars. The true safety, the true peace was wherever my purpose led. Glinta's tiny world was never meant to be a hideaway from the world's problems. It was a training ground, a lifeline, an ally to better face each problem head-on.

Section Four

Into Song

Chapter Thirty-Nine

Zieglon

Liza and I found Guilen, Steve, and President Dessidon in a secure meeting room. They were unharmed, and allowed us to safely escort them out to assess the damage.

Back in the entrance hall, broken sculptures and the things they'd struck littered the whole area around the corpse of the giantess. Many men lay badly injured and surrounded by their families. Others fared worse. Guilen stared at the carnage in horror as Steve jumped into action, healing the critically wounded. Liza joined him, healing others with some pointers from Steve.

Man after man rejoiced, seeing his injuries healed in moments. And uproarious lines quickly formed before Steve and Liza.

I stayed close to the President's side as we surveyed the area. Near the stairs to the second level, a group of the folk guarded what looked like the monad, floating above the tile floor.

I pointed it out to the president. "We'd better check that out."

As we approached, Dessidon asked, "What's going on here?"

One of the folk bowed and answered. "I saw it myself, Mister President. That Shran Mattian, he killed a giant from inside its belly and disappeared. Lady Haldra was running down the stairs, and you wouldn't believe it. He appeared right in front of her, appeared out of nowhere, saying there's a plot against your family. Then they both vanished into this orb."

Even as the man spoke, Shran appeared, silently, along with Thordin's daughter, Nella. "Lady Haldra is safe and secured," Shran said, looking at me.

"Good work," the president and I said at the same time.

"No," Guilen said in disbelief. "That's unthinkable! It's... how could she do this to our own home?"

"We'll save that for her trial," Dessidon said, then addressed the crowd, listing off the names Liza had identified as members of the Keesec and asking for their whereabouts.

I hurried over to Hothen, who looked as pallid as a pillow case. "You look horrible," I said, scarcely fighting back the tears. "Steve will heal you at once."

"I just need another minute, my friend. Plenty of these folks need help more than I."

"Steve! Liza!" I called. "We need some healing, fast." The man and my wife ran over in a heartbeat. "You can grow back limbs, right?" I asked.

Liza felt Hothen's arm, then stared sadly. Who could blame her if she didn't fully understand her abilities yet?

"From scratch?" Steve shook his head. "I'm sorry. We would do more harm than good."

"Don't fret about it, Zieglon," Hothen said, breathing heavily. "Now I'll have a roaring song ready for everyone I meet."

Nevertheless, Steve touched the man's arm. The stub at the end of his elbow sealed itself cleanly together, and some of the ruddy vigor returned to his face. Then Hothen was on his feet, and I pulled him into a tight embrace. "That you will, Hothen. You will indeed."

* * *

By Monday morning, the mayor had carted off most of the wreckage from the courtyard where the people of Newmund now assembled. We draped two curtains in the red and white presidential colors where the oaken doors had hung the day before. Below that, each of the remaining Stohvan families lined either side of the steps, along with me and mine on the lowest level. We each wore the presidential colors in our own way: Steve in a special red robe of his own, Shran and I in ornately buckled coats with sharp, white sashes, and Liza wearing a new red dress with elegantly braided white hair flowing over her shoulders.

At the top stood President Dessidon the Second, adorned in full presidential attire. "People of Newmund," he said, "I came in disguise, not knowing what I would find. I found a mayorship full of men ready to face what no one could have prepared for. Many gave great sacrifices yesterday. Many were injured or lost their lives defending me, their mayor, and all their folk. Yesterday, you all showed great strength and even greater courage.

"What else did I find? Grave folly. The human-like monstrosities we overcame yesterday were no works of nature. Rather, the legends appear all too true: before the Storm, our ancestors learned to distort and combine elements of living creatures, even with human beings. Rather than healing and uplifting their people, those in power preferred to redesign men, women, and children alike into bizarre forms as it suited their whims. And remnants of their machinations have survived up to the present day.

"Why do we sculpt our heroes and aspirations in stone and metal, and why do our bards always require the classical songs to be word-perfect? Merely for our enjoyment?" Dessidon paused, looking across the unanswering crowd. "Ask any pupil, and they'll tell you, 'certainly not!' In truth, we do it to solidify the true and the beautiful for generations to come, so those immovable objects drive our imaginations rather than the reverse.

"What if we sculpted them instead from sand or mud? The winds and rains would quickly return them to dust. My dear people, when every truth is made questionable, every good fungible, every beauty merely fashionable, we lose our very selves. That loss disintegrates the harmony, casting adrift each of our minds in a sea of self-serving 'isms.'

"My daughter, your own Lady Haldra, sits in custody now, standing accused of instigating yesterday's attack along with a dozen others. They did so in hopes of forming such a world, no matter the cost. Though I pray it be a lie, those to blame will surely pay for the blood they spilled with their own.

"But I found more still. Four persons in particular."

President Dessidon called up Steve, along with my family, so the four of us climbed the steps between assembly of nobles. As Liza and I shared contented glances and smiled at our fast-growing son, I noticed Steve, too, looking on the three of us as a proud father would.

Dessidon continued when we'd taken places beside him. "I present to you, the family Mattian. Through their efforts, ingenuity, and acts of courage, they saved incalculable lives and helped apprehend those responsible for yesterday's deadly attack. Far from least of all, Shran Mattian has shown more promise than any youth I've met, single-handedly destroying a giant and personally saving my granddaughter in the act.

He addressed us as he continued. "Though I have no authority to bestow Newmundian nobility, even that title could not capture the gratitude we owe you. Rather, I will endeavor to give you a place in the Othark canon. Not a sculpture but sculptures will be made, not a song but songs will be sung by bards across Othark, for I believe your greatest deeds are still to come."

As the people applauded, I motioned to Guilen, who was standing nearby. "May I have a word?"

"If you wish," the mayor said and gave me the floor moments later.

I stepped forward and cleared my throat as I surveyed the audience below. There stood my great friend, not in fine clothes but decked in mayoral armor and gripping his tasseled spear in the left hand, the rest of my men behind him.

Then I addressed the crowd. "I would like to recognize Hothen, personally. He showed such courage defending all of us that he regarded his own life and limb as a small price to pay."

Some cheers broke out, and then I continued. "I, for one, disagree. The Keesec are the sort of enemy no one should have to endure. Mortal enemies dwelling within our own folk? Our own families even? I tell you, if but one of your fingernails was damaged by the schemes of such enemies, that price is too high. My dear wife, Liza, heard it from their very lips. The Keesec, these keepers of secrets claim they are merely the tip of the iceberg. Therefore, from now on, I will endeavor to hunt down these destroyers of nations, these breakers of bonds and harmony, to the last man and the last woman."

Steve too requested a word, which the president also obliged. The red-robed man motioned for attention and the courtyard quieted until only the sprinkling of the central fountain and distant chirps of birds broke the silence.

"May All Father's blessing be with you now and forever," Steve said. "Call me Steve, or Steven if you wish. Of all the generations I've been on Tew, few of them have been so encouraging. And after many centuries of dormancy, I think you all ought to know,

323

my bloodline has reawakened here and now. I pray all of you choose to benefit from what we can offer, while the opportunity is yours. Once again, you have friends in the Tower of Tew."

To my surprise, Mayor Guilen approached Steve, arm outstretched for a handshake as he spoke in a voice only we atop the stairs could hear. "You healed so many of my folk after I treated you worse than an enemy. Somehow, those around you managed to save even more. All that to say, you have my apologies, Steve. Please forgive me."

Steve smiled and shook the president's hand vigorously. "That I will, Mister Mayor. That I will."

And as the assembly carried on, I recalled one thing I had left to do.

Chapter Forty

Liza

Monday's assembly left me shaken and confused more than anything. My smiles would only fool the others for so long. By some fortune, I managed to tear away from the crowds for a period of solitude. All afternoon, I wandered wherever people were most scarce, pondering everything that had transpired. The questions and worries simply wouldn't clear away.

All too soon, the sun hung down close to the horizon, casting down its brilliant golden light as I strolled through the garden maze.

Then I spied one narrow sunbeam peeking through the hedges. It met a perfect white rosebud, enveloping it in a light that stood out against the shady background. I knelt beside it reverently and inhaled the first pleasant breath in a long while.

The day before, I had drained my reserves dry once again, healing the injured. Yet, when I woke up, they were refilled, filled with the pure vibrance of starlight. I knew its rhythmic flavor well. But with each beautiful motion of the starlight melody, another strange statement circled around in my head. *"You don't deserve this,"* it repeated: sometimes a call to self-pity, other times an accusation.

I wanted to share what I'd received. I stretched out a life-infused finger, reaching for that precious flower bud.

325

"I wouldn't do that if I were you," came a familiar voice from behind. I turned to see Steve emerge from an adjoining path in the hedges. The look in those knowing eyes sparked a flashback, the memory of myself dying beside him only two days prior. He took a knee by the budding flower, and I leapt to my feet uneasily in response.

"Sorry to startle you," Steve said.

I nodded, wanting that to be the end of it. But then, I had to say something, the first words I'd spoken in hours. "Everything going on, it's just too much. One minute I'm actually on top of the world, the next minute I'm fighting for my life, against the very monsters I helped create. They ought to lock me up with the Keesec, and instead the president wants me in the Othark canon. I never asked for this."

"Of course," Steve said. "And there's something you should know about that. Shall I tell you now?"

"Alright."

"Everyone who joined the ranks of the Eldenvolk had precisely zero choice in the matter, until you."

"You were forced into it?"

"Not by any human hand. I believe I was the first to experience it. While I was in a very large vessel, in upper space, a certain window shattered. The depressurization trapped me alone and completely unshielded for some minutes. That simple event bathed me in that wonderful, terrible starlight as the air fled from my lungs, and my vision dimmed. In short, when a crew member resuscitated me, I awoke like this. One way or another, we, the Eldenvolk, got unintentionally exposed to upper space, and nearly died. We never had a choice."

"Well, you chose for me. Now this changes everything, my whole life."

"I had a directive I dared not disobey. What you have is a gift and a calling: a calling you answered, to your credit. Those foolish enough to try joining us on their own initiative received nothing but cancerous wounds when the process didn't kill them."

"Then I answered another 'calling'" I said. A few tears whetted my cheeks, but I stilled my jaw which very much wanted to quiver right about then. "Now people are dead, good people. Even Zieglon's best friend is maimed because of me. You tell me, Steve. What do I do about that?"

"Aye," Steve said, "but healing will come."

"Hothen's arm isn't growing back. The president told you about Penna, right? She isn't coming back. No matter if it was self-defense, I killed her with these hands. When I was stealing their... all I wanted was more."

Steve nodded solemnly.

I spoke in a hushed voice. "Down there with the Keesec, we spoke to an entity made of mist. They called it—"

"Usually better not to speak the name, I find. It can draw unwanted attention."

"Well, the entity asked if I'd joined them. I told him I had, and—" A shiver went down my spine at the memory of that inhuman voice. "It looked at me and just said, 'You will.' Was it reading my mind, or telling the future, or what?"

Steve thought for a moment and finally said, "It means they dearly want our gifts used for their designs. Never give them that privilege again."

"It's horrible. How can all Othark canonize me after the things I've done?"

"So that they may learn from them. So that they can watch you learn from them. Look here. This rosebud will be beautiful in its time." He touched the flower bud, making it bloom immediately.

"You just said not to do that," I scoffed.

"Exactly. This blossom is here today, and gone tomorrow." When he touched the newly bloomed flower, the petals stretched out to full breadth, wilted, and browned away. The little flower bud hadn't done anything to deserve that.

"You wasted it."

He rose to his feet. "I *rushed* it. Do you take my point?"

"I suppose you wish me to be patient with myself before you kill more innocent flowers."

Steve chuckled. " 'Patient,' yes. *Present*, so much the more. The point is, you will be in this world a very long time, longer than you can imagine, time to grow in goodness, to grow in wisdom. Putting your gift towards nothing but the highest good, the highest beauty, takes practice."

"It wasn't a question of practice. I knew exactly what I meant to do. I should have known what would happen but was too weak. I was too selfish, and now I'm just waiting for the day it all catches up with me."

"It sounds like there's one thing you need right now more than anything."

"Perspective?"

He shook his head. "Forgiveness."

It made no sense. Too many of my victims had already met the grave. Weren't they the ones I'd need to ask most of all? "I can't get that unless someone else gives it."

"So, ask for it. By All Father ask for it, Liza."

I hadn't heard him swear before, hadn't thought him the type. Was he being rude on purpose, ordering me around like that? Each response I started to mouth slipped away one after the other. Perhaps I had missed something.

The sun was just touching the horizon when Steve sighed and started back in the direction he came from. "Think about it. And find me whenever you need me," he said, cheerfully.

"Where are you going?" I called after him.

"Back to the Tower, I think."

"Will it let me in now too?"

His voice carried through the hedges as he disappeared around the corner, "When you're ready, come and see."

I did keep thinking about it, what I really needed. Gradually, gradually, the thought wrapped itself round and round the morass of worries, compressing them into one dense droplet. The fear of punishment and the terror of humiliation were replaced by one simple longing to find forgiveness.

Chapter Forty-One

Shran

T he mayor had concluded Monday's assembly with one last proclamation. "People of Newmund, nearly all of you obediently held to the ban on approaching a certain tower to the present day. Yet now I see, pride misled me to call it sinister. Upon examination, yesterday's events showed that that mysterious, impossible tower is more than the dark shadow it casts. Look no further than the Mattian family to see it rather serves as a giver of gifts for the benefit of us all. For that reason, I can no longer uphold the prohibition on visiting it. From now on, anyone may approach the Great Tower freely."

The mayor took one deep breath and resolutely nodded to the trumpeters. They played the presidential anthem to the beat of marching drums, and everyone began to disperse.

I stood there on the steps with Father, Mother, and Steve, pondering how so much had changed in so little time. How many people of every rank and craft would go to the Great Tower now? Perhaps they'd meet Steve there, or even go inside. What other ancient mysteries would we uncover there? I only knew I wanted to return very soon.

I absentmindedly touched the amulet hanging from my neck. What was happening inside it that very moment? The monad had held Lady Haldra long enough to prepare one of the mayor's holding cells, where she now sat, awaiting the trial. How long she could delay her execution, remained to be seen.

Glinta would have seen the whole assembly through the amulet's eyepieces, and I'd soon tell her what everyone had said. It was a strangely pleasant feeling, the two of us alone connecting these very different worlds. And I had the sneaking suspicion both worlds would come to depend on each other more than either of us knew.

When Mayor Guilen, Thordin, and Gilda, with their families, started going back into the palace, Father gave me a friendly nudge. "Well, Shran, since schoolyard is canceled today. Better come with me."

"Where to?" I asked.

"To teach you a little something in the meantime."

We passed through the crowds and found a secluded spot in the gardens, overlooking the fields and villages scattered across the countryside. "Oh yeah. We said you'd teach me the songs for recitations, right?"

"For recitations?" He shrugged. "Who cares? They won't do you any good until you truly know them—live them! Which song does Falen start with?"

"First, we need to recite 'the Mighty President', and then come other important ones from there."

Father raised an eyebrow. "He reigned a few short decades ago."

"It happened before you were born, though," I said.

"That's yesterday in the scheme of history. You ought to start as far back as possible and build up from there. What else is due?"

I named the rest of the songs for recitals, and Father started by listing them in chronological order. Then he began to explain the background story and the significance of each one in vivid detail. He made concrete images come to life in my mind, until I could almost touch the events seen through the eyes of those long-dead. There it all was: the worldwide famine after the Storm, the appearance of legendary men rebinding people in fellowship, the development of song-craft and sculpture, the discovery of purrium-splitting, and events leading up through the Peltern dynasty. The Stohvans had all but wiped out the Pelterns, until Dessidon the Second and the Third Lady.

We continued late into the afternoon. The stories stacked, every one upon the others, until the present day emerged, clear and vibrant. For the first time, I felt that I truly knew both when and where we stood. It struck me: the grandeur of the land spread out before us. Even the stray villages in the distance took on a special gravity. They were the seat of a people, *our* people.

After explaining the songs, Father sang through each one in a soothing baritone voice, me keeping up as best as I could. The flowing rhythms and rhymes gradually started to seep into my very bones. Through repetition, each line began to creep its way forward from the back of my mind until it emerged as precise words. They were no longer merely words but rather substantial, meaningful. Line by line and verse by verse, I eventually came to know them, knowing them like brothers I never had.

The sun just started to droop down below the distant hills when Father sighed and said, "That's about enough for one day."

"Yeah. I think I can remember them well enough now."

"Remember them, yes. More importantly, meditate on them wherever you go. Relive them day by day. Grow into them."

"And then I won't forget them?"

"And then you'll become like the best of the heroes therein. It's positively criminal I haven't taken the time up till now to show you, but one day, you'll pass on these and more to your children."

"When I've got some, I will," I laughed. And another thought came to mind. "If I'm going to be canonized—to have songs about me that people have to learn—I've got to do more things worth singing about."

"What do you have in mind?"

"I don't know yet. But I want to know how to fight like you, to be ready for anything. Could you teach me that?"

With a wide and toothy grin, he said, "I thought you'd never ask!"

Mother emerged from an opening in the hedges, smiling with hands on her hips. "There you are. They'll be serving dinner soon, you know."

My stomach growled as I realized we'd skipped lunch altogether.

"Right you are, my lady," Father said, and we headed her direction. As we did, he spoke in a voice only I could hear, "Take care of her, Shran. When I'm gone."

"I will," I said.

We wove our way through the hedge maze towards the palace.

"Zieglon," Mother said, "there's so much I have left to tell you."

"You will," he said, "in time."

She nodded, reassured. "I've been thinking. Everything is going to be different now, isn't it?"

"Well, let's see," Father said. "Tomorrow, All Father will bring us a sunrise. Some men will work for the good and others for ill. Some poor soul will undoubtedly stub a toe on the leg of a table or slam his fingers in a door. Others will discover old beauty from a brand-new perspective, and you two," he briskly squeezed me and Mother to his sides. "Whether from here or from the stars, I will still love you. No. Some things never change."

The whole entrance hall lay spotless, with silver-laced pine trees set up wherever a statue had stood. Processions of the most finely dressed servants lined either side of a gold carpet leading into the mayor's court. Each servant bowed reverently as the three of us passed. The doors to the mayor's court hung wide open, guarded by spearmen in sparkling armor. The guards parted to let us through, and the doorman announced us each by name.

Hundreds of candles flickered on the long tables, each one surrounded by people who rose and turned to watch our entrance. At the mayor's lower table stood the young nobles I had spent so many days avoiding. On that night, they gazed on us with no hint of malice, and I thought Nella smiled at me. In my eyes, remembering the line from whence those young men and women descended, how it had nearly been snuffed out, even Jaldane looked almost... precious.

There, at the mayor's high table, stood glorious figures draped in royal robes: President Dessidon Stohvan the Second, Mayor Guilen Stohvan, his nobles and high officers all around. The mayor glanced at three high table seats still waiting to be filled and beckoned us forward.

The End

Acknowledgements

The help of my friends has been invaluable in the daunting process of writing and re-writing, and re-re-writing this book. Thank you so much, Ben and Henrik, for your feedback on early stages of the manuscript.

Thank you, Gunnar, for all your support and feedback on multiple drafts, as well as finding me a cover artist!

Thank you, Anders who continually met with me, week by week, giving occasionally blunt yet necessary advice.

Thank you, Nicholas for creating the cover: the first and foremost mode of judging any book.

Thank you, Abigail, one of my favorite mitten-people(let the reader understand), for holding me accountable to finish this book.

And all the other friends, family, and others who supported me in innumerable ways throughout the process.

Last but not least, thank you, dear reader for getting this far! I sincerely hope you've enjoyed this, my first full novel, and if you did, please recommend it to your friends, join us at The Upper Horizons Community of Facebook, or check out my website at AlexanderPatten.com

Peace be with you and yours,
—*Alexander Patten*

www.ingramcontent.com/pod-product-compliance
Lightning Source LLC
Chambersburg PA
CBHW032139190626
46814CB00005BA/1763